D1102260

INSIDE THE CAGE

INSIDE THE CAGE

MATT WHYMAN

SIMON AND SCHUSTER

For Wilf

SIMON AND SCHUSTER

First published in Great Britain in 2007 by Simon and Schuster UK Ltd,
A CBS COMPANY.

Copyright © 2007 Matt Whyman

www.mattwhyman.com

This book is copyright under the Berne Convention.
No reproduction without permission.
All rights reserved.

The right of Matt Whyman to be identified as the author of this work
has been asserted by him in accordance with sections 77 and 78
of the Copyright, Designs and Patents Act, 1988.

Simon & Schuster UK Ltd
Africa House,
64–78 Kingsway,
London WC2B 6AH.

This book is a work of fiction. Names, characters, places and incidents are either
the product of the author's imagination or are used fictitiously. Any resemblance
to actual people living or dead, events or locales is entirely coincidental.

A CIP catalogue record for this book is
available from the British Library.

ISBN: 1-41692669-0
EAN: 978-1-41692669-6

1 3 5 7 9 10 8 6 4 2

Typeset by Rowland Phototypesetting Ltd,
Bury St Edmunds, Suffolk

Printed and bound in Great Britain by
Cox & Wyman Ltd, Reading, Berkshire

www.simonsays.co.uk

This story is based on real events.

Despite the evidence, the authorities responsible for what happened will insist it is pure fiction.

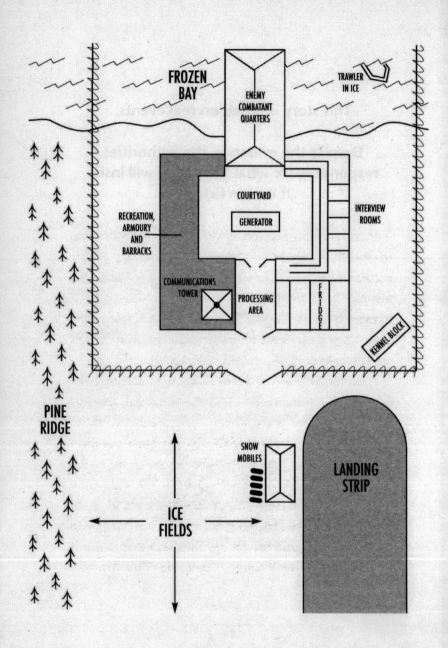

1

Nobody got hurt because of what I did. Not a soul was maimed or injured in the making of my crime. People got *rich*, I imagine. The word is millions of dollars went missing. Now the finger of blame is jabbing at me. I have even heard whispers that my actions funded arms deals, drug deals, most probably mafia meals on wheels and all manner of crimes and misdemeanours.

I just don't know. I couldn't say who cashed in or how much anyone made. All I did was sneak my way into a system network where I could call the shots. My orders may have opened the door to America's most revered vault, but I do not consider myself to be a bank robber – let alone an enemy combatant. The regulation clothing I've been issued with might condemn me as an enemy of the state, but no terrorist network put me up to the job, nor paid me for my time and skill. I did it out of curiosity, and from the other side of the Atlantic.

Operating from the computer in my bedroom, I did it because I could.

The money meant nothing to me. I knew it wasn't mine, so I didn't take a dime. It was the security measures I wanted to beat. When an institution claims to be virtually impenetrable in this day and age, you *know* it's only a matter of time before someone starts testing the firewalls. If it hadn't been me, another script kiddie would've done the same thing. I just wish I'd known the spooks would track me down. It meant every keystroke, call and command I'd made could be used by the security agencies as evidence against me. Online, I worked my way onto closed networks with swagger, confidence and even a little cheek. Right now, a long way from any keyboard, all I can do is keep my head down and pray nobody notices that this boy is totally out of his depth here.

Ping. The illumination goes off on the seatbelt sign overhead. I glance up, drawn from my thoughts, and figure the trigger for it must be hardwired into the aircraft's system. For there aren't any passengers on this flight at liberty to stretch their legs. Our leather seats and headrests may be designed for comfort, but I very much doubt that anyone on board is feeling relaxed. This isn't because the upholstery is worn and scuffed, with tired springs underneath guaranteed to bring on backache – frankly, that's the least of my concerns. I tell myself to stop looking around, just in case I catch anybody's eye. Instead, I study the pressure marks that circle my wrists.

I only wore the plastic tie restraints for the short walk from the terminal to the plane, but that was enough to make an impression. Apparently it's against safety regulations to fly anyone with both hands bound. I don't really understand why it's acceptable to be handcuffed to a special agent instead, like I am now. If a plane went down at this height, we'd all die regardless. And should my body be recovered, dressed like so many others on this flight, I can't help thinking it would be said that I had got what I deserved.

'Problem, son?'

This is just about the first thing the guy accompanying me has said since we took off from Heathrow. I had tried to find out more about my situation. I figured that was entirely understandable. The course of events has seriously shaken me up, after all, but it doesn't seem to concern him. It's only now that he tunes in to me, in fact, which makes his question feel a little loaded.

'No problem here, sir,' I say, and exchange a glance with him.

Like all the Men in Black on board, he's dressed in a casual suit – open at the throat – with a badge clipped to the inside pocket of his jacket that opens doors as soon as he flashes it. He's forty, maybe forty-five at most, and married for some time. I also guessed that he had gained some pounds since he walked up the aisle.

His wedding ring gave all this away. A platinum band so tight it had squeezed his finger out of shape behind the knuckle. I couldn't help but notice, what with time to kill and the handcuffs linking us. It wasn't exactly information that could earn my freedom, but I knew not to ignore even trivial detail. Often, personal stuff like this can help you crack passwords and PIN numbers, which makes it invaluable.

I hear him clear his throat just then, and worry that he knows what I'm thinking. So I turn to him once more, sensing the cuff that binds us tighten.

'It's just you look a little green,' he tells me. 'Scared of flying?'

I wanted to reply that I had no fear of being in the air. It was what I faced on *landing* that made me feel so sick with nerves. Instead, I look at my lap and tell myself he must be watching every move I make.

Some minutes later, we hit turbulence. The aircraft starts to shake and judder. An overhead locker springs open like a dropped jaw. The agent underneath reaches up to close it, which obliges the prisoner shackled to him to stretch from his seat uncomfortably.

In response, like a cruel taunt now, the light blinks on once more, advising us to buckle up.

2

Right now, I should be in lectures. It's Friday morning, which means Design Technology. Computer Studies is what really interests me, but it's actually Drama that I do best. I have a genuine flair for character acting, so my teacher says. Without her support, I would never have been permitted to combine such different subjects. You didn't get many vacancies for system software developers who could also do improvisation, but I knew other uses.

I also have an essay to deliver today, I remember. I hadn't even started it. My plan had been to work through the weekend and deliver it first thing on Monday. Most likely my tutor would mark me down as a result, but I could always tweak the grade. One of my first online conquests on starting college was to access the central database. With every student record stored here, I found I could subtly manipulate anything from notable achievements to attendance rates. Not just for me, of course, but anyone I could trust not to give the game away. I never made money from this kind of thing either. Instead, I earned the kind of favours and respect that ensured I never got a hard time for having a connection with computers.

Even if some people did quietly consider me to be a geek, I was well aware of how to turn that to my advantage. Like those who came to me for help, I would've improved my essay results by no more than half a grade if necessary. I didn't want to draw attention to myself, after all.

Which is why it had come as such a shock to be quietly picked up by the police on my way out of college yesterday.

The car had appeared out of nowhere. One moment I was walking along, quietly considering who I might find online at home. The next thing a dark saloon with smoked out windows was purring along behind me.

In my view, drivers who make out that they're too important to be seen are generally crying out for attention. Our college recently dealt with a cocaine dealer who did business at the back gate from a motor just like this. As caffeine was my drug of choice, I figured they would drive on by when it became clear I wasn't interested. So I pushed on, turning left into my street.

The car stayed right with me.

I remember wishing I had remained on the main road

all of a sudden. In public view, in case I was about to become the victim of a crime. I didn't turn around, however. Even when the vehicle doors opened and footsteps joined my own. I could actually see my house, midway along the terrace. I even decided that if I could make it to the gate these goons would walk on by. Just then, my home seemed like the safest place I could be. All I wanted to do was close the door behind me, check my email and a message board I used, and then get on with clearing my homework.

'Carl Hobbes?'

It took a moment for me to register my own name. And another to click that the person on my tail was talking to me. I switched around, unwilling to stop moving, and then faltered on seeing a couple of suits.

'Can I help?' I asked, somewhat uselessly.

I knew they weren't trying to sell me drugs. They were too old, too well dressed and well spoken for that.

'*Are* you Carl Hobbes?'

I looked from one of the two men to the other. In response, the guy asking the questions snapped a wallet open at me. I only caught a glimpse of a badge before he closed it again. It could've been anything. A day-pass to Disneyworld, for all I knew. Even so, it was enough to bring me to a stop.

'What's the matter?' I asked. 'Has something happened?'

I lived alone with my dad. This close to home, and

judging by the look on both guys' faces, I worried they had stopped me with some bad news.

As it turned out, I was right. But not in the way I had feared. Nor did it have anything to do with my activities on the college database. What I went on to hear was the last thing I expected, and the most shocking.

A third figure appeared from the front passenger seat just then. He clasped a walkie-talkie handset to his chest. From the car, I could hear radio chatter. And that's when a voice through the speaker mentioned Fort Knox.

'Come with us,' he said, as the man who had shown me his badge stepped around to stand at my side. I felt his hand grasp my upper arm from behind. Just then it felt as if I might fall down like a rag doll if he chose to let go. As they took my bag away from me, I thought about the books and papers inside. For some reason, I panicked that without them I'd be unable to complete my homework. The guy at the car held the rear door open for me. He was staring at me as we approached, reading the wrong thing from my stricken expression. 'It's over for you now. This thing is finished.'

3

Nobody has called me Carl for the last twenty-four hours. Ever since they picked me up, I've had to answer to Hobbes. My father was the last person to address me by my first name, and that was through the glass partition in the visiting room. 'Don't worry, Dad,' I assured him, despite feeling utterly dazed by what had happened, but he was in the same mind state as me. Frankly, nothing was going to shift the disbelief from his eyes. I knew he was thinking of my mother. Even if he didn't say as much, I could sense him question what she would have made of all this. I was taken back to my cell before he departed. I left him staring at the plastic seat. He could still be there for all I know.

My solicitor clearly hadn't dealt with a case like this before. I didn't hire her. It wasn't like that. I was simply read my rights at the station desk, and advised to get some legal representation.

'How?' That was my first response, which came out in barely a whisper. For I'd never been in trouble with the law before, as I tried to tell them then. I had no idea where to begin trying to appoint a lawyer, nor did I have any funds to hire one. The officer behind the desk said I should try to relax, handed me a laminated sheet with some numbers on it, and told me I qualified for legal aid.

'What does that mean?' I'd asked. It didn't sound good.

The officer had glanced at a colleague, who was sending a fax from the side-counter, and exchanged a playful glint. 'It means you are entitled to free professional advice,' he said, 'from an expert in dealing with drunks, drug addicts and wife-beaters.'

An hour later, I faced a tense young woman with mousy hair and a Biro that kept on failing as she scribbled down notes. Her name was Ms Lorna Greene. It said so on her badge.

'I'm sorry,' she kept saying, whenever the Biro stopped working. The third time, I began to wonder if Ms Greene was apologising for being so nervous, or because she knew more about why I had been brought in. She didn't ask me too many questions. Just the basics, I suppose. Finally, she stared at her notebook as if she couldn't read her handwriting, and then stood up to leave.

'Is something wrong?' I'd asked. I wasn't just lacking confidence in Ms Greene. I wanted someone who knew how to cut through paperwork *and* get me out of here. 'You are coming back, aren't you?'

She shouldered her bag, open at the clasp, and forced a smile. 'A lot of people have been called to this station because of you. Some of them have asked to speak to me.'

Five minutes later, and looking a lot more assertive, my solicitor returned to explain that an offer had been made.

'It's from the American authorities,' she began, as if this made it something I couldn't refuse. I'm not sure what I'd expected to hear. When Ms Greene finished, I had to ask her to repeat it so I could be sure I hadn't missed some kind of catch.

According to her, I had actually been invited by the Americans to *fly out* and answer some friendly questions. This wasn't an order, she stressed. It was a *request* for me to come voluntarily. Once they understood exactly how I had managed to hack into such a high-security financial institution, they would put me on a plane home again. I wouldn't be arrested or earn any criminal conviction. Not a caution or even a fine. As part of this package, my father would be forbidden from talking to the press, as would I on my return. In fact, they proposed that the whole thing would be kept completely off the record.

If word got out, of course, I would be known forevermore as *the hacker who broke into Fort Knox*.

It was the coolest thing I had ever done, and also the most reckless. Nobody was supposed to be able to compromise the Kentucky-based gold bullion depository. With almost five thousand tons of gold bars locked away inside the vault, it had earned its reputation as being the most secure location on earth.

Until now, that is.

I would be notorious, if people knew. Most probably I could even profit from the story for a while. And yet no interview or lecture fee could ever compare to the high price I'd pay for ruining the reputation of an institution the American people regarded as a national treasure. That's how my brief saw things, anyway. Ms Greene's delivery was designed to make me think she had really thought this through. Given the state she'd been in when I first met her, it simply helped me to conclude that someone had treated her with great respect out there. Someone who also clearly knew how to soften a hard sell. She even confessed that the offer 'broke every rule in the book and then snapped the spine clean in two', which clearly hadn't come from her. Even so, she strongly suggested that I accept.

My first response was obvious.

'I'm only seventeen.' I'd said this like she needed

reminding, even though she had all my details on the pad in front of her. 'Can they do this to me?'

'Technically, you're still a minor. So, your answer is no. They can't touch you until you turn eighteen.'

'Which isn't until later this year,' I'd pointed out, and then realised where she was heading.

'Do you know what you're getting for your birthday?' Ms Greene addressed me quite firmly this time, and gave me no time to reply. 'Because if you don't agree to come voluntarily it will be a very public arrest. I'm sure I can get you out for the time being, but you'd only be counting down the weeks and days until they come for you. And when they do, they'll want to exact some revenge on you for being so slippery.'

I remember shrugging at this, like a fool, because I was pretty sure she could tell I was frightened underneath.

'It would be quite a party,' was all I could think to reply, and then apologised immediately. 'I'm listening,' I promised, and sat up straight while she spelled it out. If I refused to accept their invitation right now, so she told me, the Americans would do it the official way. First, they'd haul me through the British courts, prosecuting me as an adult, of course, and then extradite me to face full charges across the water. Yes, I'd have a defence team, but at this level the prosecution would make sure the evidence against me was watertight. I could be looking at a very long term in a

13

penitentiary, she warned, and spared no detail on what a fresh-faced Brit boy might encounter in that kind of jail environment.

I told her I would sign the agreement immediately. She told me they were refusing to provide any paper-work, and then left to confirm my decision before I could change my mind.

4

At first light this morning, under a grey winter sky, I was driven to the airport by three police officers.

The handover was carried out in an interview room adjacent to the Customs and Excise Hall. All it had to offer was a desk, two plastic chairs and a mirror on the wall. This was when I met the special agent who would accompany me on the flight. He was a little heavyset, leaning on the desk with his back to me. I could see his face in the mirror, however, which reflected eyes pinched by years of either sunshine or laughter, but with dark bags underneath. The guy looked jet-lagged, in my view, but not unapproachable, which came as a relief. I had woken up long before they came for me, with a sick feeling in my guts about what I faced, so this very human face was kind of reassuring. I noticed he was looking at me, and so I braved a smile. He turned, asked for my full name, but didn't introduce himself. Instead, he addressed the officers, and just sort of shot

15

the breeze for a bit. He asked after their superior, claiming to have once played golf with him, before asking them to pass on his regards.

I should've started asking questions as soon as he dismissed them. I was alone for no more than thirty seconds before he returned with a jumpsuit, a pair of slip-on pumps and a transparent zip-lock bag. He placed the bag on the table, folded the jumpsuit over the back of one of the chairs, and then asked me to get changed.

'You can keep your socks and underpants,' he told me, turning to leave again. 'Everything else goes into the bag, including your wristwatch.'

'Why?'

'Procedure,' he said simply, and left me alone once again.

This time, I heard a lock turn from the outside.

I didn't move for a beat. I just stood there in a daze, like someone informed of a sudden death. I half expected him to bounce back in with a prankster's grin and a camera crew behind him, but all I could hear beyond that door were distant, muffled flight announcements. I looked at the jumpsuit, finally. It was bright orange, which made all this so hard to take in. People were paraded across the news in orange jumpsuits if they had done something very bad, or something very bad was about to be done to *them*.

Friendly questions. That's all I was facing. So long as

I told them everything they needed to know, I'd have my own clothes back in no time.

I barely recognised myself in the mirror. The jumpsuit was a size too big, and made me look scrawny. I fastened the press-studs from the bottom up, feeling like they must have mixed me up with someone else.

The week before I'd had my shaggy hair cropped close. I'd wanted to upgrade my appearance, but still wasn't used to the way it had reshaped my face. Studying my reflection in that room, with the jumpsuit collar scratching at my neck, my jaw line seemed harder somehow. My gaze more intense. I stared into those eyes, motionless under thick black slugs, and found it hard to connect with the convict staring back at me. Just then, it struck me that the mirror might be two-way. If so, there was a very good chance that I was being observed from the other side. Despite this, it didn't persuade me to turn around or act differently. It was as if I had been imprisoned in someone else's body, unable to think or act freely. Even when the man came back with wrist restraints, I simply held out my arms as directed, and bit down on my molars when he pulled them tight.

Everything will be OK, I kept telling myself, as he left the bag with all my stuff in it and led me through a warren of corridors. *This is just procedure*. It was only when he pushed through a side door onto the tarmac that I wondered out loud what on earth was going on.

He didn't reply. Just took me by the arm and escorted me briskly to the steps of a waiting plane. I knew nothing about aircraft, but this one didn't look cut out to cross the Atlantic. It was about six sizes too small for a start. The sort of private jet reserved for people you wouldn't normally encounter in your humdrum, everyday life.

'Where are we going?' I asked at the top of the steps. The engines had just started up, and the noise was hard to talk over. My legs felt weak and unstable all of a sudden. 'This wasn't what was agreed!'

He thumped on the door hatch with the side of his fist.

'There are some things I am authorised to tell you,' he said finally, like it pained him to string words together. 'Firstly, we're not operating in violation of any international treaties.'

'What?'

'In the interest of both British and American security,' he continued, raising his voice over the engines now, 'you will be taken to a third country and debriefed with full respect for your human rights. Now don't freak out on me,' he warned quickly, as if he had just departed from the script in a bid to keep me cool. 'We want to work with you on this. Understanding what you achieved could really be of benefit to us, which means hooking you up with military personnel at the top of their game.'

The special agent stopped there, as if giving up against the jet engine. Then the hatch door slid open, and he motioned for me to step aside.

Inside stood a pumped-out, shaven-headed suit. He could well have been under orders not to smile. If we were standing at the entrance to a nightclub, I wouldn't have given him a second glance. Instead I watched him slip the button on his jacket, and glimpsed a holster strapped inside.

'I got carried away with a computer!' I protested, reeling from it all. 'I'm not a terrorist!'

The special agent with me didn't reply. He just reached for the badge inside his coat. 'You don't need to worry about a passport,' he said next, and flashed it at the meathead with the handgun. 'This is a ghost flight.'

'Meaning what?'

'Put it this way,' he replied, coming closer to be heard, and jabbed a thumb at the main terminal, 'it ain't showing up on the departures board.'

I followed him through the hatch, into some warmth at least, and gasped at what I turned to face. There could have been no more than a dozen rows of seats on board, but in half of them sat men cuffed to their guards and dressed in the same colour jumpsuits as mine. Despite the regulation clothing, they could've come from all four quarters of the globe. Some were Middle Eastern, Asian or North African in appearance, but several faces looked Eastern European, I judged at a glance. The only other Western-looking white guy wearing orange was much older than me. He was kind of rangy looking, with straggly, slicked-back hair and one of those long bandit moustaches like he'd been plucked off a horse to be here. Everybody was looking at me, but only this one flashed a grin, like he had picked up on my fears and was relishing it.

'I don't understand,' I whispered, feeling tightness in my throat and chest. 'I thought I was flying to America. I want to speak to my solicitor.'

The agent took the window seat behind the guy still grinning at me. He'd had to practically drag me from the aisle before hissing at me to shut up. 'This is an extraordinary rendition,' he said under his breath. 'Your brief can't help any more. Now take it easy, Hobbes. If you cooperate you'll be home before the weekend is over. You won't need any representation, then. Just a hot bath, a decent sleep, and you can get on with your life.'

'Hold on!' I reached in vain to touch my temple, forgetting about the cuff. 'An *extraordinary rendition*? What *is* that?'

The guy looked like he was about to tell me, but a voice from the row in front cut in, with words that left me cold. 'It's a one-way ticket to hell, my friend. The Guantanamo Bay of the North awaits us all. Best you buckle up!'

5

Without my watch, I can only guess how long we have been in the air. Ninety minutes, perhaps. Two hours. Maybe more. After take-off, once I'd calmed myself as best I could, I had tried to track our direction by the position of the early-morning sun. It was easy to do, because we flew over an endless expanse of churned-up cloud, directly into the light. This meant we were heading east, not north, which gave me some hope that the moustachioed man in front of me was just some wise guy hoping to scare me. Then we banked several times and my bearings slipped.

After that, I found the time on my hands hard to kill. There was no in-flight movie. No refreshments, attendants or announcements. All the luxury fittings had been stripped out, in fact. The headrest in front quite clearly once housed a TV screen, and I imagined the pocket underneath used to be stuffed with select magazines for the rich and famous to read about themselves. Even if these distractions were here now, nothing would put me at ease. The seatbelt sign continues to flick on and off, but the turbulence can't compete with the real reason I'm so on edge.

What the moustachioed man had said really rattled me. Everyone knew Guantanamo Bay was a detainment camp for terror suspects. I followed the news. I just didn't want to be a part of it. The American government might have quietly admitted to the existence of other camps, but they didn't exactly host open days for them. Right now, I wondered what it was they had to hide.

I think back to everything the special agent has told me so far. It hasn't amounted to much. Even so, his unofficial assurances have spoken volumes. They told me I was in the care of someone who didn't just follow orders but could speak off the record if it meant getting the job done. Back home, when it came to gaining information I could use to achieve my aims online, this would be the kind of person I worked on. I wasn't exactly trying to sneak onto a server here, but something told me it might still be worth gaining his trust.

For even if I really *was* among America's most wanted, I had to believe what he'd shared with me. I wasn't like all the other guys in orange jumpsuits, after all. I had no war to wage with anyone. I was just being flown in with them to speak to their people. There'd be no need for them to put the squeeze on me. I'd tell them everything, no problem. They'd learn from me how I'd outwitted the vault's security measures, mark me down as a reckless idiot, maybe, and then send me packing. I had nothing to hide. No big secrets whatso- ever. This made me feel a little better, though I didn't stop twitching my feet. I felt wired. Restless. Holed up in my own world until a moment ago . . . when I realised we had begun a slow descent.

This time, the seatbelt light blinks on and doesn't go off again.

'Is this it?' I ask my partner in handcuffs.

'Just stopping off,' he says, and clears his throat. 'A pick-up.'

The fuselage continues to shake as we drop through the cloud canopy. I sense my hearing thicken. Pinching my nose doesn't clear it, and nor does swallowing. The crazy guy in front complains that his ears are really hurting, but the agent beside him says nothing.

With a clank and then a whine, the undercarriage can be heard unfurling. Even so, I can't work out how close to the ground we must be. The view through the port window is just one dirty white maelstrom. It looks like white noise on a TV screen. I settle in my seat. With nothing better to do, I even close my eyes. I stand no hope of sleeping, but feel so wrung out by what's happened that I should steal any moment I can to relax.

Behind me, just as my lashes mesh together, someone howls in pain.

My agent twists around in his seat, and I can't help but look as well. Three rows back, an agent is pressing a hand to his right ear, much to the surprise of the prisoner chained to his wrist beside him. The poor guy in the jumpsuit tries to edge away, as if to demonstrate he isn't responsible for whatever has happened.

'Goddamn this bucket!' the agent complains. 'I think I just burst an eardrum!'

'Take it easy,' the agent beside me instructs him, sounding like his superior. The edge to his voice also makes me think this isn't about seeing him through the pain. Certainly some heads begin to turn in interest.

'But Williams, the cabin pressure is a problem.'

'I said, take it *easy!*'

I glance at the man beside me, knowing his name now. Special Agent Williams settles back, tugging at an earlobe as he does so. My own hearing is still blocked, and I too can sense an ache building. I'm about to say something when the tyres nudge the runway. We lift again and tip to one side, then thankfully come back on a level. From the window, through the sleet, I make out airport buildings and hangars. A hoarding crowns the central terminal, but we are too far away to make out the lettering. By the time the plane has come to rest, in what appears to be a remote corner of the airfield, I feel like we're on board some kind of plague flight. The pressure in my ears has eased by now. It's the tension on board that remains as tight as ever. Turning to the window opposite, I see only conifers behind the perimeter fencing, thick with snow.

'Where are we?' I ask, overcome by curiosity.

Through the gap between the seats in front, the minder accompanying the crazy guy cautions him to keep his mouth shut. Williams spots it too, catches my eye and grins. 'Sweden,' he says, and then frowns theatrically. 'Or maybe Denmark, Norway, even Finland. I'm never sure of my bearings in this part of the world. Some day they might let me stretch my legs and look around.'

I can see that he is playing with me, which just makes me feel more determined to find out. I ask if he knows where we are heading. In response, Williams turns to the window once more. It signals an end to the questions. We're nowhere near the aircraft stands, I notice. What's more, the jet engines continue to spin. A police wagon speeds out to meet us, with its blue light revolving. Williams tuts to himself, 'Well done, fellas. Low key as ever.'

I face forward, feeling scared all over again. Every time I think I have got a grip, something shakes me up. It isn't the police wagon this time, even if I did just think on instinct that it was coming for me. It's the sense that the special agent at my side clearly makes this kind of journey on a regular basis. That he could purposely withhold so much information suddenly seems desperately unfair. It may be no big deal to him, but can't he see that I need some reassurance? I'm on this flight by invitation, or so I thought. Had I known that I'd be travelling with terrorists, chained up just like them, I might have opted for the court case.

'So, how far north are we heading?' I dare to ask, and turn to face him side on.

He pretends not to hear. Then I notice his jowls pinking. It tells me I have at least got through to him and even provoked a response. 'Do you need to visit the restroom?' he asks eventually. 'You're entitled to take a leak.'

I think about this for a moment, wondering how my question could've led him to this, but go along with it anyway. 'Does that mean you have to come with me?'

He nods, but despite his solemn expression there's no disguising the fact that we're fooling with each other here. 'In that case I'll pass, thanks all the same.'

'OK, but you should know that we have another *two* hours' flight time ahead of us. You'll have to go at some stage.'

'Right,' I say, and take this as the answer I had been holding out for. 'Thanks.'

A small victory, I think to myself, and settle into my seat. Not only do I know the name of my escort, he has just confirmed how much longer we have in the air. In front of my computer screen, I always made it my business to gather as much information as I could about a security system before I attempted to punch through it. I may have made some mistakes lately, but I would learn from that. The two facts I had picked up here didn't exactly help my case, yet. As a way of controlling the situation, however, I could at least consider it a start.

Just then, my attention is drawn further up the aisle. After several knocks on the fuselage the bald agent at the door hauls open the hatch. The elements howl outside, which makes me sit up smartly. Amid the swirling snowflakes, a voice barks out an order, upon which several guards appear with a single prisoner in their care. This one is wearing the regulation jumpsuit and plastic restraints, but his dead, hollow-eyed expression makes him stand out from the other faces on this plane.

'*I know you,*' I whisper to myself, as the crazy guy whoops and whistles at this new addition to the passenger list. It isn't someone I've ever met, but his appearance triggers a strong sense of recognition. He's unusually tall, a little stooped, with bone-white skin and greasy, crow-black hair that licks around his ears. His presence turns every head, but we're not looking at a rock star here. I know he's made headlines, and figure he must've done something nasty to earn his ticket on this flight. I draw breath to ask Williams, but freeze when those eyes rise from the gangway and find me.

In the skip of a heartbeat, I wonder if *he* knows who *I* am.

6

All good hackers must know how to deal with data. If they're going to achieve their objective, and overcome every ring fence that stands in their way, they'll need an ability to collect, store and retrieve information on the fly. Memory tricks can work wonders here, which basically tap into the way your brain is constantly coding and translating everything from objects and images to colours, smells and tastes. Personally, if I need to remember an item, name or face, I'll associate it with a card from a tarot deck. In my mind, each of the twenty-two major cards represents a small group of physical, mental or behavioural traits. It's basically much easier to summon a card from memory and serve up the information that way, than it is to scratch your head and curse the fact that it's right on the tip of your tongue.

The hollow-eyed man calmly accepts his seat across the aisle from me. The door is closed against the snowstorm, and a hush returns to the plane. I know for sure that I have never encountered him in my life. In my head, however, and much to my surprise, those tarot cards begin to turn.

That my recall isn't instant tells me I haven't purposely memorised his name. It isn't unusual for me to summon the name of a movie star or a band I like in this way. Certainly this guy isn't famous for the right reasons, as confirmed by the kind of cards that come to mind.

Judgement . . . Justice . . .

I dismiss each card in turn, working through them as they come. If I wasn't so distracted by his presence I'm sure I could think quicker. There's something deeply detached about him, I notice. He doesn't even *blink*, which makes me think he might have been sedated.

The Hanged Man . . . Death . . .

'Hobbes?' The voice beside me cuts into my thoughts. It makes me realise I have been openly staring at the new arrival. Special Agent Williams isn't even looking my way but at the view from the window as the plane begins to taxi once again. 'A word of advice, son. Your welfare is my priority. Now you got to help me do this,' he says, and turns to glance briefly across the aisle. When he speaks again, he leans in close to my ear. 'Keep your business to yourself, understand? Don't be concerned with what other people have done to win themselves all these Air Miles. Because at some point my back's going to be turned, like for example when you need the can.' Again he stops there, allowing his point some space to breathe. At the same time, the plane squares up to the runway, awaiting clearance for take-off.

I feel my cheeks heat at this, and figure his advice must be worth taking. Even so, as the plane accelerates all of a sudden, I can't help but notice that the man remains in his plastic tie restraints. Either the agent accompanying him has simply forgotten this, despite sharing a handcuff, or he's opted to overlook procedure for his own peace of mind.

I'm scoping my neighbour from the edge of my vision, straining so hard that my eye muscles ache. All I can really see are his bound hands resting on the clip of his seatbelt. I notice how slender and angular his fingers seem, meshed casually in his lap. Just as I'm thinking I should quit looking altogether, something about his posture changes. It's only a slight twisting of his spine, perhaps, but it's enough for me to glance up and realise that I now have his full attention.

A gasp dies in my throat. I snap my gaze to the front, only to be drawn back by his sheer force of presence. I meet his stare directly. Immediately, one card comes to mind and remains there: *The Devil*.

Associating anyone to this card speaks for itself, and in a blink his name forms soundlessly on my lips. It's *Grimstad*. Thomas Grimstad. He nods in response,

30

a mere tipping of his head, and suddenly I am left with the feeling that I know too much about this individual already.

This time, I face the front and stay that way. For his crimes have made headlines, which is how I came to file his name away unconsciously, along with a press picture that fitted his face. The plane lifts into the air just then, which makes me feel even more uncomfortable. Finally, I sense that I am no longer the subject of his unshakeable stare, and breathe out as quietly as I can. From the seat beside me, I hear Special Agent Williams murmur, 'That'll learn you,' but pretend not to hear. Instead, I focus on getting through the next two hours without making a bad situation much worse for myself. I might know what kind of atrocity Grimstad is capable of committing, then again, as I remind myself now, he's no longer in a position to repeat it.

I close my eyes as we climb, feeling every shudder through the fuselage pass through me. My ears begin to play up again, but I'm determined not to make a fuss. I wonder how the agent behind us is doing. The one who complained earlier. I figure he'd made a big song and dance about nothing. I don't know much about burst eardrums, but I'm sure it would cause more than just a sharp intake of breath. I make myself yawn, hoping to clear my hearing. If the pain would only go away, I'd be thankful for the fact that my ears have muffled the drone of the jet engines. By shutting myself away inside my thoughts, I feel like I'm in the one place where nobody can touch me.

Given the conditions, I half wonder if the flight crew in the cockpit have been ordered to fool with the cabin pressure. I try swallowing several times to make everything good again, but it doesn't help. Maybe, I think, this is how they begin to work on breaking down the resolve of some of the more determined detainees. It certainly didn't sound very legal. I dwell upon what would stop me from going public about this on my return. I had been made to swear a vow of silence, as had my father, but none of it was in writing. I picture myself sharing the story with people at college, and then wonder whether I'd been requested to stay quiet for my own good.

It isn't funny, imagining how people would lift their eyebrows questioningly, and maybe even humour me, whilst not believing a word. Even so, I can't help smiling at how ridiculous it is that I am considered dangerous enough to be handcuffed. Instinctively, I hide my mouth behind my free hand, and am surprised to find my top lip is wet.

I open my eyes, but it takes a beat for me to realise that the dark jammy stuff on my fingertips is blood. I swear under my breath. Weirdly, it sounds like I'm speaking from behind a closed door. I take a breath to alert Special Agent Williams, but somehow my lungs don't respond as they should. Alarmed, I try again, and realise that the air is lacking somehow. Then I hear a clenched, muffled curse from the front of the plane, not the back this time. Special Agent Williams springs forward in his seat, searching for the source of the outburst, and that's when I know that something is very wrong indeed. For a trickle of blood has beaded from Williams' ear onto the collar of his shirt. He looks down at me, and then reaches for his lobe in bewilderment.

'Oh no—'

The way my hearing is working makes me feel like I am two steps behind what's happening. People are out of their seats now, mostly agents but some of the prisoners are panicking and one further down is gulping for air like a landed fish. I can't tell if we're continuing to lose air, but it's certainly growing colder. I want to leave my seat, like Williams, but he orders me to stay put.

'Take steady, shallow breaths, understood? Is that clear, Hobbes?'

He shows me the palm of his free hand, and then barks across at the agent accompanying the detainee called Grimstad. I switch around to see what's going on, clinging to the idea that somehow Williams would never allow us to die. The guy in front isn't laughing any more, I notice, but cowering in a crash position. Only the prisoner in the aisle seat opposite appears unconcerned.

This time, I'm the one who stares unashamedly. Grimstad doesn't register me, but faces forward like he's lost in some imaginary in-flight movie. The agent beside him is yelling into a walkie-talkie now about a *situation*, and clearly struggling to make himself heard. I can see that Grimstad must be suffering as we are because a black bead of blood slips from his nostril, and yet not once does he stir. A horn goes off from inside the closed cockpit, just then. Whatever it means, the noise alerts the pilot to what has to be a major fault with the cabin pressure, for immediately the plane see-saws into a steep descent. The engines max out, and I feel myself lift against the seatbelt. For a moment, everyone falls quiet. When the oxygen masks tumble from the overhead consoles, the chaos resumes in the scramble to breathe freely once more.

It's only when the pressure in my ears begins to ebb that I start shivering. Maybe it's a delayed response or a result of the plunge in temperature, but I am not alone in reacting like this to what's happened. As soon as the plane begins to level out, I snap off the mask, as does Williams, and swear in relief under my breath. I hear some of the agents act to keep their charges calm as much as themselves. Even Williams tells me to watch my tongue. The only individual needing no such attention is Grimstad. There isn't a trace of blood on the oxygen mask hanging in front of him. The kinks still present in the cord make me think he hasn't even

34

tried to stretch it to his face. He's wise to the burst vessel in his nose, however, because he's dabbing at his nostrils. There's no concern on his face when he inspects his bloodied hand. Instead, by bowing his head closer to his bound hands, he daubs a strip across each cheek like war paint. Despite the turmoil, when he sits back an expectant smile crosses his lips.

And with a jolt, I realise it's this exact smile that had made his picture in the press so disturbing. Captured on a mobile phone, it was one of those shots that made headlines for what it *didn't* show.

The plane sinks through storm clouds as I think about what must have been going through his mind at that time. It's a manoeuvre that feels more like a 4x4 bottoming out on a mud track, such are the bone-jarring shakes and bangs we endure.

'Hang in there, Hobbes!' Special Agent Williams rests a firm hand on my shoulder. 'Didn't I say you're safe with us?'

Despite his tone, and the fact that the pilot appears to have the aircraft back under control, I sense that Williams is as rattled as I am. It's understandable, having just dropped rapidly to an altitude that wouldn't tear us apart at the seams. I wonder if we're simply going to press on at this level. We might be able to breathe again, but the turbulence is terrible. Despite everything, Thomas Grimstad is still smiling. While everyone around him is struggling to gather their wits,

7

Touchdown, when it arrives, brings little sense of relief. If anything, it just changes the nature of the tension on board the plane. For an hour or more we've had to fly closer to the ground than the cloud cover. It commanded the kind of silence on board that made me think every single passenger was holding their breath.

'Just relax,' Special Agent Williams kept saying, without once shifting his gaze from the headrest in front of him. 'Everything is good.'

From there on out, I'd spent much of the time looking down upon a rolling expanse of snow and pine forest, praying that we wouldn't end up ploughing into it. Sometimes the plane would lift and tilt a little, and the terrain rose and sloped accordingly. If we were forced to fly this low because of a problem with the cabin pressure, I had thought to myself, the comfort zone must be desperately slim. I knew that I was way out of mine, and hurtling further from it with every mile we made. It didn't get any better when the plane headed out over open sea. Wreathed in mist, the grey and choppy water seemed way too close for comfort. I could see foam topping every lick and swell, which was more than enough detail. It didn't tell me anything about our location. All I could take in was that we were too low for comfort but lucky to be alive.

Nobody needed the oxygen masks. They'd simply swung over our heads as a constant reminder of what we had been through. My throat felt horribly tight, and my nose itched as the blood inside it dried. I also couldn't stop thinking that I really needed to move around. I'd been sitting in the same position for ages and wanted to stand, if only for a moment. I thought about asking Williams, but remained quiet all the same. I figured if I was going to need some favours from him, this one was not important. Even when one of the flight crew eventually approached him for a quiet word, I didn't dare ask what it was about. I'd watched Williams nodding as the man spoke into his ear, and then tip back smiling as if he'd just been promised an upgrade on the flight home.

Flying so low made me think we were about to land at any time, and nobody likes the feeling that brings. Even when you're on board an aircraft making a textbook approach it's natural to question whether these are your last few seconds on earth. As conditions worsened outside, obscuring the ocean below, that sense of dread had plenty of time to eat into me.

By the time the landing gear actually locked into position beneath us, I had already sweated into the fabric of my seat.

'Here we go!' The guy in the row in front of us is the first to break the silence. He sounds all fired up again, and breaks into a giggle when the plane banks steeply to one side. He may *sound* unhinged, but judging by his physical presence he isn't too crazy to work out on a regular basis. Through the blizzard outside I see a rugged shoreline take shape, with a canopy of trees massed on the slopes behind it. The rise is so steep it appears to reach up towards us. I feel the plane lift again, continuing to turn, and as it clears the ridge a vast, snow-bound peninsula opens out underneath us. Very briefly, on account of the plane's scything manoeuvre, I glimpse a makeshift-looking landing strip. Running parallel with the ridge, it's marked out in the snow by a long funnel of flares. This tapers towards the shoreline, which must tuck around the forested rise to create the headland here. I spot a sizeable outpost at the water's edge, but my view is robbed as we straighten out to make our approach. All I can see now is a white-fringed grandstand of pine trees, scored by trails and rocky outcrops. As we descend, so the line between this ridge and the sky slowly climbs up my window. I sense there's no going back. A shift in the sound of the slipstream tells me the ground must be metres away. I press into my seat when the wheels connect, bouncing once before the pilot drops us squarely onto the surface. I reach for the armrests, braced for the worst, only to find Agent Williams has already occupied the one between us.

'At last,' he mutters sourly over the roar of the air brakes.

We trade a single glance. Despite the earlier bravado, he's evidently relieved to be on the ground. He releases his grip on the armrest now, and twists his wedding ring with his other hand. It tells me the guy is stressed, far from his family, and yet in this brief moment he's glad to be alive. Above all, it means his guard is down. If I'm going to make a bid to build on this fragile bond we've made, now is the time to strike.

'I think the worst is over,' I say. Williams ignores me, but I don't turn and face the front. 'I just wish that applied to me as much as it does to you.'

Immediately, his lips tighten. But he can't disguise his amusement. I'm in no mood to be this upbeat. Still, I smile along with him, praying I have done enough to draw the man from the harsh formality of his role. Finally, at long last, he shakes his head and grins outright.

'A flight like that can't do much for your nerves, I guess. I'm thinking you'd never have come voluntarily if you'd known it would be this bad.'

'I'll survive,' I reply. 'But maybe I'll find my own way home.'

Special Agent Williams chuckles once, and then regains his composure straight away. He glances outside as we taxi down the runway, and for a moment I think I have failed. A second later, as if having just consulted his thoughts, he comes back around. 'These are sensitive times,' he begins, using the engine noise to prevent being overheard. 'We can't just make a flight like this in a military aircraft. Many countries simply wouldn't permit us to cross their airspace, let alone touch down to pick up persons of interest to us. So, in their wisdom, the powers that be hire commercial planes like this. The advantage is we get to sit in buff seats, which frankly beats the benches you'd find inside an air force transporter. The downside is that we place our lives in the hands of private contractors. Obviously, the administration want to avoid unwanted attention, and so they tend to assign us a worn-out pair of wings like this. If the pilot wasn't one of ours, we'd have vanished from the radar just as soon as this hunk of junk lost cabin pressure.' He checks his watch, and then leans across me to peer through the glass on the opposite side. 'We use sites like this one for the same reason. We're out of sight and out of mind, in places that no longer serve a useful purpose to anyone else. Some nations accommodate our needs without question. Others require diplomacy and persuasion, of course, or register their position by offering us desolate hellholes.'

Listening to this, I wonder if he really had told me so much because I'd tapped into his relief that we've made it in one piece. Then I think perhaps it's because we've arrived somewhere so remote that such information is useless to me. 'But no matter how lousy some detainment camps can be,' he finishes, and smiles wryly to himself, 'at least a camp can't fall out of the sky.'

He might be joking, but a jolt runs through me when he says this. Until now, my only clue that we were heading to a detainment camp was from the clown one row in front. Now Williams had referred to it directly, and the hairs on the back of my neck immediately lift and prickle. It's hard to see much through the needles of snow, however. The forest slope forms a dark band over there, while the flare closest to us is beginning to taper and smoke. I see no other sign of life, which simply makes me feel like we've arrived in the back of beyond.

'Stay in your seats, people.' With the engines killed now, Agent Williams turns to address his team. 'Let's do this by the book.'

Immediately after the plane comes to a halt, the shaven-headed agent leaves his seat. Once more, he hauls open the hatch in front of the cabin, and again an icy rush of air greets us. This time, it is joined by the sound of attack dogs barking. I may not be able to see much from my window, but I can tell that they are straining at the leash. The agent at the hatch stands aside now, making room for the first of two soldiers in white battledress: one male, one female. They enter carrying an olive-green container between them with a number code stamped on one side. I try to see what's inside when they crack open the lid. This only becomes clear when they begin tossing pillow-sized plastic packs to the agents accompanying each prisoner. Williams catches his pack with both hands, and sets it on his lap.

'Welcome to your weekend retreat,' he tells me quietly, turning the pack over in his hands. 'The good thing is, this tells us they're expecting you.'

I am not sure whether to look out at my surroundings once more, hoping to get my bearings, or simply stare at the pack. It's covered in a transparent plastic wrap, which Williams snaps away in one go. Other agents have already broken open their packs, which all contain the same things.

'So, this is where we get off?' I suggest, eyeing the sleeveless jacket and pull-down hat. Both are blood orange in colour, a darker shade to the jumpsuits, and made from a synthetic-looking fleece.

'It's just to get you into the compound,' says Williams. 'The cold has teeth out here, and you do have some rights.'

He lets the jacket fall open, keeping the hat on his lap.

'What about you?' I ask, eyeing the suit he's squeezed into.

Williams shifts his attention to me for a moment, and grins. I draw breath to ask if there should be gloves in the pack. What I really want to point out is that these pumps I've been made to wear aren't going to protect me at all. As it is, I say nothing. On hearing the sound of rifle bolts locking into position, I look to the front and immediately forget about footwear.

There, the two soldiers who have just unloaded the box now stand with weapons poised. I have never had a gun pointed at me before. It feels like a very bad joke and a terrible mistake all rolled into one. Then I wonder whether they're here to kill us all. I try to shrink in my seat, but find I can't move a muscle. I sense my stomach knot, and just try to breathe through it. Williams continues to shake out the creases in my fleece, seemingly oblivious to what's just happened. Then our shaven-headed friend steps forward, and I see him refer to a clipboard in his hands.

'McCoy?' he calls out. In front of us, the agent accompanying the crazy guy responds by lifting his hand. 'OK,' he tells the agent wearily, and strikes something off the list. 'Bring out your dead.'

I hear two seatbelts unclip, one after another, and then the man called McCoy is led into the aisle. Having only really heard random bursts of chatter from this guy, I get a good look at him at last. His shoulder-length hair is receding at the temples, with generous eyebrows over pale blue eyes. What's most noticeable about him is the moustache. It forks way down both sides of his mouth, doing little to counter his long, chiselled face. Nor is there any disguising the gleeful grin he directs at me. Immediately, I look away. This combatant might be revelling in the attention he's receiving, but I'm not here for that. All I want to do is keep my head down, clear my name and go home.

'How do you want me?' I hear McCoy say. 'This is fun!'

Beside me, Agent Williams tuts to himself and shakes his head.

'I want you to shut up and follow my orders,' the agent in the aisle replies. 'Now, I'm going to unlock the cuff so you can climb into the coat. Just don't go forgetting that if you so much as *breathe* aggressively, we will respond with a bullet between the eyes. Is that clear?'

'Very good, cap'n. I'm your bitch now.'

I can't place the man's accent, but it's rough and kind of salty sounding. It's neither English nor Australian, but something midway between. Aware that McCoy has turned away from me to face the agent, I dare to look up once more. The two soldiers command my attention. They're still poised with their fingers curled around the triggers, braced for one wrong move. Once again, I think to myself that there has been some big mistake.

Any moment now, the shaven-headed agent will find my name on his clipboard, screw up his brow and get on the radio to find out how the hell some wetback kid could've wound up on board the flight. I watch him for a moment, but he doesn't seem at all concerned by his list. He's observing McCoy with total contempt, waiting for this clown to zip into his jacket and tug the hat over his ears. As soon as he's done, the agent tests a fresh plastic restraint for strength, and asks McCoy to show him both wrists. This is the cue for the bald agent to order both soldiers to stand aside. They do so without once taking their sights from the detainee, who is marched to the front of the plane now, and then out into the blizzard.

The agent with the clipboard consults his list again, pawing his dome as he does so. He reads out another surname but it doesn't register. Not until the soldiers swing around, and level their rifles at me.

'It's your turn, Hobbes.' Agent Williams unclips his seatbelt with his free hand. He must notice that I've frozen. Even my breathing has halted as I stare at both barrels. I feel his hand close over my wrist, and then unlock the cuff that binds us. 'Nothing bad is going to happen,' he says, and motions for me to release my own seatbelt. He takes one look at my face and adds, 'It's just procedure. Trust me.'

8

Special Agent Williams directs every move I make. I am privately grateful to him, because as soon as I am up on my feet I feel weak at the knees. This has nothing to do with being seated for a long period of time. It's down to the simple fact that two marksmen are watching me, as well as a band of individuals who are clearly considered to be a major threat.

Thomas Grimstad has barely blinked since the plane dropped down to a height that stopped all the bleeding. For a man whose actions have caused international outrage, he really is unnervingly calm. What rattles me more is the blood daubed across his cheekbones. A sign, I think, that things are still ticking over inside that mind of his – primed to go off at any time. Just knowing that I am struggling into a sleeveless fleece beside Europe's most infamous would-be suicide bomber is badly distracting. I fumble with the zipper, assured only by the guiding voice of the agent before me.

'That's it, Hobbes. Now the hat . . . your wrists . . . we're done. OK, just stand quietly for a moment.'

I do exactly as I am told. With rifles pointing at me, I'm conscious of every breath and move I make. I don't take my eyes off Williams as he reaches for the overhead locker like the agent before him and hauls out a full-length jacket for himself. The charcoal grey colour, not to mention the fine wool tailoring, makes me think he looks more like a businessman dressed for a cold snap. I don't dare to look around when he turns to lead the way, even though many eyes follow me as I pass row after row.

The shaven-headed agent fails to look up from his clipboard when we reach him. He simply stands aside for us, then calls out another name: *Thomas Grimstad*. As a result, I leave the plane feeling as uneasy about what's behind me as I am about what's outside.

'Move on, Hobbes. We're not here to admire the view.'

It's the clear ferocity of the barking that has stopped me at the hatch. I have always been wary of dogs. I don't like to admit that being near them makes me nervous, but it's a fact, and one I find hard to conceal on facing my welcoming party.

Despite orders, my feet instinctively stop moving, I look around, and find I have to squint to see anything in this blizzard. The sudden plunge in temperature makes my eyes smart. It also hits the back of my throat as I breathe. Even the air is a shock to my system. It feels as thin as it had before the plane was forced to drop. Despite the force of the wind gusting across this terrain, there's no mistaking the guard dog awaiting me at the foot of the aircraft steps. It's an Alsatian, straining hard against the leash. Judging by the handler's stance, this black-and-brick-coloured demon would go for my throat if permitted. I simply stare for a moment as it twists, snarls and snaps in my direction. Then I become aware that the path from the plane leads to a single-storey building. It's only a short distance, twenty metres or so, and yet it's marked by half a dozen more dogs and their handlers.

'Don't let me down,' says Williams, sounding gruff all of a sudden. We're still at the top of the steps. He backs up to clear the way for me, flips his collar up against the snowstorm, and stretches on the gloves he's just pulled from his pocket. I watch him work his fingers in snugly, wishing I could do likewise. 'I know what you're thinking,' he says next, raising his voice to be heard. 'You're looking at me and asking yourself "why does this fat ass get to wrap up warm?" and it's a fair point. You just have to trust me when I say this isn't personal. Every detainee is processed in the same way, but I don't draw up the rules, OK?'

'Whatever you say,' I reply, thinking at the same time that if they're hoping to provoke me into some kind of confrontation then they've picked the wrong person.

Yet more barking draws my attention. Right now it isn't the cold that troubles me as much as the dogs. I tell myself they're here for show, and focus on just getting down to ground level. This time, I sense Williams close behind me. He presses one hand into the small of my back, guiding me, it seems.

The handler, wearing the same white fatigues as the soldiers on board the plane, drags his dog away to make some space at the foot of the steps. I don't stop moving this time. I just turn into the headwind as directed and make my way towards the hut. The surface of the airstrip is really just ice and grit. As soon as my pumps hit the ground I can actually feel the terrain through the thin rubber soles. The snow that has been shovelled away forms a bank on each side of the airstrip. It also borders the loop at the far end where the planes must taxi and turn around. Beyond it, through the fragments of this blizzard, I glimpse the shoreline. I can't see much, but the ocean beyond looks strangely static. In these conditions, I'd expect to see foam-tossed waves and crashing breakers. It's only when I notice ice debris littering the surface that I realise this body of water that cuts around the headland has entirely frozen over.

We might be thousands of miles from home. So far from civilisation that the seaward horizon could mark the edge of the world. Even so, the hut we're approaching reminds me of one of those temporary classrooms they used to drop in by crane at my old school. It's really just a long, corrugated metal box with meagre windows and a ramp in front of the door. I glimpse a row of snow bikes, half buried in a drift behind the hut. In the snow beside it lies a dark shape that demands a second glance. I can't just stop and stare, but that's exactly what I want to do. My knees go loose as I take it in, and all the breath leaves my lungs involuntarily. *For I'm looking at a corpse.* I am sure of it, despite the blizzard: a body frozen in the snow. I try to turn so I can alert Williams, but his hand comes down on my shoulder, steering me onwards. Immediately, I question whether this means he is aware of it. Because if he is then death must be a regular feature here.

For the first time since I left England, I am overwhelmed by a sense of panic. Online, if I ever got out of my depth, I could simply sever the connection. Even on the plane I had managed to keep myself reasonably cool under pressure. Williams must pick up on it because he doesn't let me go, just frogmarches me forward a couple of metres. Now what I see tells me more about my state of mind than anything else. For that body in the snow is, in fact, a twisted tarpaulin cover. I feel no relief, however. Just shaken up and overwhelmed. I walk on as directed, aware that I must *not* lose it like that again, and grit my teeth to stop them from chattering.

9

Inside, I find McCoy and the agent minding him. They stand in front of the far wall, foregoing the bench bolted to the floor just behind them. McCoy marks my arrival with a wink, and shows me a gap in his teeth. A streak of blood has dried under one nostril, which makes him look like he's been in a fight. The agent with him has zipped his jacket up so high against the cold that his chin is hidden from view. The room is divided in two by a simple partition and glass hatch. We're on the under-furnished side, with not even a potted plant or a picture in sight. The soldier working at the desk on the other side seems oblivious to our presence. That his coat is slung over the back of his chair makes me think it's altogether more inviting in there than this chill, bare space we're in.

If this were a dentist's waiting room, you'd take one look and walk right out again. But then I wasn't here to have a tooth extracted. It was information they wanted from me. And if the special agent at my side would only listen, I'd tell him everything right now.

Without a word, Williams encourages me to cross the floor and stand next to the agent beside McCoy. When I turn around, I find two more soldiers with their weapons locked on to me. It feels like I'm facing a firing squad. Even so, having walked off the plane without incident, I feel sure that simply keeping my nerve will keep fingers from squeezing triggers.

Grimstad falls in, accompanied not just by his special agent but one of the soldiers from the plane. I look to the open door, stupidly wishing my dad would show up, but the next figure in wears the same regulation fleece and hat as the rest of us.

'Ain't this shaping up to be a fine beauty pageant,' McCoy mutters. 'So many pretty faces in one room!'

'*Silence!*' At once the agent with him is bawling at the man to be quiet. 'The prisoner will shut the hell up until he is spoken to, understood?'

'Yessir,' McCoy replies, sounding drastically humbled.

The outburst serves to still those detainees who had been shuffling from foot to foot, or shaking their arms in a bid to get warm. I'm aware that I am trembling. I just can't be sure if it's from the cold or the situation I'm in. I grit my teeth, and focus on the worn linoleum that covers the floorboards in here. Wet boot prints fan out from the door, and continue to spread until every detainee is present.

The last man to come through the door is no prisoner. He's wearing the same winter camouflage as the soldiers, but has stripes all over his lapels and a peaked cap pulled low over his eyes. He is dark-skinned, with a close-cut grey beard. The way he stands before us is so calm and measured that it makes him seem almost presidential. He clasps his hands behind his back, then requests one of the agents to close the door and join him at his side.

'Gentlemen,' he says next. 'I understand it's been a tense flight, so let's make this orientation brief.' He pauses there, which is evidently a cue for the agent beside him. For he addresses us now in Arabic, translating for those who do not speak English. Following this, he switches to a tongue I don't recognise, and appears to ask a question. Nobody answers. I figure everyone present must be familiar with one of the two languages.

'My name is Commander Stagger,' the ranked officer continues. 'And if there's one thing we have in common it's this: I don't want to be here any more than you. None of us consider this to be a dream post. As you will appreciate, conditions are extreme and unforgiving,' he adds, with a nod to the window behind us, 'but they also guarantee your safety.'

The agent picks up with the translation then, but I don't stop looking at Stagger. I place him in his fifties, perhaps. A little older than Agent Williams, but in good

55

shape. 'I imagine some of you might be wondering why you haven't arrived here wearing blacked-out goggles. This is a classified location, of course, and the last thing we want is for details to leak out about our whereabouts. But let me ask you this.' He pauses there, and draws our attention to the open door. 'Do *you* know where you are?' Outside, the blizzard is so intense that even the runway is hard to see. 'This is the middle of nowhere,' he continues. 'And I mean that quite literally. Out here, we are cut off from the rest of the world. It's an ice-cold Alcatraz, my friends. There are no roads or footpaths, and the terrain is treacherous. The nearest settlement, one with global communication facilities, is one-twenty-five kilometres from here. Without adequate protection or transport, you'd stand a better chance of reaching Mars.' This time, he continues to speak as the agent chases behind with the translation. 'As for the sub-zero temperatures, on a good day it can sink to minus twelve. By night, it drops another ten. Factor in the windchill and you're talking very negative numbers. Enough to freeze the blood, in fact. In short, you'd be dead by dawn. It means we can be guaranteed that you're not going anywhere. More importantly, we can be sure that nobody will be coming for *you*. And judging by the activities that brought you to our attention, it's reasonable to assume that many people in this world would want to see you six feet under.'

Commander Stagger paces the room again while the

translation takes place. Not once does he look at me, or any other detainee. It's as if he's come here to inspect the floor. All I can think is that I'm here because I'm guilty of highlighting weak points in a secure system. I hardly see why anyone would want to kill me over something like that.

'Now that you're officially under my care,' he continues finally, 'I see no further need for restraints. That's not because I *trust* any of you,' he adds quickly, raising his voice to make the point. At the same time, Williams gestures for me to raise my bound wrists. I see the other agents do likewise, including one who unfolds a penknife from his pocket. From the corner of my eye I watch him step up to the detainee at the end of the line and snap the blade upwards through the plastic tie.

I turn away as the agent with the knife makes his way along the line, and just look right through him when he comes to sever mine.

'If you want to make a break for it then go right ahead,' Stagger goes on, as if this is an open invitation. 'Be my guest, fellas. The door is wide open. You won't get a better chance than this. For one time only I give you my word that we won't come after you. It should be remembered by one and all that you're easy to spot in orange. We'll just watch you giving it your best shot while the elements close in and shut you down. You should also be aware that out here hypothermia is never far away. When the shivering stops, that's when you should start to worry. It's your body's way of signalling that it's lost the battle to keep your blood warm. But by then, you'll be too weak to retrace your steps. Chances are you'll be so confused and disorientated that you won't even recall what it was you were fleeing in the first place. All you'll want to do is lie down in the snow and close your eyes.' As he speaks, I think about the tarpaulin I had mistaken for a corpse. I even wonder if it had been arranged like that as a warning to the new arrivals. 'Death, when it comes, won't be painless,' stresses Stagger. 'If you've reached the point where jagged ice crystals form in your cells, you'll be grateful for the heart attack it can trigger. Otherwise, you could spend your final minutes feeling like you're being sliced up from the inside. In short, gentlemen, the cold is all you have to fear here. Some of you may be seasoned killers, but for sheer cruelty you're no match for Mother Nature.'

He steps to one side at this, giving us all a clear view of the atrocious conditions outside. Nobody moves. We just listen to the agent complete the translation. Even if anyone here had failed to understand the Commander, they don't break the silence that follows.

'In a moment from now, we'll be making the short walk to the main compound.' Stagger fills the space with his voice. 'It's a matter of minutes from here at a brisk march, but it's going to be cold. *Very* cold. As a rule, every detainee who is required to step outside is entitled to wear insulated gloves, headgear, jackets, pants and boots. Before this requirement comes into effect, of course, we have to sign you *in*.' He lets the translator speak freely here, though I can't help thinking he's stopped on purpose so we think about what this means. 'I guarantee that in a few minutes from now those of you who were thinking of escape will realise I just saved your lives.' This time, he faces the translator, waits for him to finish and then circles an upturned finger at the guards. 'OK, let's get these people inside the cage.'

I turn to Williams, as if to check that I understood, but he seems tuned out of proceedings. I think twice about talking out of turn, in case I get the same tongue-lashing as McCoy. Even so, I want to know more about what I can expect during my time here, in case I have a problem with it. I have played nicely ever since they took me in, despite the fact that nobody has been entirely straight with me. Now this talk of cages, death threats and perishing from the cold just took it all a step too far.

'Can I ask you a few things?' I say finally, as the last detainee to enter the hut is ordered to lead the way. 'Just quickly?'

'Not now.' Agent Williams doesn't even look at me when he says this. He's just fished out his mobile phone, and is studying the face with a frown. 'No signal whatsoever. Not even a goddamn bar.' He rubs the display against the fabric of his jacket. It doesn't change his expression, however. 'Every time I'm despatched to this dump, I might as well cease to exist.'

'It's important.'

'It can *wait*, Hobbes!' The force of his response takes my breath away. Increasingly, Williams had appeared to warm to me. Suddenly, he lays waste to my efforts by blowing up like this. Even so, I'm not sure I'm completely to blame. It's as if I just bothered a man with much on his mind. He shuts down his mobile, and returns it to his inside pocket with a curse. 'At least *you* can hear me loud and clear, son. Now, fall in behind the others. You'll have time to ask questions later. And in return we got plenty for you.'

10

This is serious. As I follow the order to file out into the snowstorm, I begin to tremble once again. It isn't just the cold that's eating into me now. I feel like a small child who has just witnessed a parent flare up. It's a natural response, I think, when an individual you've trusted with your life shows a hint of being a monster inside.

All I know for sure is that I'm caught up in something that really shouldn't be happening to me. I want to turn around and tell Williams that all of this is just so unnecessary. He could've just shown up at the police station where I'd first been taken and got exactly what he wanted. All he would've had to do was sit down with me in an interview room and I'd have spared no detail. He'd have learned everything without resorting to pressure or threats. Instead, I feel tricked into coming to God knows where, and I'm not coping well with it. The elements outside help to hide how I'm really feeling; such is the howling wind, the snowfall and the temperature. It means I can hunch low, pinch up my eyes and battle with my streaming nose. In fact *every* detainee looks like they're snivelling in these conditions, which is no surprise given our clothing. With little in the way of protective layers, I can actually *feel* my body-heat deserting me. Even so, I wonder if Williams has picked up on what's causing me such anxiety.

'You can do this, Hobbes,' he says, sounding like he's back on my side again. Having seen what he could be like underneath the team-talk, however, his words don't do much to reassure me. 'All you got to do is get through those doors, and the worst will be over.'

'You told me nothing bad would happen at all!' I remind him, aware that we can't be heard over the blasting wind.

'Nothing bad *is* going to happen. Now focus, Hobbes. Quit busting my balls!'

We're following a path through the snow that must have been shovelled out just before our arrival. It cuts between the hut and the airstrip. This time, despite the blizzard and the caravan of orange-clad figures ahead of me, I have an unbroken view of the water beyond. I am close enough now to see how the frozen surface has clashed against itself, fracturing in places and throwing up sheets and splinters in all directions. Some have been shaped into points by the wind, others have sheared off completely, but it's the big trawler boat that grabs my attention. There it is, scuppered in the shallows with its back end submerged and sealed under the ice. It could've been there for decades, judging by the rust and decay.

Up ahead, one of the dogs marking the way lunges at the leading detainee. His handler makes no effort to tighten the leash, which forces the detainee to shrink sharply to his left. The agent at his side keeps him upright by the scruff of his fleece, but it's only when the detainee behind follows in his path that I realise we are being forced in this direction on purpose. At the same time, I clear the front of the hut. My eyes might be stinging, but I see where we are heading at last. Williams seems prepared for this, and takes my arm as if to keep me focused on moving.

'What *is* this place?' I ask over the gale.

'Camp Twilight,' he replies, an answer at last. 'Chances are you won't see the sunshine here. It rarely lifts from behind the horizon.'

I say nothing, thinking that the commander summed it up better when he referred to the place as a cage. For we're heading towards a compound on the shoreline with wire fencing so high it could've been designed to restrain some prehistoric beast. With observation posts marking the front corners, and finished at the top with coils of barbed wire, this isn't exactly a holiday destination. Nor do I feel like I'll be safe from harm inside. Such a grand-scale perimeter dwarfs the pre-fabricated buildings way back at the water's edge. But what grabs my attention is the warehouse on the wharf behind it.

The first thing I notice is that there are no windows to be seen. With high walls and a pitched roof, hammered together from what looks like corrugated metal sheets, this church-like structure juts into the shallows on stilts. I know it's unreasonable, but it makes me think we're being shepherded into a slaughterhouse. Just as I feel I'm getting a grip on my nerves, so a sense of panic rises up again and forms a catch inside my throat. As much as I would like to turn and flee, I also want a big hand to reach down and extricate me from this nightmare in the making. The only hand I feel, however, belongs to Agent Williams. Again, he steers me onwards, walking close beside me now.

'Used to be a fish cannery,' he says. 'Mostly cod, so I believe. The trawlermen would bring their hauls here to be gutted, tinned and then transported away by boat again. I guess you could say it's still a processor of sorts.'

'I'm scared,' I tell him, without thinking.

Agent Williams hurries me along. 'The cold really is all you have to fear, Hobbes. Believe the Commander when he says it.'

The cold. There's no escape from it out here. At first it felt like a short, sharp shock. Now it is turning into sheer torture. With every step I take it becomes more formidable than the dogs. With no leash to hold it back, all I can do is keep reminding myself that I *will* get through this. I claw my toes inside these feeble, soaking pumps, and bunch my fingers into my palms. I feel it seeping through the collar of my jumpsuit, which makes me shiver uncontrollably. I remind myself that this is a good sign. I may be helpless here, but my body's defence system will not be beaten. Through the gates now, I pass more guards without once looking at their snarling dogs.

The grounds within the perimeter could fit two soccer pitches. To my right, we pass a compound for the dogs. It's a long kennel block, with grilles over the windows and a row of cages set at the back. As we march by, I notice that each cage is fitted with an overhead heat lamp. The bulbs glow like setting suns, which are blocked out from time to time by canine inhabitants clearly fired up by our arrival. The din coming from inside may be muffled, but it still sounds terrible. Even so, there isn't much more that can unsettle me now. The closer we come to the main building, blocking out the wharf behind it, the more formidable it seems.

The entire structure is mounted on piles to clear the ground ice, and fronted by a steep, wind-carved drift of snow. A path has been cut through it to keep the entrance clear, with a single-storey tower mounted just to the left of the main doors. Smoked-out windows on this upper level go all the way round, while a mast is only visible through the snowstorm by the beacon flashing at the top. Judging by the blooms of rust around the bolts that keep the whole thing together, this place could have been here for as long as the wreck out in the shallows.

Under such a bleak and unforgiving sky, however, and with the rising sense that I can't take much more, it does at least look like it has something to offer. The detainee at the head of our ragtag procession reaches the main entrance and a queue begins to form. By the time I join it, some of the men behind me are beginning to mutter and curse.

'Stay cool,' says Williams, as one of the doors finally cracks open. 'They have to bring you inside in turn.'

I shift my weight from one foot to the other, watching the first detainee and his minder step inside. It seems so unfair that we are forced to wait out here. If the aim is to illustrate how futile an escape bid would be then they've already done a terrific job. I am scared, chilled to the bone, and just so frustrated to feel this helpless. If I have to wait another second, I might as well just give up the fight.

'Get a grip,' I mutter to myself, and suddenly I'm furious because I know I'm about to let myself down. 'Get a *grip*!'

'What's that . . . Hobbes? Oh, man!'

I wipe the tear from my cheek with the sleeve of my

jumpsuit. I assure him it's the cold, but as soon as I do so I choke and gasp. 'I'm fine,' I say, and clear my throat hard. 'I'll be fine.'

'Are you sure?'

The grip on my elbow tightens.

'*Please*. Just give me a moment.'

Williams considers me, less than convinced.

'So now we're processing *kids*,' he says, looking pained. 'What did they expect?'

Through the glass in the door, cross-hatched with a steel mesh, I see a soldier standing with his back to us. He doesn't look like he's set to turn and summon the next pair inside any time soon. There are four men in front of me, each one hunched away from the gale, and I wonder how long it'll take. I don't have to think for long, however, for Agent Williams leads me out of the queue now, and escorts me to the front.

'Hey!' This is McCoy, who's been behind me all this time. 'What's with the special treatment? We're all freezing our asses off back here!'

As Williams thumps on the doors, appealing for the soldier to open up, more voices join the protest. I can't understand them all, but the feeling is clear: the English kid who had hoped to keep his head down is now the centre of attention for all the wrong reasons.

11

My emotions had got the better of me. Under the circumstances, as Williams himself must have realised, it was understandable. From my point of view, however, it feels humiliating beyond belief.

'*This way, Hobbes. Ignore them.*'

I just wasn't used to letting my composure unravel, even if I'd only let it slip for a second. It certainly didn't come naturally. When I was much younger, I'd spent some time wondering why relatives would turn away and dab their eyes whenever they showed up to visit Dad and I. It wasn't so much the weeping that shaped my attitude. It was the fact that they tended to hide their mourning for the loss of my mum, as if somehow that was a source of shame or embarrassment.

'*Keep going, kid! Coming through . . .*'

The tipping point had come when Williams held my gaze. It was what caused my eyes to fill at the rims, even if I had been able to stop it there. The last time I'd even come close to cracking was when my girlfriend had let me go. The split left me reeling, and for a while I just bottled it up. My dad was aware of the situation, but we never did talk on that level. We'd always been more like lodgers in the same house than father and son. I guess there were people I knew at college who would've been sympathetic, but because of my interests and my coursework, I tended to forge connections online – in chat rooms and on message boards.

'Back off and let the boy through!'

In the virtual world, you can offer as little or as much about yourself as you like. People can't even look into your eyes and see it for themselves, unless you're dumb enough to have a webcam trained on you. Personally, I prefer the anonymity, which is perhaps what drew me to the hacking community in the first place. There, preserving your identity is an art form. You don't just invent a screen name. If you want to really impress, you route yourself through several servers around the globe so that nobody can trace you. I did this a couple of times on a board I like to use, but it seemed like showing off to keep finding fresh ways to fool everyone. Besides, once I'd got to know the regular users, I was more interested in sharing and debating the best techniques to compromise a secure system. Sometimes personal stuff crept in, of course. One regular script kiddie who I often chatted to late at night even learned I'd just been dumped. It felt like a weight off my mind,

69

just putting it into words, but I didn't go into great detail. I may have been heartbroken, but as far as that code cracker was concerned my first love would always be hacking. And that was what I went on to devote myself to as a way of moving on.

'We'll see you on the inside, Hobbes! Don't go taking the best room in the hotel now!'

At first I thought that Agent Williams had decided to get me inside quick because he felt sorry for me. It was only once the doors had swung shut on the detainees outside that I wondered if he was simply trying to hide my vulnerability from *them*. Either way, I think to myself, it had helped me to move on once again. This time, however, I'm unsure if this is for better or for worse.

'Dry your eyes,' Williams tells me now, sounding gruff and awkward. At the same time, the soldier who appears to be in charge of the small army present in this processing area squares up to us both.

'Sir, you're causing a disruption.' He slings his clipboard onto the counter he's been standing behind, as if preparing for a fight. Behind him, a set of spiral steps lead up to what must be the smoked-out tower I had seen from out the front. Judging by the radio chatter spilling out through the hatch, I figure this must be the communication centre. The soldier notes me scoping it out, and glares at Williams. 'Get him back behind the blast doors and await your turn.'

'He's just a kid,' Williams says. 'Cut him a break.'

'Rejoin the queue, sir. We can get them in a lot faster with some order.'

'That you're calling me "*sir*" suggests you need to think about this, soldier. Just buzz us through and let me do my job.'

My hands and cheeks feel hot with this sudden change in temperature. I want to rub my palms to stop them from prickling, but don't dare move without Williams' say so. I wonder if the soldier can tell why this agent has just insisted that I skip to the front of the queue. I look straight ahead, determined to keep it together, and feel a small sense of relief when he steps aside for us and orderss the next man outside to enter.

'Thank you,' I say under my breath, as Williams leads a path to a fire door on the opposite side of this space. I don't know if I should be grateful, given the animosity I have left behind me, but it feels like the right thing to say.

Williams doesn't respond. He strides across the floor, still clutching my elbow but only nominally now. Wood-panel walls, thick with varnish, make this space feel a bit like a run-down school reception. One under military occupation, in view of the number of personnel crisscrossing it. Two big windows, both strengthened with wire mesh, flank the door at the far end. It reveals a view of a broad courtyard in the half-light outside, clotted with snow and dominated by the cannery behind it. In the centre of the courtyard stands a power generator. Raised from the ground on breezeblocks, the motor inside this hulking, corrugated container sounds hard at work. I spot fuel drums roped away underneath the blocks, which look as if they're huddling together for warmth.

Laughter draws my attention to the left. Through an open door, I see two figures ambling away from me down a corridor. One of them is wearing khaki army trousers and a vest. He's bouncing a ping-pong ball with a bat as he moves. I hear laughter from another soldier, and decide this must be their recreational wing. On impulse, I look in the opposite direction. The door there is identical, except it's shut and stencilled with a sign insisting upon 'Authorised personnel only'.

'Brace yourself, Hobbes.'

I look back at Williams, find him ready to swing the door open.

'For the cold, or something else?' I ask.

He smiles to himself, nodding now like we have an understanding. 'Maybe both.' Agent Williams grasps the bar to haul the door open, and then pauses as if struck by a sudden thought. 'Just don't cry on me again,' he warns. 'If you so much as shed another tear, I'm going to leave you outside until you stop shivering and go into shock. At least this way you can make an entrance with your head held high.'

I've only been in the warmth of the processing area

72

for a minute or so, but stepping out once more feels twice as tough. My hands are raw, as if stripped of skin, while the downdraught within this confined space is incredible. Williams yells something to me, but I can't hear him over the generator and the gale, so I just follow as he hurries towards the cannery. I work out that the wing to my left must contain the soldiers' living quarters, or some extension of it, while the one across to my right remains a mystery. Judging by the security cameras bracketed to posts at each corner of the courtyard, however, every step I make is being watched from somewhere. I look up and around. The rear windows of the communications tower are visible above the building we've just come through. The treated glass makes it look like the space inside is thick with fog, though I'm sure people are observing me from the other side.

This side of the cannery offers two doors. One is set within the other. You could launch a cruise ship through the biggest, I think, but it's the secondary door that opens when Williams flashes his badge at the camera closest to us. I have to dip my head to fit through, which makes the cavernous space on the inside seem all the more heart-stopping when I finally lift my eyes.

'Well, here we are.' It's as if I've arrived in his own private home, except this is hardly welcoming. Oblivious to my gasp of surprise, Agent Williams steps

73

aside so I can take it all in. Despite the vast size, it's home to two simple rows of cages. There has to be at least twenty of them on each side, spaced like soldiers on parade, and with a man contained inside almost every one.

Then I take in the empty cages, and feel an overwhelming urge to cut and run.

Agent Williams slams the door shut behind us. It deadens the sound of the generator, but also highlights an oppressive kind of quiet. I might've come here voluntarily, but this really doesn't look like the kind of place I can leave at will.

'My God,' is all I can say, and find my attention turning from one detainee to the next. All of them are dressed as I am, in the same regulation jumpsuit. Most of them are sitting with their legs tucked to their chests. One or two lie on mats, and could be dead for all I know, while a prisoner at the far end is kneeling in the corner of his cage, swaying to and fro. Several guards pace the floor between them, carrying rifles over their shoulders. Lost for words, I look around for a moment. The interior of the building is constructed entirely from timber, but for two metal gantries slung between the roof joists front and back. Yet more guards look down from these elevated positions. The one at the far end leans into the rail with both hands spread wide, clearly watching me. Beneath him, at the back, a short set of steps lead to a metal trapdoor fringed by rust. Judging by the winch above it, I figure once upon a time the catches would be hauled up through there.

I hear voices from the gantry overhead just then, mostly walkie-talkie chatter, but the echo slamming around in here makes it impossible to work out what's being said. It isn't just the scale of the place that strikes me, though. The stink is so bad that my face pinches up just as soon as I remind myself to breathe.

'It's fish,' remarks Williams, though I'm well aware of what's behind the smell. 'This place hasn't seen a catch in years, of course, but no amount of scrubbing is gonna shift the stench. It'll always be a cannery at heart, even if we call it a detention centre.'

'It's suffocating,' I say, because it isn't just fish guts, but sweat. The odour of unwashed bodies, stewing in what feels like an over-heated, under-ventilated environment.

'Look at it like this,' says Williams, turning to look at me. 'I don't suppose you'll be here long enough to get used to it.'

Movement on the gantry overhead draws his attention first, and then mine. I glance up, and see the guard there is now looking down his rifle sights at me.

'There are fingers on triggers everywhere you look,' says Williams. 'Now that's something you *never* get used to. Doesn't matter what side of the gun you're on, it's guaranteed to give you pause for thought.' The guard up there could be frozen through. It's clear he's got a bead on me as Williams says this. Somehow, in the company of Agent Williams, I don't feel like his finger would dare squeeze the trigger. Even so, it isn't something I want to test.

'Let's get this done,' I say. I meet Williams' eyes this time. 'Any information you want from me, it's yours. I just want to tell you that now.'

He graces me with a half-smile, only for the sound of boot-steps to draw his attention. I turn to see one of the two guards from the centre of the cannery crossing towards us now. He's staring at me as he approaches, with tight, piercing blue eyes. I look away quickly, and find Agent Williams again. 'Whatever you've done is not my business,' he tells me. 'I'm just here to look after your welfare, so you're fresh for the interrogators. As long as you don't come to harm in our custody, Hobbes, I will have done my job.'

At this, the guard arrives and salutes Williams. He's evidently pumped up inside that uniform, judging by his build and thick neck. He doesn't even look at me now. Williams assures him that I'm good, whatever that means, and that's when I realise he's leaving me.

'Hey,' I say, as he turns away. 'I'll see you again, right?'

I don't expect him to answer me, and sure enough his silence tells me he'll be back. He may have played it gruff with me on the flight here, but I had drawn enough from him to know that deep down this was

76

someone who could show warmth and compassion. If Agent Williams was going for good, he'd have let me know.

At once, the handover guard steps into position. He's wearing a canvas name-strip over his shirt pocket that reads NORTH. I only have to glance at it for him to shoot me a venomous glare. He doesn't hide his hostility from Williams, who seems helpless all of a sudden. He just shrugs, one hand on the door, and tells me to relax.

'North here will take good care of you,' he assures me.

'*Sir!*' Everything about this guard makes me jumpy. He's just so quick to acknowledge Williams. He matches me in height, but everything from his uniform to his upright manner leaves me feeling like a troublesome pupil.

With a final glance at the gantry, Williams tips a salute of sorts at me. Next he switches his attention to North. 'The boy is here voluntarily. I know you've been briefed on this, so go easy.'

'*Yessir!*' replies North, without taking his eyes away from me.

12

From the moment Agent Williams closes the door behind him, I feel isolated and under threat. North doesn't move a muscle. He just continues to stare right through me. His skin is pitted with deep acne scars, like someone has just shoved a handful of gravel into his face. I realise I'm staring and look to my feet, soaking and numb in these stupid pumps. When I dare to look up again, I doubt he has even blinked.

'Hi,' I say eventually, thinking somehow I have to break the silence. 'I'm Carl.'

'Carl.' The guard appears to chew on my name. North speaks with a Deep Southern drawl, I realise, which is ironic given his name. 'You're the thief, right?'

The question leaves me lost for words. 'Well . . . not exactly,' I begin, only for my explanation to trail away as his glare ignites.

'Turn around,' he growls. 'Turn around *now!*'

I face the other way without a second thought. Even

before I've had a chance to draw breath I feel a twisting pain travel from my right wrist all the way to my shoulder. The guard has forced me into an arm lock, and there's no escape from it. I throw my head back with a gasp, and find him breathing into my ear. 'Your sugar daddy's gone now, boy. From now on, you don't talk or even *look* at me without permission, understood?'

My upper arm is in agony, but another twist persuades me to nod in agreement. 'OK,' I say weakly. '*OK!*'

The pressure doesn't ease at this. Instead, North cranks it up another bar, which forces me to swing around to face the central space in a bid to stop him from breaking bones.

'Walk on,' he orders, which I do without question. I notice some of the detainees watching me. Nobody seems even remotely disturbed by my treatment. They simply stare as I am marshalled towards an empty cage along the left-hand flank. It's constructed from a steel frame and thick mesh, with a door swung open. Which must be in readiness for me, I think. I know I'm going to have to crouch in order to enter, and can only look forward to the moment I am safe inside and free from this gorilla. 'Mind your head, Hobbes!' As he says this, North uses his other hand to grab the back of my neck. He then thrusts me forward, slamming my head into the meshing above the open gate, before shoving me hard into the cage. I am left reeling from the impact. I want to clutch my skull, but it's my arm that's suffering more. Instead of letting me go, he decides to make things even worse. I feel muscles tearing inside my shoulder socket as he winds the limb into an un-naturally straight position; a needling sensation that spreads like a wildfire. Even then he doesn't release me. Instead, North stands tall, places the sole of his boot on my ribcage, and yanks my arm upwards.

'*Hey, North! Look at you, man! Nice move, but haven't you forgotten something?*' I hear the voice address North from across the cannery, sounding horribly cheery, but it means nothing to me. For I feel like I've just been struck by a lightning bolt. '*Your guy in the isolation cell was due out half an hour ago. They'll be queuing them up outside, but you know the drill. You sign 'em in, you sign 'em out.*'

Next I feel a ghastly jolt go off deep inside my shoulder, and yet despite the appalling pain, there comes a sense of release.

'My guy can *wait*,' says North under his breath. 'I'll get to it when I'm done here.'

My arm is free at last. Despite this, on top of the agony I'm in, it seems rotated in a strange way. North is still standing over my cage. I see him turn around, which is when I realise that the other guard from the floor has come across. He draws level with the man, with both hands behind his back and his mouth bunched to one side like he's considering marks out of ten.

'He looks all bust up to me, buddy. Unless you're thinking of breaking his other arm?'

'It's a *dislocation*, Cortés. I'm not dumb enough to cause permanent damage. Though I gotta tell you, anyone who arrives here in orange deserves what's coming to them. Even if they're under no charge, it cuts no ice with me. Now give me some space, so I can take care of things.'

The guard called Cortés is olive-skinned, with dark hair and trim sideburns. He seems totally unconcerned that I'm here voluntarily. He's also in no hurry to leave. He looks at me, and then across at the man beside him who has done this. I guess they're of equal rank, though I am beginning to suspect what's happening here is something Cortés would stop if only he had the authority. All I can do is lie there, stunned and useless, as if my arm has turned to lead. Finally, with a sigh, Cortés backs off by a step. 'Just remember your other guy, OK?'

In response, North turns, sees me grimacing on the floor, and frowns.

'Don't you dare start whining on me, Hobbes. Be a man!' Judging by the state I'm in, it's clear he's done some damage. I just don't get a chance to respond because he's crouching before me all of a sudden, and dragging me out into his arms. I want to struggle but

81

he's too quick. Too assured. At first I think he's going to haul me out and carry on the onslaught. I scream as he grabs my upper arm, feel tremendous pressure driving into my shoulder. Then, with a pop, and just as I think I might pass out, the pain begins to ebb away.

'Why?' is all I can say as he withdraws from the cage, slamming the gate shut behind him. '*I haven't done anything!*'

North snaps a padlock into position. I'm aware of the hush that consumes this vast space. All the murmuring, coughs and movements have ceased. Everyone is looking at me. North tests the padlock, and then straightens out his uniform.

'You're a Brit,' he says matter-of-factly. 'Brits are supposed to look out for their allies, like they look out for you, but clearly you have a problem with that. Now I told you to keep your head down, but did you listen to me? No, you did not. Too busy plotting how to steal from us again, most probably. So, to be sure you stay focused, from here on in you do exactly as I say. Otherwise, accidents happen.'

I want to see Agent Williams. I figure he can't be far away. I even wonder whether he might've heard the whole episode from the courtyard. In which case, he could be back here at any moment to tear strips off this guy.

'May I sit up?' I ask.

82

North shrugs.

'If you can.'

I haul myself upright, clutching my shoulder. I still can't believe what he's done. One moment I was in unbearable pain. The next it just felt like a dull cramp.

'I'm good,' I mutter, aware of the locked gate between us. If he's going to come at me, I think, he'll have to find his key first. North responds by squatting before me. I flinch, dragging myself back, but realise quickly that he's there to talk and nothing more.

'Let me familiarise you with the fixtures and fittings we got to offer,' he begins, and nods at something behind me. 'Firstly, you have a pot. Just lift the lid, do your business, and hope it don't smell too bad because the cleaning detail only come around once a day. The bucket is for washing. Don't get the two mixed up. You'll get warm water at breakfast time only. Inside it, you'll see a bar of soap, toothbrush and toothpaste. If you want me to treat you right, don't be an animal and let your hygiene slip. Finally, the two mats there are for your comfort. Any questions?'

The rate at which he has just rattled through this leaves me way behind. I look at the pot, recessed into the floor with the toilet roll inside it, the bucket containing the washing items, and the two mats in question. One is rolled up, but clearly long enough for me to stretch out on. The other one is a quarter the size, and a mystery to me.

'What's this for?' I ask, testing my arm with a grimace as I draw the mat closer.

North's expression brightens, like I've just amused him. 'What this is for is to say your prayers,' he chuckles. 'I think you'll find it comes in very useful in here.'

He turns to Cortés, who has witnessed everything without a word, eager to share the joke. 'You can use it as a pillow if it helps,' North suggests, sounding almost sympathetic now.

'I'll see how it goes,' I say, nursing my shoulder still. 'Hopefully I'll be out of here soon.'

North falls quiet at this, only to explode, fleetingly, with laughter. It comes out of nowhere, and is gone just as quickly. 'I do apologise,' he says next, mocking my accent. 'Ignore me, and just hold on to that thought, won't you?' He moves to leave, gesturing for his colleague to follow. Cortés remains where he stands, even when North purposely barges past him. I have him down as Hispanic and in his early twenties. If North has the pitted skin, oversized muscles and temperament of a gym junkie with a taste for steroids, his fellow guard seems like he could be altogether more human if permitted.

Cortés stirs, shot of his colleague at last, and curses irritably under his breath. At the same time, he glances at the guard on the gantry. The guy up there is leaning against the rail with his rifle at rest across his chest. It's clear he's seen what happened, but doesn't appear at all concerned. Cortés returns his attention to me. This time, he doesn't seem entertained by what he sees. I want to speak, but I'm in shock and way too scared. All I can do is lie there, aware that every effort I make to draw in my arm triggers showering sparks of pain. I meet his eye. He shakes his head and turns away. The next thing, he comes back around with a foil pack of pills from his top pocket, and pops two into his palm.

'Take these,' he says with great reluctance, and flicks them through the mesh. 'North gives me a migraine so often that I always carry them with me.'

I claw the painkillers into my hand, and knock them back without water.

'Thanks.'

Alongside my shoulder, it's my feet that are giving me grief. The walk to the cannery had left them numb with cold, but now the heat is playing hell with them. I reach for my pumps with my good arm, and peel them off along with my socks. My toes are pink and swollen. I try to wiggle them, and draw the air between my teeth.

Through the grille of my cage, Cortés watches me inspect one toe after another.

'Don't you breathe a word about this,' he warns. 'If I hear you bleating, so help me I'll break every bone in your body, and *then* let North take his turn.'

I shift my focus from his face to the wire of the cage, feeling strangely cocooned from harm.

'I won't,' I tell him, and gingerly straighten my arm to prove it. 'Feeling better already.'

Without another word, Cortés heads for a side door to the left of the main entrance. I realise this leads to the mystery wing, and wonder if I'll get a glimpse of it when he walks through. But then, as Cortés clears the space in front of me, I become aware of the detainee in the cage opposite. Our eyes meet, and stay that way even when the two guards make their exit, but I can't be sure whose jaw falls first.

13

The prisoner rocks forward, grasping the mesh as if to gain a steadier bead on me. It isn't someone I've ever seen before. And yet somehow it feels like I'm faced with an individual who really didn't expect to find me here.

From my point of view, I am simply shocked to find myself looking at a *girl*.

'Oh *great*!' she says, and rolls her eyes.

At any other time, under very different circumstances, I'd be curious to find out why a total stranger should greet me like her worst enemy. As it is, I'm too shaken up by what happened with the guards to do anything but avoid her glare.

Like most guys my age, I've made attempts to get to know girls and been met with utter scorn. It's all part of the learning experience, I guess, just like finding yourself hung out to dry from a relationship when you least expect it.

Having crashed and burned as I have, I guess that's one more reason why I withdrew yet further into my online world. There, I could reinvent. Not just polish the rough edges of my personality, but mould and shape an entirely fresh identity. I could be someone else. I could be *someone*.

Right now, as a direct attempt to make a name for myself via a virtual visit to Fort Knox Bullion Reserve, I am nothing more than a rat in a cage. I have a military-issue jumpsuit to show for it, a traumatised shoulder and zero control over my immediate future. In fact, pretty much the only thing in my life that remains the same is the look of contempt my presence can inspire from the opposite sex. I tip my head, searching my mind for clues to this girl's identity. I figure Thomas Grimstad probably isn't the only one here to have earned media coverage for his crimes. Then again, if I have seen this girl before I wouldn't have forgotten it in a hurry. Despite the distance between our cages, she looks about the same age as me, with a crow-black bob cut high at the fringe, and a striking, expressive face that clearly mirrors her inner feelings. It means she doesn't have to curse under her breath again for me to know my presence is unwelcome. I just can't figure out what I've done to invite such scorn. I try to shrug as best I can, as if I should apologise for any mis-understanding. In response she turns to face the other way, and lies down in apparent despair.

I glance at the marksman on the gantry at the back. He's still observing me through his rifle sights. Careful not to make any sudden moves, I poke my socks through the wire to dry. He doesn't move a muscle. I wonder what he must be thinking. Whether he knows more about the situation than me. I'm hardly in a position to ask. Then he swings the rifle towards the main door as it opens, and I feel I can breathe a little easier. I turn to see one of the special agents from the plane. He leads a figure inside, clad in the same orange jumpsuit as the rest of us. The detainee is wearing wrist restraints again. Immediately I feel responsible. I imagine that by jumping the queue I kick-started some unrest. I'm being paranoid, I realise, as the man is handed over to another guard, who leads him to his cage. Yes, I'm in a very serious situation, but it's hardly likely that these guys would want to harm me. Even if they *were* able to break free from their confines, I figure they'd have bigger scores to settle.

Before this new arrival is locked away, the next one arrives at the door. His wrists are also bound, behind his back this time. He takes one look around, appearing utterly overwhelmed. Without warning, he backtracks by a step and then bolts for it. The agent accompanying him grabs him by the elbow, yelling at him now. A guard from the gantry steps rushes to assist, but the detainee is beyond reason. He's bellowing wildly in Arabic and twisting like a bear in a rage. I hear an order

89

to fire from the gantry, at which the agent snaps around and screams at the guards up there to back off.

'Nobody's getting killed on my watch, soldier! Just radio me the punishment squad right now!'

'Already on their way!'

As he speaks the detainee switches from retreat to outright aggression, and tackles the agent around his waist. At the same time, I hear yet more noise from the courtyard. Within seconds, two, four and then six guards pour through the cannery door. These guys are scrambling to brandish their batons, which they brace to hammer down blows on the guy at the heart of the spectacle.

There are so many of them my view is obscured, but the assault continues long after the detainee has fallen silent.

'OK, fellas,' says the agent finally. He's standing over the motionless man, nursing a thick lip. 'You can deal with this wise guy later. Let him come round in the cage.'

Several guards duly haul the detainee by his ankles across the floor. The man is out cold, which is perhaps a small mercy given the brutal indignity he's suffered. Without word, this so-called punishment squad disperses. Nobody talks or seems at all fired up. It's as if this kind of thing is a regular event, and a tiresome one at that.

I look around, astonished at the subdued silence.

Not a single detainee seems even slightly horrified by the act of brutality that has just occurred. Such indifference is exactly what they showed when North came for me. Still, it makes me realise how vital it is that I keep my head down from here on in.

Avoiding the attention of the girl opposite won't be hard, I decide. For she's sitting with her back against the gate of her cage. It at least gives me a chance to ponder her again as the next detainee comes in from the cold. She's slim, with long legs and a curving hip that gives some form to the jumpsuit. My attention is only drawn from her when Grimstad is led across the floor between us. I catch him looking at me, a trace of those blood smears still present under his eyes. His wrists are bound, and though he appears quite calm this transfer requires a five-guard escort. As soon as he is secure inside his cage, however, they rush back to the main door, where the next detainee to arrive has just made his presence known.

'Sur-*prise*!'

McCoy's voice is unmistakeable. It isn't just his accent but the fact that few men in their right mind would dare to make a mockery of such a serious situation. Sure enough, his outburst is met by some sharp yelling from the special agent at his side and the soldiers who rush to subdue him. Even North crashes back into the cannery to assist, as if duty bound to be at the heart of any trouble. 'I've lost mah boy!' McCoy

91

bawls out next, tossing his head back to make himself heard. 'You can't miss him: he's whip thin, a little tearful, and goes by the name of Hobbes!'

I feel my heart seize inside my chest. Even my breathing stops short when the girl in the cage opposite twists around to find me again. McCoy is really playing up now. He's digging in his heels as they hurry him across the floor. Two guards hold him in the same vicious arm lock I suffered. Despite their efforts, the look on his face leaves me thinking that he's revelling in the pain as much as the attention. I see him scanning the row I'm in. Instinctively, I drop my eyes to the floor. And that's when he spots me.

'There you are! We were worried!'

McCoy's words finish with a muffled cry of pain. I dare to look up to see the guards have closed into a scrum around him now. The detainee can be heard protesting, but it isn't clear what he's saying. They practically fling him into the cage beside Grimstad, lock it down and then disperse without a second glance. McCoy picks himself up from the floor, clearly winded. He reaches around to the small of his back, which is where he must have been hit, but seems too dazed to concern himself with me again.

In the silence that closes upon us, broken only by the guards as they patrol the floor, I realise that the painkillers are beginning to take effect. The ragged ache in my shoulder has eased, and yet nothing numbs the realisation that it isn't just the inmates who should be feared here.

14

In our regulation orange jumpsuits, it must be easy for her to look across and mistake me for someone else. In every cage I see someone with a dark and difficult past, and I guess it must seem that way from her side of the cannery too.

From time to time this arresting girl stirs from what appears to be deep thought. She then steals a glance in my direction, only to look away so quickly I know that I'm at the centre of her attention. I even run through the tarot pack in my mind, just to be sure she isn't someone else who has made headlines, but come back with nothing.

The next time she looks up, I offer her a small smile. She turns away, unlike McCoy, who catches sight of the exchange and lights up for me.

'Are you gonna let her treat you like that, Hobbes?'

He hauls himself to the front once more, eyes pinched and glittering. Within seconds, two guards are on his case. North is the first to slash a baton across the face of his cage, followed swiftly by a second strike from the guard with him. McCoy recoils from the assault, snapping his fingers away and howling.

'Do you have a problem with the concept of silence?' North demands.

'No, sir.' McCoy nurses his fingers now, but the sheepish look doesn't wash with me any more. Nor with North, it seems, who reaches for his walkie-talkie and mutters an instruction into it.

'Are you bored, McCoy, is that it?'

McCoy regards him quizzically. 'Just passing the time, sir.'

North takes a step away from the cage. Awaiting a response from his walkie-talkie, he swings his baton idly, like a baseball player warming up at the plate.

'If you're tiring of your own company, we can find plenty of ways to keep you occupied. I can't offer you no movie, but how about some music?'

It's hard for me to see how McCoy takes this. Judging by the pause before he speaks, however, my guess is that he can't be sure if the guard is being serious.

'Sure,' he says eventually. 'Do you take requests?'

'Not right now,' replies North, as if ready for a wise-crack like this. 'We got something very special lined up for you first.'

I watch the other guard stride away with a private

smile made very public. He looks at a marksman on the gantry, who tips him a salute. A moment later, the very foundations of the cannery are shaken by the sound of a grinding guitar. It comes from some very big speakers somewhere, and is basically an introductory riff to what sounds like the gates of hell swinging open. Everything from the bass and the drums to the growling vocals contribute to one almighty wall of sound. It's intense enough to disturb every detainee here. Some shift position, others cover their ears, and yet there is one guard who is visibly pleased to hear this track ring out. I only have to listen to a couple of bars to know exactly why North has selected it. He even uses his baton to play out an imaginary guitar riff before grinning at his colleague. It isn't something I'd ever choose to listen to for pleasure, but I have heard it before. Anyone who has tuned into the news over the last few months would know that this is the signature tune of a black metal outfit called Dødsengler. The band, from Norway, were infamous the world over. Not for their music, I should say, but for what it had inspired.

Only one detainee appears to be totally tuned out from this onslaught. It makes me wonder whether he's yet to come alive about what he has done.

Having identified Grimstad on the plane, I now find myself considering his past. Being subjected to music I had heard before helped summon yet more details. I knew how to make it work by association, much like visualising the tarot cards. In this case, his story had been retold so many times in the media, and from every different angle, that I find myself picking through what seems like the kind of dossier the military must have amassed on him.

One evening before Easter, on what would become an infamous night for Norway, this young man caged across from me had caught a tram from his home in a suburb of Oslo. A great deal was made about how he had purchased a single, one-way ticket, and travelled to the centre of the city. Those who rode in on the same tram said his appearance was striking, but no real cause for concern. With his unwashed tresses, studded neckband and buttoned-up leather trench coat, even I'd have marked him down as just some regular kid rebelling from his safe, suburban upbringing. You saw it on every street in the Western world. It was all about posture and shock value, but ultimately harmless.

I consider myself to be a pretty good judge of character. In this case, I would've been terribly wrong.

Thomas Grimstad had just turned twenty-three. He lived alone in a tenement block on the city fringes, and held down a regular job in a videogame store. Nobody reported him as a problem there. Going by the guy's potted profiles, he was courteous and knowledgeable to customers who knew their games, and trustworthy enough to hold a key for the store. That evening, Grimstad was on his way to a rock venue, known for hosting acts outside the mainstream. Top of the bill was Oslo's own Dødsengler or Death's Angel. This bristling, antagonistic four-piece had a reputation for slinging buckets of offal into their audiences, and verbally abusing them from the stage. You wouldn't take your grandmother to one of their gigs, but you might be drawn in yourself as a way to escape the grind of your humdrum life.

Inside the venue, Grimstad ordered a mineral water from the bar at the back, where he watched the support act impassively. A sound technician in the wings proved to be the most reliable witness of events from there. He recalled seeing our man squeeze through the hordes when the curtain opened on the main event, and then mouth the words to the first three songs. An image from a mobile phone was released some days later. It captured a gleeful Grimstad, dodging a goat's severed head that had found its way into the hands of the crowd. It was a mesmerising shot. I remember it well. He just looked like a regular kid from the fringes having the time of his life.

A minute after the picture was taken, as strobe lights strafed the stage, Thomas Grimstad unbuttoned his trench coat to reveal a torso strapped with white packages and wires.

If I'd been in the technician's shoes, on seeing something like this I'd have flown into a panic as he did. People assumed it was part of the act when he scrambled into the spotlight and started yelling uselessly over the din. By this time, Grimstad had a nine-volt battery in one hand and two wires in the other that he'd calmly teased from his sleeve. Desperate now, the technician grabbed the singer's microphone and screamed at people to move. *The boy there has a bomb!* Whether this was the right thing to do is irrelevant now. Despite the crushing stampede away from him, Grimstad had already touched the wires to the battery.

The reason why it hadn't gone off was never clearly explained. That the explosives were matched to a batch seized from an Al-Qaeda cell in Paris a month before generated as many headlines as questions. According to newspaper sources, the cell had been days away from obliterating the American Embassy and several members remained at large. Could Grimstad, a young man who had renounced Christianity, like so many black metal disciples, have become a fundamentalist for a very different religion? It didn't seem likely. So how had he come into possession of such lethal equipment, what was his purpose in targeting his fellow fans, and why did he just stand there passively awaiting the police?

Thomas Grimstad confounded the Norwegian authorities. One week on from being taken down by Taser gun in the abandoned concert hall, he'd refused to explain himself to anyone. Then evidence surfaced that linked his explosives to other terrorist activities on the European continent. When presented with this,

just survived a car wreck. Other detainees gather themselves like me, while the quiet is just so loaded and unreal. It also serves to amplify the slightest squeak in the timbers, for the storm winds outside continue to test the cannery. Someone coughs, and a guard on the gantry shifts his weight from one foot to the other. Only Grimstad remains as detached from his surroundings as ever. If this was planned to provoke him into acting up, it hasn't worked.

I want to unroll my mat, but I'm too scared to draw attention to myself. I glance at McCoy. He's picking over his toes now, looking like a child unable to break out of a sulk. I wonder what he has done to be here. Possession of a bandit's moustache and sideburns isn't a crime in any country after all. I find myself thinking about this while looking at the girl in the cage beside him. There she is, flanked by the two men in this cannery that I would least like as my neighbours and yet she looks totally unruffled by their presence. I wonder how long she has been here, and who it might be that she's confused me with. She's lying on her side again, asleep I think. Then she opens her eyes, as if reading my mind, and narrows them at me.

This time, I find nothing to stop me from concerning myself with my mats. I make some space to unroll the long one, but choose not to use the prayer mat as a pillow. It seems a bit disrespectful, and the last thing I want to do is make even more enemies. So I lie down

101

as best I can, stare at the vaulted ceiling high over-head, and wonder how I've managed to get myself into this. I haven't taken any lives, after all. Then I think that if every caged prisoner has committed crimes like Grimstad then I really am different from all of them. Williams had said I was simply here to hook up with personnel who would understand how I'd com-promised such a high-profile gold depository. All they wanted to do was improve their security measures, and by talking to me they could do just that. It was like being a consultant in some ways. Maybe North just assumed I had done something far worse. It would explain his aggression towards me, even if it couldn't ever be justified. Just like being housed within a cage unfit for any human being.

I consider telling Williams about North and my treatment here, or even the people scheduled to talk to me, whenever that might be, but then dismiss the idea. I just want to pass through here like a ghost spirit, with the minimum of grief and disruption.

I am over the worst, I tell myself. Then, with a final look around, I cradle my shoulder and dare to close my eyes.

15

'Back of the cage, Hobbes. C'mon now.'

When Agent Williams speaks to me, it serves as an abrupt alarm call. I sit up with a gasp, surprised that I have actually been asleep. I recognise his voice, even if it does sound abrasive, but my surroundings take a moment to make sense.

'What time is it?' I ask.

Williams looks less than impressed. 'Just get yourself away from the gate. I can't open up until you do so.'

My back is aching from being on such a hard surface, my shoulder has stiffened considerably, and my hearing is still muffled. I do as I am told though, hiding my discomfort from him. As soon as I am upright, Williams unlocks the gate and swings it open. The first thing he does after that is turn his attention to the pot in the corner.

'There's nothing for you to take away.' I keep my

voice down, despite the fact that almost every word exchanged within the cannery can be heard.

Agent Williams frowns, but in good humour, I think.

'What am I?' he asks. 'Your chambermaid? I'm not here to empty your toilet, Hobbes. But if you got a problem you should tell me.'

I shake my head, and yet all I'm thinking is that despite everything we have a *dialogue* here. Maybe it's the hacker in me, but I'm sure Williams must know the timetable for my interview. In my world, knowledge is power, even if I'm not in an immediate position to do anything with it.

'It's embarrassing,' I tell him, thinking if I play up my vulnerability along with a sense of play I might just disarm him. 'If I was a dog in the kennel block out there you'd at least let me out for a pee.'

Agent Williams guffaws, and then stops himself when heads turn in our direction. I bite back a smile, and once more sense his defences dropping.

'I guess I can allow a voluntary detainee to use the can,' he says. 'Just this once.'

I look over at McCoy, who is watching me from his cage across the cannery. 'The last time you did me a favour,' I whisper, reflecting on my preferential treatment at the main doors, 'I don't think it went down too well.'

Williams glances over his shoulder at McCoy.

'What's he going to do about it, Hobbes? *Look* at you funny?'

McCoy may be caged, but I can tell he's just waiting for a chance to intimidate me again. Then I think of my bladder. I must have been here for some hours now, because it's practically squeaking every time I breathe in and out. Aware of my options if I stay here in the cage, I agree to take up Williams' invitation. The way I see things, it isn't just a chance to relieve myself in private. This is an opportunity to work on this guy's habit of speaking to me off the record. At the same time, North and Cortés appear at the main door. A flurry of snow follows them in. Cortés is holding a small tray with some dispensary bottles on it. North has a clipboard, with a pencil tied to a length of string.

'Medication time,' Williams tells me quietly, watching the pair step in from the cold. 'Prayers keep some detainees calm. Others need to take a pill.'

'Really?' I wonder why he's telling me this. If he's serious, it seems like the kind of information that should be classified.

Williams reads my surprise just as soon as he turns back to face me.

'Interrogation is a delicate art,' he says next, drawing closer to the meshing. 'The last thing we want to do is drag in terror suspects kicking and screaming. Not *every* time, at least,' he adds, grinning now.

I watch North and Cortés head for a cage on my

side, about six down from me. 'I don't need anything,' I tell him. 'As soon as my interview starts, I'm happy to talk.'

'You aren't *getting* anything,' Williams replies. 'Unless you got a condition you didn't share with the doctor when they first brought you in.'

The GP was one of the first people who had visited me in the police cell. She had asked a few questions, checked my pulse, my scalp and the inside of my mouth, and left with plenty of ticks on the form she'd filled in throughout. Had I known that I was about to be flown out here, I suspect she would've found my heart racing.

But no, as I tell Williams now with my eyes fixed on the pumped-up psychopath in guard's uniform, there is nothing wrong with me.

North is first to cross the floor between the two rows, having finished with the first detainee. McCoy watches his approach with great interest.

'What have you got for me, boys? I'm feeling one of my headaches coming on.'

Ignoring him, North heads for Grimstad's cage. There, he turns and glares at Cortés, who hurries to join him with the tray. Cortés is the first to speak to Grimstad. His tone is overly gentle, almost polite, and Grimstad duly backs off to the rear of the cage. Having opened up the gate, North then hands him a small cup. Grimstad knocks back the contents obediently, and hands it back without even a nod.

Agent Williams watches the exchange with great interest. 'I'm guessing you keep up with the news,' he says under his breath.

My first thought is to make out that I don't know what he's talking about. As a hacker, appearing to be ignorant is a good position to adopt when it comes to gleaning information. In this case, however, I'm not coming to Williams cold. I suspect he must know, from my interest in Grimstad on the plane, that I am aware of what he has done. If I lied, I decide, it could just break the bond I'm building here.

'His face made headlines,' I say, as the padlock is returned to Grimstad's cage. 'A jumpsuit isn't going to disguise who he is.'

'Or what he did.'

'*Hey!*' This is McCoy once again, cutting out our conversation. North and Cortés have just turned for a cage further along the row, but stop now and face him. 'I'm talking to you two nursemaids! Haven't you read my medical report? I got some epilepsy problems!'

Cortés faces North, who consults the clipboard. 'Nothing here, McCoy. I suggest a long sleep might help. Not just for your sake but for everyone here.'

McCoy glares at the guard balefully. 'I got a headache, asshole, and it won't go away on its own.'

'Boo hoo!' North spins around on his heels, ignoring the volley of abuse that breaks over him. I watch Cortés back away in the same direction, as if in retreat. A

107

moment after the pair clear Grimstad's cage, I catch sight of Grimstad quietly dropping a blue pill out of his mouth and into the palm of his hand. He looks up to find me watching, stares at me for a beat, and then draws his mouth into an amused smile. I snap my attention back to Agent Williams.

'I'm not sure I can hold on much longer,' I tell him, crossing my hands in my lap. 'Can I use the restroom now?'

Agent Williams retreats from the gate, creating a space for me. I am ready for McCoy to turn his vitriol in my direction, but ignore him this time. I just keep my head down as I had told myself, and follow Agent Williams to the side door across the cannery.

16

You know sometimes when you're really desperate to relieve yourself, but something holds you back? This happens to me, right now.

'I can't go,' I say, and I'm quite genuine about this. I'm also content to come across as vulnerable as I sound. It always brought down barriers online. I just hoped it would do likewise in the real world. 'I can't go because I'm being watched.'

I'm standing at a grubby urinal, wide enough for six men, with a window above that's frosted on the inside and out. I'm alone at the pipe, however. Williams is at the door away to my left, as I'm only too aware.

'I'm not watching you in *that* way, Hobbes. When you're out of the cage or the interview room, and no guards are present, I'm duty bound to keep you in my sights.'

'So when will the interview happen?' I ask, and focus once more on the task at hand.

'Whenever they're ready. It could be they're waiting for you right now,' he adds. 'So if you spend any more time at the plate they might just put you to the back of the queue.'

'I'm trying,' I say. 'It's just so off-putting.'

Williams tuts and sighs to himself. I figure this is the last time he'll give me a break. Then I hear his shoes on the tiled floor, and suddenly there he is at the far end of the urinal, unzipping himself.

'Hey!' he says abruptly, and I find him glowering at me. 'I don't like being watched either. Keep your business to yourself, Hobbes, like I told you on the plane. I'm helping you out here. Trying to make you feel better by taking a leak. Eyes to the front, soldier!'

'Sorry,' I say hurriedly. 'Sorry.'

Maybe the shock of seeing him there is what does the trick. Either way, I am pleased I have played up to his image of me as a kid in a spin. I haven't gained a great deal from it yet, but here he is taking another small step to make things easier for me. For a moment, we stand there in silence. Doing our thing. Williams finishes first, and is back at the door having rinsed his hands before I can close up the press studs on my jumpsuit. When I turn for the sink, I find him grinning at me.

'If that was a pissing contest, Hobbes, I just won outright.'

I twist the tap. There is only one. The water is ice

cold. 'But I lasted longer than you,' I say, chuckling now. 'Doesn't that make me the victor?'

I shake my hands dry. In doing so, my bad shoulder twinges. I wince, just for a beat. When I recover I find Williams considering me.

'Be careful in here, huh? If you want to be a winner, go into that interview and tell them everything they need to know. Don't get smart with them, or hold anything back, because they'll be wise to it. They're highly trained bullshit detectors. And believe me, Hobbes, if they pick up on the slightest whiff, they'll do everything they can to wipe your face in it. You may only have been here for a short while,' he adds after a pause, 'but I'm sure you know what I mean.'

I am mindful not to move my arm, in case it gives me any more grief. If Williams is wise to the fact that some of the guards operated above the law, he isn't going to admit it directly. Even if this is because he is powerless to stop it, I am grateful for the advice.

'I'll be careful,' I tell him.

Williams finds the door handle behind him. As he does so, the light bulb above us flickers and goes out. At the same time, I notice a background hum fade away. It has to be the generator in the courtyard, but I figure it might be best if he spells this out for me. After all, I didn't want to look like a detainee who had paid too much attention to his environment.

111

In the flat, natural light from the window, Williams curses and drops his hand from the door. 'Whoever thought it would be a fine idea to turn this tin shack into a military camp is fit for little more than flipping burgers. It might be more secure than the bank you busted open, Hobbes, but nobody considered that the elements would work *against* us as well.' He stops there, as if reminding himself that he's sounding off to a prisoner.

'So will the power come back on?'

Williams regards me, as if making an evaluation.

'The downdraught in the courtyard can blow hard sometimes,' he continues after a moment. 'If a gust has knocked out the pilot light it'll need restarting. Either that or someone forgot to switch the fuel drums. Don't worry. If it isn't fixed in the next five minutes then the backup will kick in. Until then, we're in a lockdown situation. If it's really serious, we just have to hope that the cavalry will come before we freeze to death.'

I sense a long-standing frustration being vented here. I also note he's fretting with his wedding band once more. With nobody here to listen in, I seize my opportunity.

'It's times like this I guess you really must miss home,' I suggest. 'I'm certainly missing my dad. He's about your age.'

Agent Williams meets my eyes once more.

'My wife,' he says, with softness now. 'My wife made me swear I'd hand in my badge this year. It's the first time in thirty years we haven't disagreed.'

I smile with him. 'Any kids?' I ask, and watch him closely as I unroll questions, one after the other. 'Let me guess. I'm thinking a boy. Just one son. A good lad. A player. The kind of kid who makes you *damn* proud. Am I right?'

This isn't mind reading. If anything it's all about interpreting facial expressions with confidence, and then dressing it up as something deeper. So long as you're braced to change direction in a blink, with practice it's easy to please.

And once you've gained the confidence of your target, you can begin to direct the agenda.

Watching Agent Williams brighten with each statement, I just know my guesswork has hit the spot. I don't need him to confirm that I'm right. He remains tight-lipped, but his face can't keep it a secret. Turning his attention to the dead light bulb in a bid to hide it from me, he begins to drum his fingers against the door behind him.

'Where is that power backup?' he asks. 'This is taking too long.'

'I've never been trapped in a restroom before,' I tell him, and prepare to steer him in a different direction. 'I'm sure McCoy will give me grief about it later.'

Williams catches my eye this time.

113

'Christian McCoy is harmless,' he replies. 'At least he is now we have him.'

'What did he do?'

Williams frowns. For a beat I think I've blown it. I look to the window, and then to the ground. I even wish the generator would come back on, but forget all about that when I hear him take a breath.

'If McCoy's case ever makes it to court,' he tells me, 'Pitcairn Island will make a name for itself again for all the wrong reasons.' The name is familiar, but Williams gives me no time to think about it. 'Pitcairn is where the *Bounty* mutiny took place in the eighteenth century. Like everyone on that tiny island, McCoy is a direct descendant from one of Captain Bligh's crew. He's genetically primed to cause trouble, in my opinion. What marks out McCoy from his brethren is that he chose not to live peacefully off the land. Maybe growing up on a remote island in the South Pacific gave him itchy feet, because for years he's been giving us the slip the world over. Chechnya. Colombia. Sri Lanka. Afghanistan. Iraq. He's a mercenary, Hobbes. A *merc*, like mostly everyone here. If there's trouble, McCoy is at the heart of it. A mercenary will fight for any cause, so long as he's paid enough dough, and McCoy has made plenty of it. If you want him to join a holy war, that's fine if the price is right. In his time, he's fought for every known terrorist group from the Tamil Tigers to the IRA. Lately, of course, Al-Qaeda has been offering him plenty of employment opportunities, and they turn to McCoy because he delivers without conscience. Money is his god, Hobbes. In our view, that makes him worse than a terrorist. At least the terrorist genuinely believes what he's doing is righteous and just, no matter how appalling the consequences.'

'Is that why *I'm* here?' I ask. 'Because you think *I'm* a mercenary?'

Williams shrugs. 'You compromised Fort Knox. That's a national *institution*, man! In my view, that doesn't make you a mercenary. It just makes you a dumbass.'

'Thanks,' I say, flatly.

'Our top tech guy is out here at the moment,' he says, levelling with me now. 'That's why you're here, just like I told you in the first place.'

'I believe you,' I say. 'I'm just finding it hard to take it all in.'

'Well, don't take too long,' he replies quickly. 'We got a decommission team flying in the day after tomorrow to inspect the camp. So long as we can demonstrate that we're operating with full respect to human rights, despite the lousy conditions, with luck they'll close us down.'

Agent Williams looks around as he says this, shaking his head a little, and comes back to find me looking at him quizzically. 'For some time now, we've been crying out for better facilities,' he explains after a moment.

'The administration is confident the inspectors will take one look at this old fish house and recognise that we deserve some place better. It means you could be one of the last detainees to be processed here, Hobbes, and in such infamous company.'

Immediately, I think about Grimstad. Then my thoughts turn to the detainee who had mistaken me for someone else.

'Who's the female prisoner?'

As I say this, the humming sound strikes up again. Williams watches the bulb glow brightly, and nudges the door open with his back.

'After you,' he says, ignoring my question.

I do as I am told, heading into the corridor once more. It's only as we approach the door to the cannery that I stop and ask him something I just can't keep back.

'Why did you just tell me all that?'

In my experience, pressing anyone in authority for information might earn you one or two vital titbits. What I had got here was a feast, from the question mark hanging over the camp to the lowdown on McCoy, and yet the fact that he'd remained tight-lipped about the girl convinces me that he knew just what he was doing.

Agent Williams draws to a slow halt, nodding to himself now.

'Intelligence is a valuable commodity,' he says simply. 'I shared some with you. Soon it'll be your turn to share some with us.'

17

Come nightfall, there are no lights out. The cannery has been fitted with flood lamps, and these are simply dimmed.

I know it's late because when North came around to collect my supper tray, I stole a glance at his digital watch. Eight thirty-six, it read, and that was hours ago. Judging by the fact that most of the detainees are lying motionless on their mats now, I figure it must be gone midnight. The weirdest thing is that whenever military personnel come in from the courtyard, as one does right now, an eerie natural light stretches across the floor. At this time of night you'd expect it to be moonlight, but it doesn't have that bleached-bone quality. This is grey and indeterminate. It's as if a distant sun is still hanging on behind the horizon line, just as Williams had said. If night really doesn't follow day here, I think to myself, then we really are cut off from the world as I know it. Having travelled so far

117

from civilisation, in fact, to what is clearly a sub-zero wilderness, it could just be the last place on earth that anyone would think to find me: *the Arctic Circle*.

As soon as I reach this conclusion my mind just races all the more. I might be physically contained here, but I can't say the same thing for my thoughts. The figure at the door crosses the cannery floor now. I recognise Commander Stagger by his upright frame and the low-slung bill of his cap. He salutes a guard on the rear gantry, and then continues to walk with his hands behind his back. I watch him passing the cages on the other side. Some of the inmates stir. Others sleep or ignore him. Only McCoy picks himself up onto his elbows, and rubs his eyes like he's just been rudely awoken. Stagger doesn't change his pace. He simply moves on to the girl in the next cage, continuing what must be an inspection. She is curled up like a woodland animal, unlike Grimstad, who is laid out, corpse-like, on his back with his hands clasped over his pelvis.

I wish I could sleep as freely. Everything I've been through has left me so exhausted it's all I want to do. I guess that I'd shut down earlier this afternoon from shock. What happened with North has left my body in need of some recovery time, though it serves to stop me from getting any shut-eye now. I'm lying on my good side, with my head resting in the palm of one hand and the ground beneath my mat grinding into my bones.

Agent Williams hasn't helped matters. It isn't what

he revealed about McCoy that unnerves me. It's his concerns about the camp I can't shake off. The wind continues to howl outside the cannery, and though the flood lamps are dimmed deliberately they occasionally flicker as if threatening to go off completely once more. If the backup system fails, taking the heating with it, I wonder how long we'll have before the cold creeps in and claims us all? And if we *are* inside the Arctic Circle, on the uppermost cap of the world, would a rescue team be able to reach us in time?

'Trouble sleeping, Hobbes?'

The voice takes me by surprise. I snap out of my thoughts to find Commander Stagger addressing me. He's standing square in front of my cage. I look through the top to find him awaiting a response.

'Just thinking,' I tell him.

'Guilty conscience, huh?' He speaks quietly, almost in a whisper, and yet there's no hint of charity in his voice. 'I realise this is tough for a boy your age,' he continues, 'but don't go making extra trouble for yourself.'

I sit up, curious as to what's on his mind here.

'What extra trouble?'

Stagger seems disappointed by my response. 'North told me what happened on your arrival. I heard you kicked up about your accommodation here. Let me say this just the once,' he presses on, before I have a chance to protest, 'you're here voluntarily, I recognise that, but

119

there is no scope for dissent. Do I make myself clear, Hobbes? You're here to explain yourself to our security guy. If there's any trouble throughout your stay, we will send you back in *pieces*.'

Stagger stops himself there, having raised his voice to a degree where some of the other detainees have begun to stir. He studies me for a moment longer, both eyes focused tightly beneath the bill of his cap, and then moves off as if he's just been looking right through me.

I watch the Commander continue with his inspection. On reaching the final cage, he faces up to the guard on the gantry once again. In quick succession he holds up his index finger followed by all five digits on that hand, and then salutes the man by touching his temple. Returning the salute, the guard watches Stagger leave through the same side door I had used earlier. Whatever signal I've just witnessed, it simply adds to my rising sense that I am not safe here.

Above all, I am left dwelling on the kind of mindset that drives someone like North. Yes, he is a thug, but there are brains there as well as brawn. My shoulder hurts like hell, but he hasn't left a mark. Not a bruise, graze or swelling. I also think he knew that nobody who witnessed the assault would back me up if I dared to speak out. And from what Stagger has revealed, the guy was clearly out to stamp on me in more ways than one. It wasn't just the fact that he'd spun a story that had effectively earned me what felt like a warning. Even before Stagger stopped to speak to me, I'd been dwelling on how North had already succeeded in intimidating me once again, this time by forcing me to go hungry.

I hadn't exactly been looking forward to supper. Even so, when it arrived earlier I knew that I should eat. A big trolley had been wheeled in, and from there the guards on duty picked off trays packed with identikit meals. North had made a beeline for my cage. He then ordered me to back away from the gate, barking instructions like he fully expected me to leap at his throat. I had done exactly what I was told, and didn't even peel away the plastic cover until he gave me permission. But instead of going back to the trolley to serve the next detainee, he had dropped down on his haunches and stayed there.

'Vegetable stew and brown rice,' he'd said, as if the two dollops on my plate needed explaining. 'And that bar beside it is multigrain. We remove the wrappers so the jokers don't use them to jam the locks.'

I had just one plastic spoon to eat my food with. The meal was lukewarm, I found.

'Thanks,' I'd said, hoping he would leave me alone.

'Mah pleasure,' he'd replied, in that drawl of his, still watching me closely. 'Make sure you swallow it down, boy.'

Something about his interest had unnerved me at that moment. I saw him summon some saliva between his lips, which he then pointedly spat between his

121

boots. My chewing had slowed to a halt. In response a grin broke out across his face, and I just knew it was because he'd tampered with the food.

I'd had a driving urge to spit out my mouthful, but was also very frightened that it would bring me more trouble. So I did as he requested, struggling not to gag, and then pushed the plate away.

'I'm finished,' I'd told him.

'If I was the chef, I'd be mightily offended.'

'It's left a nasty taste in my mouth,' I'd said, reaching for the plastic cup on the tray. 'I take it this is clean water?'

'Pure as the driven snow. Just like me.'

After that, I'd taken myself to the back of the cage without being ordered, and avoided his gaze when he collected my untouched meal.

'Thank you,' I'd forced myself to say.

'Don't you want the bar?'

'Not any more.'

North had shrugged to himself and removed the tray. For a brief moment I had wondered if he really could've spat in my food. I hadn't seen him dip down towards my tray as he crossed the floor, or make any move to tamper with the meal's plastic cover. Once again I'd begun to question whether my nerves would hold out on me. I didn't feel calm. I felt like I was sitting in a space that could heat up underneath me at any moment.

Then came my brief exchange with Stagger, and with it a sense that the temperature was rising.

I am rattled, which goes against my nature. It doesn't help that I'm beginning to question whether these guys are conspiring against me. I even wonder whether much of what has happened so far could be some kind of test. I may have tried to tease information from Agent Williams earlier, but what he had gone on to share made me think *he* was the one playing *me*. Now I have the Commander to consider. If Stagger is wise to the truth about North's assault on me, perhaps he had just come to sound out whether I am the sort of detainee likely to keep his mouth shut. Not that I want him to suspect I'd hold anything back either. I think about this, and find myself worrying that perhaps I *should* be telling him all about the abuse and intimidation handed out by one of his guards.

I reflect on everything Commander Stagger said, searching for clues about the military's view of me . . . and then stop myself at once. For I'm being ridiculous, I realise. North is simply a loose cannon. Whether or not his superiors know is irrelevant. As soon as they sit me down to talk about Fort Knox, they'll swiftly realise that I am happy to cooperate. And besides, if I complain about my treatment here, it's only likely to delay my return home. Right now, it's all that matters to me.

I'm not surprised that my anxieties are running riot,

given my surroundings are designed to literally rattle my cage, but it still doesn't help to calm me. All I can do is shift my body on the mat to find the least uncomfortable position, and try to get some sleep.

Only this time I reach for the prayer mat, still rolled up in the corner, and lodge it under my head.

Immediately, I feel better, and close my eyes. This lasts for a minute at most, before the main door opens once again. I look across the floor without moving, and see several guards striding towards the first cage in my row. The first guard to reach it draws a baton from his belt and bangs it against the wire. I catch my breath at this crashing end to the silence. Judging by the way the guard responsible then barks an order at the detainee to back against his cage, I figure the poor guy must feel like he's woken into a nightmare.

I'm not alone in sitting up to watch. I recognise most of my fellow passengers from the flight take notice. Only Grimstad remains at rest.

'Step out of the cage, Sadeq. Don't make a scene like last time!' I watch the detainee do exactly as he is told. He stands before them, looking groggy, and then howls when two guards lock their elbows under his armpits. The man puts up no resistance. Even so, one of the guards unclips his baton from his belt and then whips it across the back of his knees.

'Do as you're told!'

With a cry, he just collapses into their control.

Immediately they rush their prize towards the side door, forcing him to hobble. I try to stand, shocked at this sudden upswing in noise and drama, but can only crouch in the cage, with my fingers grasping the wire.

The door swings closed behind them. I hear the sound of the lock turning on the other side, and look to my fellow detainees for some kind of explanation. The men in the cages on either side of me remain motionless on their mats. Their indifference makes me think this is a regular occurrence. I notice that the girl hasn't shifted either, while Grimstad basically looks like someone who has died in his sleep. Then I turn to find McCoy watching me, only he's not clowning any more. He simply nods solemnly and points at me, as if he knows somehow that they will be coming for me next.

18

McCoy is a troublemaker. This time, I fear he'd just stirred things up in my mind because he's wise to the drill here. It means as soon as the side door opens once again, about an hour later, I'm braced for some attention. The Pitcairn Islander isn't in possession of a sixth sense. I knew that. He'd just interpreted Stagger's hand signal to the guard: one and then five. The guy they had taken came out of the first cage in the row. There are three cages between us, as I had counted down after McCoy pointed me out.

I was in the fifth.

The detainee who had left between the guards is now returned in the same manner. He is ordered to keep his head down as they hurry him to his cage. Unlike his departure, however, the guy doesn't make any effort to run with them. His legs are making vague movements, but the momentum is with the guards, who drag him the last couple of metres to his cage.

'Dead man walking, Hobbes!' McCoy is relishing this. I don't even have to look in his direction to know it. My heart is working like a jackhammer. I begin to prickle and tremble. I can't shake the image of what they did to the other detainee before dragging him away. If I knew where they were about to take me it might help, but I'm not dumb enough to ask any questions. As they turn their attention along the row, I find myself retreating to the back of my cage. The sound of their boots striking the floor grows louder, and then stops, just as McCoy had predicted, directly in front of me.

'Showtime, Hobbes. Let's give these people a master class in British manners, huh?'

I have seen both these guards before, I realise. One of them had glared at me when Williams first pushed his way to the front of the queue. Now he snaps the padlock open, and requests that I step out of the cage. I emerge through the open gateway, braced as best I can for them to grab me by the wrists.

Only that doesn't happen. I am shown no physical restraint whatsoever.

The silent guard simply shows me the way towards the door. I have to look at them in turn to be sure, but then do as I'm told. The pair walk close beside me, but as an escort only. I am still feeling deeply intimidated, but also just a little foolish now for showing such fright in front of McCoy. I hear him on my way out, berating the guards first of all, and then surrendering to an order from the marksman on the gantry to shut the hell up.

The guards make no conversation as we walk. We turn into the corridor at a brisk pace. It gives me little time to take much in once we pass the restroom. I count six solid doors on one side and the other, numbered from one to twelve. We stop outside door number ten. The glaring guard raps high up the door with his knuckles. I hear a muffled '*Yo*', and immediately find myself facing what looks like a meeting room. It's stark and white, with a table in the middle and a strip light overhead. Commander Stagger is seated at one end of the table. Another man is with him, at the seat facing away from me. He moves to stand up as I enter, but his chair is tucked in so tightly that he makes a bit of a mess of it. Commander Stagger remains seated, with a stack of documents in front of him.

'Make yourself comfortable, Hobbes.'

I'm directed to the only spare chair around the table, facing the Commander himself. The man on my left has sorted himself out now. He's back in his seat, pushing up a pair of oversized glasses. This guy has the kind of corkscrew auburn hair that girls would pay a fortune to gain or lose, depending on their style sense. It's really just a ball of frizz that's clipped short over his ears and at the nape of his neck. He's a big build, too, with a chin that threatens to crease in two when he refers to his own set of documents.

128

'Hobbes, this is Arty Dougal. Arty is the reason why you've agreed to come all this way.'

I nod and smile, and then wonder if that's the right thing to do. This isn't a job interview, after all, or a bid to earn a place on the computer-science degree course I had in mind. Arty may be dressed like he's just been dragged backwards from his desktop, in a T-shirt and combat pants, but I am well aware of the ranking officer before me, as well as the two guards breathing down my neck. Commander Stagger clearly shares my own need for space, because he asks them both to wait outside.

Just as soon as the door has closed, Arty Dougal picks up a pencil, taps it on the paper, and says: 'Shall I tell you what I think?'

My first response is to frown, but I stop short of asking him to repeat himself.

'Go on,' I say, sounding as puzzled as I look.

'I think we have a great deal in common. That's my opinion, based on the report I just read on you. How old are you, Hobbes?'

'Seventeen,' I say, addressing this to Commander Stagger, who is listening intently. 'I don't reach the age of criminal responsibility for a few months yet.'

Stagger hides a smile behind the back of his hand.

'When I was your age,' Arty continues, 'the phones were the biggest challenge. The Internet didn't exist, but we still had a global network in the form of cables, switchboards and exchanges. *Phreaking*, it was called, back in the late seventies. A phone phreak basically made it their mission to understand more about the telephone systems than the companies who ran them, and then used that knowledge to their advantage. Once you had an engineer's identification number, you were away. You could call up the switchboard operator, tell them you were running a maintenance check, and they'd do anything for you. I could have them set up party lines to chat with friends, make long distance calls and even set up wire taps – you name it, I pulled it off and never paid a dime for anything. I once picked up a payphone in a police precinct, made the one down the hall ring via exchanges in Berlin, Moscow, Beijing and back again. Piece of cake, my friend! I even had the company credit my account with the cost. Can you believe that?'

I don't doubt his mastery of messing with telephones, but I'm more interested in what he had been doing in a police precinct. Nevertheless, I tell myself it isn't my business, and just look suitably impressed instead.

'It sounds like a golden age,' I tell him.

'Oh, it was,' he agrees. 'Until technology raised the stakes, of course. The telephone operatives who used to make the connections for the engineers? Those friendly girls and boys were replaced by electronic switches. Now you couldn't just conduct a conversation with a switch. They were triggered instead by the bleeps and

130

squeals from a little box of electronics. All the engineers were issued with them. They'd just dial in and let it squeal down the line.'

'Like the sound of a modem,' Commander Stagger interjects helpfully, though I know this already.

What I don't expect is that the man he's just interrupted would then offer me his best impression of one linking to a network.

'*Bbbrrrrrrr . . . ddiiiiiiiiii . . . chkchkchkchkckhchk . . .*'

All I can do is sit there aghast as Arty Dougal whistles, trills and clicks at us both. I glance at Commander Stagger, who notes my expression and asks him to stop.

'I think Hobbes knows what a modem sounds like,' he says harshly.

'I do,' I say. 'We used to use one at home when I first got into computers.'

Commander Stagger refers to his notes at this, as if perhaps he has details of it right there.

'Anyway,' says Arty, unabashed, pulling at one ear lobe. 'We're getting ahead of ourselves by several years here. When the first electronic switches were introduced, they were triggered by a much more simple series of audible commands. Before the engineers' boxes came onto the black market, some of the phreakers actually mastered the exact pitches used by the phone company. Have you ever heard a 2,600-hertz pitch, Hobbes?' Arty curls two fingers to his lips and whistles briefly. 'Back then, it would get you a directory request. With the switch opened up, you could walk right into the system and speak to real people in any department you liked. One time I had the district judge's home telephone put on a blacklist. It took the company six *weeks* to work out how to bring it back—'

'What did he do?' I ask suddenly, cutting Arty dead.

'Huh?'

'What did the judge do to earn that kind of grief from you?'

My question just came out on impulse. Having picked up on the comment about the police precinct, I guess my curiosity got the better of me. It had already earned me about as much grief as I could get myself into anyway. Watching Arty Dougal shift uncomfortably on his seat, I just hope I haven't pushed things too far. He glances at Commander Stagger, who nods as if to permit him to answer.

'I got into some trouble with credit cards,' he confesses, only for Stagger to explain things more fully.

'Arty has a criminal history, Hobbes. When the cops picked him up in 1985, they found over three hundred bank statements in his apartment. None of them were in his name.'

'The credit card companies were very vulnerable at that time,' Arty protests. 'If your card was lost or stolen, you'd call a helpline to report it. I just found a way to redirect the line so those calls came to me instead.'

He falls quiet for a moment, seemingly ashamed of his actions. 'Once I'd harvested details of a credit card, I'd call up the company for real, make out I was the card holder, and request a change of address. After that, I'd wait a few weeks, report the card as lost—'

'And a replacement card would pop through your letter box, also a new PIN number if you hadn't already succeeded in extracting that, along with the statements recording your spending spree.'

Judging by the look on Arty's face, I figure I've correctly guessed the final stage of the scam. 'Things are more secure now,' he tells me. 'You couldn't get away with it any more.'

'And you didn't get away with it *then*!' Stagger points out, smiling all the same. 'The cops only came knocking because they'd been tipped off that Arty had been dealing a little dope, so you could say he was unlucky. As it turned out, the bust proved to be the making of him. It seemed a waste to let his formidable talents wither away in jail, which is why we offered him a job instead.'

Arty shrugs and spreads his hands. 'They made me apologise to the judge first, of course, but from that moment on you could say I saw the light. Over twenty years I've been working for the military now, overseeing security for their communication systems. You won't get far by whistling into a mouthpiece any more, but nor can you crack through my firewalls. Damn it, they're impenetrable. Like castle ramparts with cauldrons of boiling oil set to rain down upon anyone who attempts to get through them. Hobbes, I've built my career on keeping up with the latest developments in technology. Which is why I'm so keen to know how you broke into the bank vault. Because it seems to me you and I are on the same wavelength, but yet I can't work it out. C'mon! I told you my story. It's your turn to tell us one to match it.'

Arty Dougal slots his pencil behind one ear and awaits my answer. I return my attention to Stagger, to be sure he wants me to speak. Maybe I'm looking a little lost for words, because he refers to his documents and paints a picture of the crime scene.

'Fort Knox Gold Bullion Depository boasts one of the finest security systems in the USA,' the Commander says. 'It has to, in view of the fact that it's among the biggest gold stockpiles in the world. The vault itself is constructed from steel and encased in concrete. Two carefully selected members of staff are assigned to the dual combination locks that control the door. To open it, they must punch in codes known only to them, and do so at *exactly* the same time. And even if a civilian *wanted* to see that door open, they couldn't. The vault is contained within a granite-reinforced building, which is itself set within heavily patrolled grounds. You wouldn't even be permitted to stand at the perimeter fence. Even if you could, you'd be disappointed. The removal of gold bars is strictly controlled. In fact, the vault is only ever opened to check the stockpile hasn't been tampered with.'

He stops there, allowing everything to sink in. 'The only other sites on American soil that boast those kind of measures are the nuclear silos.'

'Which I oversee,' adds Arty with conviction. 'All military sites are *my* responsibility.'

'The bullion that went missing was worth millions,' Stagger explains. 'If every single bar had been taken, it could've threatened the country with bankruptcy.'

'But all the bullion *didn't* go missing,' I point out. 'And I didn't do any of the stealing. I just opened the doors to the vault to prove it could be done. What happened after that came as a complete surprise to me.'

What I say is met with silence. The Commander and the systems security expert simply look at me in astonishment. Overhead, the light bulb dies for a second, and then stutters back into life. The pair don't even blink.

'Then you must be a prince among thieves,' says Stagger, as if to humour me. He folds his hands on the desk, considering me for a moment. 'OK, why don't you take us right back to the beginning. I want to know *exactly* why you chose to target the depository, and what in God's name you were thinking of when you thought you could pull it off.'

19

Here's the thing about hacking: it isn't rocket science. You don't need a sky high IQ, nor expertise in computer programming. You need to be switched on, of course, but anyone can learn the tricks of the trade. It's all about understanding how a security system works, and exploiting its weakest point.

In every case, that point is always human.

A quarter of a century ago, before computers wired up the world, the phone phreakers tapped into the very same vulnerability. Arty Dougal started out by tricking switchboard operators into making connections on his behalf, and that approach hasn't changed. Maybe Arty had put so much effort into keeping up with advances in technology he'd lost sight of the basics.

It doesn't matter what kind of protective measures stand in the way of your goal. You could be faced with software defences such as packet-filtering firewalls, network intrusion detectors, or tarpits and honeypots designed to snare and trap unauthorised users: nothing is impenetrable. Even the devices that are intended to *physically* prevent you from accessing a secure area can be overcome in the same way. From titanium vaults to infrared beams, combination locks or pressure-sensitive pads, every form of protection requires one thing, and that's someone with the authority to access it.

The person with the keys and the passwords might be highly trained, but they still have to make decisions every second of the day. As a hacker, that's your target, because people can always be fooled into making the *wrong* decisions.

It might take a little persuasion, some sly trickery perhaps, but one wrong move could cost them dear. What's more, if the system is a big one, like a military installation, or, let's say, a bullion depository, then more than one individual will know how to access the system.

And the more people who know, the less secure the system becomes.

You really don't need much to make a start, which is what always surprises people. It was the same in Arty's day, as he had demonstrated by whistling a simple tone that would trigger a switch down a telephone wire. All he would have needed to achieve this was an engineer's manual, one that outlined the different tones and their functions, and engineers were only human. They could be bribed or hoodwinked, which is where the true skill lay.

Arty's account of how he could get through a telecom company's first line of defence was certainly impressive. Even so, I could have told him that one of America's most infamous phone phreakers was once rumoured to have the power to trigger a full-scale nuclear attack on another country. All he had to do, so the story goes, was call up a classified military number from a public phone booth, insert two fingers between his lips and blow gently into the receiver.

Nowadays, your average hacker can freely download a simple little software program that does the same dirty work. Like the telecom companies of old, every organisation has its own internal system. This is basically just a network of staff computers. Each organisation is different, of course, depending on their needs, and yet the system in place will always have a weak spot. Somewhere, it'll be hooked up to the Internet. This is the link between the inner sanctuary of the company and the big bad world outside, and precisely the connection that the software can hunt down.

It means with a few keystrokes you can bring up all the staff computers within a company system, including the user names for each one.

Now, this kind of information is useless if the computers on the system are password protected, as well they should be. However, you can set this software program to bring back only those systems in which one or two users have left their passwords *blank*. It might be a sackable offence in most places, but for many workers it's a minor risk that is well worth taking. When you hit your desk each morning, tired and maybe hungover, the last thing you need is a computer that won't let you in because you've forgotten your password again. Leaving it blank does away with any need to remember one at all. And besides, nobody will know, will they?

Timing is important at this stage. As a hacker, you don't want to log on to your target's computer remotely while he's actually working on it. He'll only wonder why the cursor has just started zipping all over the screen. Wherever they are in the world, work out what time that organisation closes for business, and make your move deep within the witching hour. Only you can decide what to do once you're inside, of course. Most hackers simply ransack a system and then put it all back together again before they leave. We're not crooks at heart. In general, we're driven by a hunger to understand how everything works, and exit feeling we have mastered it. So long as you delete the log file on your way out, the one recording evidence of your activities, you won't even leave any electronic footsteps or fingerprints behind.

This is textbook stuff, of course. No genius required. Just a lot of time on your hands, and a willingness to persevere. You can hack into an unprotected desktop and find half a dozen script kiddies at work in the same

20

'OK,' I say, addressing the two men at the table. 'Where shall I begin?'

'The start is always good,' replies Stagger, referring to the notes he's just made. 'Who's behind it, Hobbes?'

'Pardon me?'

He peers over the top of his documents. 'Who commissioned the job?'

I glance at Arty Dougal. 'Nobody,' I say. 'It's just something I did from my bedroom.'

'Hackers don't work alone,' he tells me. 'Hackers may *appear* to be outsiders. People who have some difficulty making friends and holding down relationships. But inside them lurks a deep-seated need to belong. To be part of a *system*.'

'I did it myself,' I say again.

Arty Dougal seems surprised that I haven't bought into his theory. 'You're asking us to believe that nobody else knew?'

'Oh, some people were aware of what I was doing,' I admit. 'But you didn't ask me that. You asked if anyone put me up to the job. The answer to that question is no. I got the idea after reading a thread on a message board.'

Both Stagger and Arty Dougal sit up in their seats. Either they didn't know about this, or they're surprised I'm being so open with them.

'Go on,' says Arty.

'The thread was about locations that were believed to be impossible to hack, and Fort Knox was top of the list, with the Pentagon at number two. Frankly, I'm surprised I was the first to try it out.'

'You weren't,' answers Stagger. 'You were just the first to succeed.'

A pause comes into our conversation. Despite the crap that's come down on me for what I did, I can't help feeling a note of pride at his admission.

Commander Stagger appears to chew on his next question before asking it. 'Tell us more about this message board, Hobbes.'

'It's just a website.'

'A hacking community.' Arty nods sagely, as if somehow I've just admitted that I belong to a system just like he had said. I face him directly again, and wait for his smile to fade away.

'It's *just* a website,' I state again. 'An online message board for amateur hackers to share software, ideas, hints and tips.'

Commander Stagger pushes his notes to one side. 'So once you decided to attempt an infiltration of the bullion depository, did you announce it on the board?'

I nod. 'Most people thought I was joking, though.'

'Most people like who?'

I think about this. 'Nobody uses their real names,' I say. 'I can give you some screen names, if that helps, but I don't actually *know* these people for real. And I swear not a single person helped me get into the depository.'

Arty Dougal leafs through his documents. '*Chimera*,' he says, pinpointing a line on one page with his pen. 'Chimera is one of the names we picked up.'

I sense my heart-rate lift a little. So they did know about the board. 'What about him?' I ask.

'Chimera is spelled here using the number one in place of the letter "i".' Arty smiles to himself at this. 'It's kinda retro nowadays for a hacker to switch numbers for letters. The phreakers were doing that back in the early eighties.'

Commander Stagger doesn't appear to register the remark. He just continues to look directly across the table at me. 'We aim to monitor every hacking community,' he says. 'We just didn't take this one seriously until after the depository sounded the alarm.'

Arty Dougal stabs at his papers. 'What we have here are the transcripts from the message board. Every conversation you had online in the week preceding the

143

job is here in black and white, which led us directly to your door.'

I glance at the document. Even from where I'm sitting, I can see line after line of chat. I clear my throat, and say: 'Chimera is the name of the guy who kept saying it couldn't be done. But I can't tell you anything more about him.'

Consulting the transcript now, Arty Dougal finds a section midway down the page. 'On January 16, at 0337 GMT, Chimera wrote: "*Man, you are asking for some trouble! Be sure to sweep for traces before you make that move, and let me know how you get on*".' Arty stops there, glances up at me, and sneers. 'Someone here really cares for you, Hobbes.'

I feel my face go hot despite myself. 'It's nothing like that!'

'Well, three days later, Chimera is back in touch, and your welfare is high up the agenda, my friend.' Arty leafs through several pages. 'January 19, at 0203 GMT, Chimera writes: "*I've been looking into the Fort Knox job, and I've had a change of heart. It's too crazy for words. You might as well be stepping on a mouse-trap. Even sniffing at that set-up is gonna bring them slamming down on you. I'm sorry, pal. I shouldn't have suggested it.*".'

I glare at Arty. 'And Chimera was right to be so cautious,' I suggest.

'So why didn't you take the advice?' Stagger is the

only one to remain quite calm, which serves to remind me that I really should do likewise.

'Because of everyone else,' I say eventually. 'A lot of people had picked up on the thread, and were basically waiting for me to give it my best shot. They said I was the best, which was flattering. I found it hard to resist.'

Arty Dougal refers to a page at the back of his documents. 'Saint Joe, Proxijunki, BitPunk, Surgeonz, BillGoats.' He pauses there, and looks at me. 'I could go on.'

I glance at the list he's just been reading from. There are dozens of screen names on it. I guess I would recognise them all.

'Out of everyone,' I stress, 'Chimera was the only person who seemed genuinely concerned that I could be caught. When all the others were daring me to go in through the front door, he was alone in suggesting that I think again. That doesn't mean he'd taken a shine to me. It's just common sense!'

Commander Stagger shows me his palms. 'Take it easy,' he says. 'We're simply trying to establish the facts.' He stops there, as if to give me some space to cool off. 'What else do you know about him?'

'Nothing,' I say pointedly. 'Chimera could be from anywhere in the world, for all I know. And I'm not daft. Hackers use a screen name for good reason. I do realise he might not be all he seems.'

'Which is what?' asks Stagger.

145

I fold my arms. 'I have no idea, and that's the truth. To be honest, I didn't give him a great deal of thought. I was kind of busy working out the best way to hack into the depository.'

Stagger appears amused at this. It's Arty who seems unhappy about my reply.

'Excuse me,' he says. 'I don't mean any offence by this, but you're just a kid. Fort Knox has been the home of America's gold reserves for the last seventy years. So, they've had a little while to test their security, and make sure it's watertight. Everything from the American Declaration to the British Crown Jewels have been stored there because, frankly, it's considered the safest place in the world. They run a thorough check on the system and procedures every other day to make sure of it. I've observed their exercises, Hobbes. The only way they could improve the set-up would be if they hired *me* to take care of it!' Arty stops there, and considers what he's just said. 'I gotta tell you, my friend, you may have done me a favour. After losing all that gold, I should imagine they've just fired their security director.'

'Maybe so.' I glance at Stagger, who seems content to let Arty continue playing with me.

'But you have to help me out here some more, Hobbes. When that call comes through, inviting me for the interview, I want to be able to tell them just how you succeeded. And right now, I'm coming up with nothing but question marks. So tell me your methods,

Hobbes. You must've cooked up some code to hijack the depository computer system. C'mon. Let's close this case right here and now!'

I shrug, not wishing to make Arty look as stupid as he sounds. 'The depository is situated within *military* grounds,' I say. 'Every week, the battalion there oversees one of those exercises you just mentioned. That information is freely available on the battalion website, as well as the name of the senior ranking officers and a number for the switchboard.' As I speak, I note the blood slowly draining from Arty's face. 'It's standard nowadays for big institutions to have some kind of public website.'

'I knew that,' he says to cover. 'But the depository guys are totally independent from us. The way they store and monitor the gold is their responsibility, not ours. We serve to protect the facility, and act as a deterrent. Our role is to make sure that whoever enters and exits the perimeter grounds has the correct documentation.'

'But you still request that the depository test the vault doors every week? I read about the procedure online.'

Arty wriggles in his seat.

'We have to be sure there are no holes in their system,' he says, sounding as uncomfortable as he looks. 'And the only way to do that is by checking it out ourselves.'

'I agree.' I smile as I say this, nodding now.

This time Arty registers my expression, and takes offence from what I've just implied.

'Now hold on. Don't you dare suggest that you hacked into their system by first gaining access to mine! Our system is *totally* secure. We got Next Generation Firewalls operating Deep Packet Inspection systems. Our Intrusion Prevention System is state-of-the-art, man! There's no way a script kiddie like you could take over a computer on *my* network. You can hunt around as much as you like. You won't find any way in without a password.'

'I know,' I reply. 'It went without saying that every one of your computers in the system would be password-protected. That's why I picked up the phone.'

21

The two men exchange a look, and then focus on me in stunned silence.

'You *telephoned* the battalion?' Commander Stagger repeats what I have just said as if to check he has heard me correctly.

'I dialled the switchboard and told them simply that I had a message to call back, I didn't give a name, just sounded vague and in need of some help. When the operator asked who left the message, I said the line was unclear, but that it had come from the top dog's office. Basically, I gave them the name of the main man listed on the website: Command Sergeant Major Daniels.'

I stop there, just in case Arty and Stagger have any questions, but they simply wait for me to continue. 'The operator suggested that it could've been his secretary who left the message. To be helpful, and because it was important for later, I said it was a male voice on my answer machine, but definitely not Daniels himself. The operator told me in that case it couldn't have been his secretary, and suggested the name of the only other man to work from Daniel's office: Communications Officer Fradera.' I snapped my finger here, and mimicked the tone I had taken over the phone. '"*That's the one!*" I said, and joked that Fradera should really learn not to mumble when leaving messages. The operator laughed and offered to put me through. As soon as the line started ringing, and the operator disengaged, I hung up.' Commander Stagger seems puzzled when I finish there, so I add, 'The operator had just given me all the information I needed: the name of a staff member who worked closely with the senior officer.'

'But you took a risk!' Arty Dougal declares this with some relish. 'Had Officer Fradera picked up his phone, you'd've been entirely unprepared. Frankly your call would have been treated as highly suspicious.' It's as if I've just owned up to a major flaw in my plan.

'You're right,' I agree. 'But as I was using a payphone on the way home from college, I wasn't too concerned about being traced.'

Arty's jowls tighten as I say this. He writes something in his notebook. 'Go on,' he mutters.

'A couple of hours later I called the switchboard again, and asked to be put through to Human Resources.'

Stagger shoots me a look. 'You make it sound like you were hoping for a job.'

150

'In any organisation,' I reply, smiling briefly with him, 'HR is the department that deals with hiring, firing, training and welfare. So, if you want to know the movements of key operatives, that's where a good hacker begins. I put on my best American accent for the call. It's passable, but the tone is what matters most. I learned that from my Drama course. Even though I had no idea what Fradera sounded like, the way to convince someone over the phone is by speaking with authority, sounding human, and keeping the conversation brief. And that's just what I did when the nice lady in Human Resources took my call. I identified myself as Fradera, and asked if I could double-check the holiday roster for the IT department staff. Now that's hardly a request that's going to sound alarm bells. I explained that we were concerned about cover over the next seven days, and could she please confirm any absences in that time. Sure, she replied, and began pecking at her keyboard. A moment later, she confirmed that I had nothing to worry about. All three team members had no time booked off in the next week. The only note she had on file from the IT department confirmed that the Operational Director and his second-in-command were scheduled to attend a lunchtime briefing on Tuesday. That's fine, I said, and thanked her for being so helpful.'

Commander Stagger is the first to respond. Leaning back in his seat, he appears to evaluate me for a second, and says, finally: 'Are you a hacker, son, or a confidence trickster?'

I'm unsurprised by the question. I just don't want to sound like a criminal by admitting that deception and manipulation are more effective than hoping to crack codes. In a small way, though, I'm flattered that my efforts have shaken up his view of what hacking is all about. My Drama tutor wouldn't exactly be overjoyed to see her student in a fix like this. Then again, without my acting training I'd never have got this far.

'I was just looking for a way in,' is all I can tell the Commander. 'Having got the lowdown on the tech team, I needed to make just one more call before I went online.'

'Take your time.' Stagger glances at Arty Dougal, who seems thoroughly unimpressed by my account so far. 'At least I understand the phone trickery.'

I rest my elbows on the table. As I prepare to continue, I feel almost relieved to be getting my account into the open.

'Come Tuesday lunchtime,' I say next, 'Eastern Standard Time, I called IT. I knew only one person would be there to pick up the call, and that he was at the bottom of the department food chain. With someone of low rank, it's important to be authoritative but also *impatient*.'

'Don't I know it,' Stagger mutters to himself.

'As soon as I heard a voice on the line,' I continue,

'I introduced myself as Communications Officer Fradera, and suggested he might know why I'm calling. The guy I spoke to sounded mystified, until I raised my voice and then he just listened. I told him I had just suffered an earbashing from Command Sergeant Major Daniels – the battalion's top dog. I said he was fortunate Daniels himself hadn't marched down to the IT department to dress down the clown who thought it amusing to deny him access to his computer. I told him Daniels was a busy man. He had operations to oversee and just how humiliating was it for him to admit this wasn't possible because he had forgotten his password, huh? As requested the day before, he simply wanted access to his desktop so he could get on with his job of running the goddamn show!'

I bang the table as I say this, adopting the same accent and abrupt tone that I had used over the phone.

'That's what happened?' Commander Stagger strokes his throat, reflecting on what I've said.

'Yes it is. I said that Command Sergeant Major Daniels was in no mood for excuses this time, and basically didn't let the IT guy on the end of the line get a word in edgeways. I was ready for him to say that he had no record of such a request, and also his plea for me to call back later that day when a senior ranking officer would be available to deal with my query. I just stopped him short, asked for his name, rank and serial number, and suggested he might like to explain his refusal to cooperate to the Command Sergeant Major himself unless he reset the damn password *fast*!'

'OK, hold on.' Commander Stagger draws himself closer to the table. 'This is his *computer* password now, am I right?'

'That's it. The password that lets him access the system so he can check his emails, write documents, search for files and use the Internet.' Stagger nods as I say this. I figure it's worth appearing to work with him on this. As the man who calls the shots around here, the Commander is someone I sorely need on my side. Arty Dougal, meanwhile, is leafing through his notes, if only to hide his rising unease. For what I've just described is really very straightforward, and totally focused on exploiting the human element of any security system. I had simply sounded off at someone with little authority, and persuaded him to execute a simple, everyday function.

'So you acquired access to the Command Sergeant Major's computer,' says Stagger to clarify. 'By tricking the IT operative to reset the password.'

'Which is a criminal offence,' grumbles Arty.

'But the password is useless without access to his computer.' Stagger waits until he has my full attention. 'I'm no expert here, Hobbes, but what good is one without the other?'

I glance at Arty, find him observing me already. For a moment I look directly into his eyes. I just know he's aware that once someone has the password the security guys might as well pack up and go home.

'Hobbes ran a program,' he says reluctantly. 'A program that allowed him to exploit any unprotected computer on the system. As soon as Major Daniel's password was reset, his computer would've appeared on the radar.'

Commander Stagger stares at me. 'Tell me about the program,' he asks. 'Did you write it yourself?'

'I got it from the Internet,' I say with a shrug. 'It only takes a couple of minutes to download.'

'Did you pay for it?' he asks, sounding increasingly tense. 'Who are your contacts?'

'It's available to anyone,' I tell him. 'You just have to know what you're searching for, and away you go.'

Stagger turns to Arty next. 'Are you aware of the existence of this program?'

Arty Dougal looks like he wants to shrink inside his skin. 'It's called malware,' he says. 'Software created by mischief-makers and shared among their own kind. It isn't something we can control, however, because people are always tinkering with the code to suit their own purposes. All we can do is react to it.'

If Arty is making excuses here, Stagger isn't listening. He might have been telling the truth, but the Commander is clearly concerned by the program's consequences, not its coding. In my case, I'd tweaked the program so it only picked out unprotected computers on a military system. Then I just inputted the address of the battalion's server, and let it come back with the only computer to have been recently relieved of its password.

'So with this program,' Stagger continues, 'Hobbes could've then logged on from the comfort of his own home, and impersonated the battalion commander? He could've accessed confidential files, and issued orders by email in his name?'

Arty refers to his notes, looking flustered all of a sudden, but just sort of gives up after a second.

'It's possible,' he says with a sigh.

'Yes or no, Dougal?'

'Yes,' replies Arty, reddening visibly now. 'Hobbes infiltrated the battalion's computer system.'

'A *military* system. *Not* the depository system. The one overseen by *you*.'

'That would be correct.'

'And so, theoretically, the battalion commander's regular request for the depository keyholders to open the vault could've been issued by Hobbes?'

'Yes.' Arty Dougal's voice seems to grow smaller every time he confirms what I have done. 'But I can assure you it will not happen again.'

Commander Stagger compresses his lips. For a beat I think he is going to explode. Instead, he calls for the two guards to return, and quietly asks them to escort me back to the cannery.

22

I am too wired to sleep. Back inside my cage, I sit on my mat and reflect on what just happened. I'm relieved to see that McCoy is all curled up with his back to me. Grimstad is awake, however, having just been roused to take his pills. Once again, he waits for the MP to walk away, and then spits them into his hand.

As for the girl in the cage between them, she is slumped against the frame at the back. She's resting there with her hands in her lap and her legs crossed at the ankles. I can't be sure if her eyes are closed because she's asleep or because she doesn't want to look at me.

Everything I told Commander Stagger and the security consultant was true. I was as stunned as they were that I'd managed to log on to the battalion system. Calling up a target and tricking them into resetting a password wasn't foolproof. Often, an IT employee would refuse to carry out such a request over the phone. They'd insist on hearing the order from that person face to face, though most crumbled if you pitched your sense of annoyance with them just right.

Arty Dougal would pay for a lapse like that, not me. There was no problem with the hardware in his security system, and the software was state-of-the-art. It was the people operating it who had let me through, but they were not to blame. Arty should've prepared every *single* member of the battalion for a scam like mine, from the switchboard up, just as Commander Stagger had realised.

I am well aware that I've caused a lot of grief, especially for the military's so-called security expert. Then again, I figure my work could also benefit their defences. Having highlighted the weak points, action would be taken to ensure the same mistakes weren't made again. You could never guarantee Fort Knox would be safe from another attack, nor any other secure environment. That would only happen when they stopped relying on humans to operate the system.

I unfasten my jumpsuit at the throat, wishing they would turn the heat down. The only time this place stops feeling like a slow cooker is when the main door opens. Every time a guard comes or goes, the cold penetrates the stew in seconds. The light out there is just as striking. Despite the fact that I'm awake for much of the night, it refuses to get dark. In fact, it's only the arrival of two familiar guards that tells me morning has broken.

'Hungry, Hobbes?' North asks, walking past my cage. He holds both hands behind his back like he's taking a stroll in the park. I don't reply. I just watch him go and hope he isn't here to serve up breakfast. A moment later, with a brief zapping sound across the cannery, the floodlights fire up to full power. The sudden brightness makes me blink and shield my eyes. I hear stirring all around me, and then voices join the mix.

A new day is here. I remind myself that I have just come through an entire night locked up inside a high security military detention centre. I feel different somehow, as if I have acquired a thicker skin.

'Hey there.' I look up from the floor of my cage, and find Cortés. Unlike his colleague, he pauses for a moment.

'What time is it?' I ask.

'I can't tell you that,' he replies, though his tone of voice suggests he'd like to. He turns and nods at the main door. There's a lot of activity going on over there, with the arrival of yet more guards. Despite this, it's the glimpse of the snowbound courtyard that holds my attention. 'Out here,' says Cortés, and I realise he is offering me something, 'we might as well be frozen in time.'

I turn to face him once more. 'I'll be going home soon,' I say, and search his expression for some suggestion that I might be wrong. 'I've told them everything I know.'

159

Cortés listens to me but is promptly drawn away by a commotion from the cages opposite. McCoy can only have been awake for a matter of minutes, but already he's drawing the sights of the rifle-toting guards on the gantry.

'I need my epilepsy pills!' he yells, slamming at the gate to his cage now. 'I got a beast getting ready to break out of my skull right now. Without my meds, *someone* will pay!'

'Calm down!' North is first to reach the cage. He kicks viciously at the gate with his boot, which prompts the detainee to shrink away. 'You don't get no medication because you don't need it! You got a headache, nothing more!'

'The doctors are lying sons of bitches,' howls McCoy, and shoots a cruel glare across at Thomas Grimstad. 'You medicate *him*, why not me?'

'Don't make me answer that,' snarls North. He wipes his mouth with the back of his hand, trading glares with the man. 'OK,' he says finally, sounding resigned now. 'I'm through with you, McCoy. Just get yourself to the back of the cage and remain there. You need to chill some.' He stops there and looks around. 'Cortés!' he yells. 'I need some muscle in here *now*. We're taking this punk to the Fridge!'

Through the morning, a sense of calm occupies the cannery. Without McCoy, the tension eases by a note.

The power goes down two more times. On the second occasion, which lasts for twenty seconds or so, one of the guards in the gantry curses his luck for being posted in a tired out goddamn tin shack like this.

Despite the blackouts, I stop being so aware of my surroundings, and just sort of retreat into my space here inside the cage. I even close my eyes for a very short while. Just enough to recharge from empty. During this time, quite without warning, one of the detainees at the far end of my row begins to sob and then howl. Within the space of a minute, the guy has completely lost it. At first, the guards simply ignore him. Eventually, one of the marksmen and even some of the detainees yell at him to get a grip, but this just prompts the poor guy to begin banging his head against the cage. I listen to all this without moving, wondering if the policy is to just ignore this kind of freak-out, and only open my eyes when I hear footsteps approaching.

'I heard they interviewed you last night. That's good. It means things are moving on.' Agent Williams drops down in front of the cage. He shoots a look at the detainee in distress and shakes his head in pity or annoyance. Either way, with all that noise going on I figure he can at least speak to me freely. I sit up, mindful of his advice that I should be entirely open and honest about how I had broken into Fort Knox. Judging by his upbeat manner, I suspect word must have reached him that I had complied in full. 'You'll soon be on that flight out of here, Hobbes. Just like you were promised. With any luck, I won't be far behind.'

I remember what he had told me about the camp being set to close down. 'When will you find out?' I ask him.

'Once the decommissioning party have filed a report following their inspection. Most of the time, we pray the generator won't fail on us. When they show up, a lot of personnel here are praying that it *does* cut out. Anything so they deem this place unfit for purpose. Just as long as everyone behaves themselves, my guess is they'll make the right recommendation and hot-foot it back to civilisation.'

'Hopefully, I'll be leaving with them.'

Williams chuckles to himself. I'm convinced by the way he relates to me now that I really won't be in this crate much longer. 'There's always hope,' he agrees. 'Although I know for a fact you'll be helping prepare for their arrival.'

I tip my head to one side, mystified. 'How so?'

'The airstrip is covered in several feet of frozen snow. It requires clearing and gritting after every blizzard, and your name is down in the detail assigned to it this morning.'

'That's slave labour,' I joke. 'A chain gang.'

'It beats trudging around the courtyard until your fingers and toes go numb,' replies Williams. 'You're not classified as a major escape risk, you see, which means they can kit you out properly this time without worrying that you'll make a run for it.'

'How can you be so sure?' I ask, as yet another detainee screams at the guy still wailing inside his cage. Even the threat of having his neck snapped in two doesn't silence him, however.

Agent Williams shrugs. 'You can try to break free,' he suggests. 'But you'd have to be confident that you could get out of range of the watchtower snipers before they find you in their cross hairs. Stagger wasn't bluffing when he warned about the cold, either. Even if you can beat the bullets, hypothermia will catch up with you eventually.'

I grin, and tell him he can trust me not to cause a problem. 'It'll be good to get some fresh air,' I say, looking around the cannery now. The gate to the empty cage across from me remains wide open. Even the mat that had been half dragged from the floor along with McCoy has yet to be rolled up. It looks like a tongue, lolling in this greenhouse heat.

A question comes to my mind. Now that I've been processed here, I see no reason why Williams might purposely ignore me as he had when I asked about the girl. So I clear my throat, and say: 'What's the Fridge all about?'

Williams follows my line of sight across the cannery floor, and finds the reason I'm asking him about it. He returns his attention to me, narrows his eyes for a beat, and I just know that what I'm about to hear means I'm basically a civilian awaiting his return to the world.

'For years now McCoy has been giving us the slip,' he says, drawing closer to the cage. 'The man knows how to stay one jump ahead at every stage of any game he's hired to play. From kidnapping to terrorist training, military coups and weapons acquisition, if the price is right then he's your merc. But everyone makes mistakes, Hobbes. Right now, McCoy is a little uptight about the fact that one error could cost him his liberty for life.'

'What happened?'

'The man dialled one of his paymasters from a Sydney hotel. The guy in question was a major-league arms buyer for Al-Qaeda. He'd just been apprehended in Pakistan, with a quarter million dollars to spend and a battery of anti-tank missiles on his shopping list. McCoy had arranged the funds for him to close the deal, and was expecting his commission. The delay was down to the fact that the arms buyer had been busted, of course. Once we'd persuaded him to work for us, it was just a question of waiting for McCoy to get in touch. What nobody expected was that we'd make such a big catch so effortlessly. Just days after we wired up our man's phone, McCoy's call came through. But instead of using a stolen cellphone, one he could ditch after making his call, he dialled out from the *landline* in his hotel room.' Williams shakes his head at this, as if such bedside phones were for display purposes only. 'The satellite trace took a matter of minutes. Within the hour McCoy was in custody, and now here he is. Far away from the sunshine, and with a sour taste in his mouth.'

I listen to this story, wondering at first why he won't be so open with me about the female detainee, and then find myself considering how McCoy must be feeling.

'I can see why he needs some space,' I say.

Williams seems amused at this. 'A detainee with attitude is no use to us. We need to crack through it so we can establish a dialogue, which is where the Fridge comes in.'

'To help them cool off?'

'To break them down,' he says somewhat abruptly. 'Where do you think we are, Hobbes, a *holiday* camp?'

Once again, this man who I felt I'd connected with changes tack in a heartbeat. It's almost as if he's just reminded himself to be like this in case the guards take a dim view. Even so, for someone coming close to the end of his career, I figure Williams must find it harder by the day to keep up the hostile attitude. It clearly isn't in his nature, after all. The Special Agent looks to the foot of the cage for a moment, aware that he's spoken sharply, I think, and then back through the wire at me. 'Listen to me, telling you all this,' he says, seemingly to himself. 'I guess I'm finding it hard to accept that a kid like you could end up on the same rack as these guys.'

'That makes two of us,' I mutter.

Agent Williams grins, and then rubs the nape of his neck.

'I'm thinking your father makes *three*.'

By now, the detainee who cracked up is beginning to sound more subdued. The poor guy has zero chance of being comforted, but at least he hasn't been beaten.

'Your son,' I say, lowering my voice so we can still keep this between us. 'I don't suppose he's the type to fly around the world in wrist restraints.'

Agent Williams grins and looks to his shoes. 'Jack is quite an achiever,' he tells me. 'A high school senior, with hopes of making it to Harvard if he gets the right grades. He wants to be a lawyer, you see.'

'That's good,' I say, wishing I could be a little more positive. 'You must be very proud.'

'Oh sure.' Agent Williams shrugs, avoiding my eyes for a moment. 'Between you and me, though, it's sorta dull.'

I come closer to the front of the cage. 'How so?'

'Well, just look at yourself, Hobbes!' I do as I am told, though I need no reminding of the orange jumpsuit. 'One day you'll have grandchildren, as will my Jack, am I right?'

'I guess.'

'So which one of you is going to have the better story to tell them, huh?'

I don't answer. He asks me not to, in fact, suggesting

instead that I think it over while awaiting the summons to shovel snow from the runway. I watch him rise to leave, straightening out his jacket as he does so. Mournful sobbing is all that keeps the cannery from silence now. I'm aware that we can no longer speak without risk of an audience.

'Will I see you later?' I ask.

'Oh, I'm going nowhere.' Agent Williams turns his back on me. 'Unlike you,' he adds, so quietly I wonder if I just misheard him.

23

Frost forms on my lashes within minutes of stepping outside. I am one of six detainees in this detail, walking in single file to the runway now. The wind and snow may have died down since our arrival, but the cold continues to make its mark. Even with the thermal head-covers handed out to us, the air out here bites into my lungs with every breath I take. Even the snow crunches underfoot like ground glass. Despite the conditions, it's good to be free of the artificial heat inside the cannery.

I blink rapidly for a moment to clear my vision, and then dab my eyes on the back of the gloves we've also been issued with. It still feels like we're on the cusp of dawn or dusk, even though we must be approaching midday, for our shadows are tapered and stretched. I have to look around to spot the sun, and find just the crest behind the pine trees that border the far side of this headland. It seems distant and burned out, but still gleams through the branches as I move.

Yesterday, having touched down in the heart of a snowstorm, it felt like I had arrived on a different planet entirely. Without the thermal clothing handed out to each of us for this task, all I could do was keep my head down and pray that the sub-zero temperature didn't freeze my bones before I made it inside. Now, having had some time to reflect and gather my wits, I look around with interest.

Walking away from the cannery, towards the compound gates, I face a vast white expanse banked by forested slopes and elongated shadows. The banks appear to meet in the far distance, which makes me think we're situated at the mouth of some glacial valley. Behind me, the cannery juts into this stretch of frozen water. It looks even more run down from the outside. Weather-beaten to the extreme. Out to sea, icebergs cut the horizon line. Closer to the shoreline, the scuppered wreck of the trawler commands my attention. Only the prow is visible, tipped back so the wheelhouse faces the big sky.

'Eyes ahead, Hobbes. We're not on a sightseeing tour!'

Two guards are flanking us, with a third leading the way. All of them carry assault rifles, while one glance to the watchtowers confirms that snipers are indeed stationed up there too. I can see one watching me right now through a pair of binoculars. We stop before the main gates, which are closed. One of the guards is repeating a request into his walkie-talkie, and glowering back at the smoked-out windows of the communications tower behind us. If that's where the gates are controlled, I figure someone must be asleep at the wheel. As we wait in line, stomping our feet to stay warm, the guard dogs in the kennel block go wild once again. This time, I feel some connection with them. The only difference between the detainees and the animals caged in there is that the latter don't wear jumpsuits.

'I will not tell you a second time, Hobbes!'

Having come through the interrogation, this kind of barking doesn't bother me so badly. I feel as if I've given them everything they needed to know, even if it *does* seem crazy that I had to come this far to do so.

The way I see things, I'm helping to clear the runway just so I can leave on the next flight out.

When the gates rock open for us at last, we trudge out and turn for the single-storey building where Commander Stagger first addressed us. Yesterday's aircraft is nowhere to be seen, however. Strangely, this comes as a relief to me. It means at least I don't have to risk my life flying home on that hunk of junk. I look around briefly, in case I've missed a hangar where it might've been taken for repairs, but see nothing but a blanket of snow.

'*Hobbes!*'

'Sorry, sir.' I look to the boot heels of the detainee in front of me. I recognise him from the flight here, along with the guy leading the way. The other three were in cages when we arrived, including the figure just behind me. I don't bother to glance over my shoulder, regardless of the guard, because I know she won't acknowledge me.

All I know about this girl is that she can bear a grudge. It almost makes me feel some sympathy for whoever she believes me to be.

We're each handed a shovel outside the building. A guard is waiting with them on the ramp to the main door, as are three dogs and their handlers.

'That's a dangerous weapon you have there.' I turn around, and find the guard who has been keeping us in line all the way. He shows me the rifle he's holding. 'But *this*, my friend, is lethal.'

He steps up so we're nose to nose. He's not much older than I am, I realise, and sporting a fierce glare. 'Don't you forget that, OK? Because I'm watching you, punk. North said you were trouble.'

I'm not stupid enough to break his stare with a smile, but privately I am sure North can't touch me now. Not with my interrogation behind me. Another guard with a dog sweeps between us just then, both of them barking at us in different ways in a bid to assemble us properly. The guard with the rifle fixes me for a moment longer, and seems almost disappointed when

171

I fall into line as instructed. And so, with each detainee assigned a section to clear, I chisel the edge of my spade into the snow as instructed, and make my first sweep across the runway.

The girl is working the neighbouring section. I might as well be invisible, for all the attention she has paid me, but I'm determined to change that. As strangers, we have shared an intense experience here. And I will not leave until she knows this is the only time and place that our paths have ever crossed.

After ten minutes or so, I have completed two thirds of my section. The snow I've piled on each side of the runway is dense, like wet sand, but the effort it took to shift has helped to keep me warm. The girl is about halfway through her job. I try to catch her eye as she turns to clear the next strip. She simply grits her teeth and pushes on. Even so, she is forced to look up as the sound of another spade strikes the snow within her section.

'Hi,' I say, mindful to keep working as I speak. 'You know I can safely say we've never met.'

She drives her spade onwards.

'Is that a fact?' she mutters finally, which I take as a small victory.

At last, she's speaking to me! The guards have split up to cover the length of the runway. Right now, the nearest one is observing the detainee two sections down from us.

'My name is Hobbes,' I say, working towards the girl now. This close, despite the half-light, I notice how dark her eyes are. 'You can call me Carl. Which would be a first around here.'

Her attention is on the guards behind me as I say this. Then, her shoulders drop a little, and some resignation comes into her expression. 'As soon as they brought you in,' she says, in a strong Southern drawl, 'I just knew you'd blow it by talking to me.'

'You're *American*!' I reply in surprise.

'Jackson, Tennessee.' She leans on her shovel now, considering the icebound horizon. 'I'm a country girl, not a goddamn Eskimo.'

I smile at this. Even if she doesn't return the gesture, I'm relieved that we're making progress. I also realise we don't exactly have time for small talk. 'Look, I don't want to poke my nose into your business,' I say finally. 'But you've got the wrong guy.'

'I am *not* mistaken,' she says, addressing me directly now, and so close the vapour from her breath hits my face with her every word. 'I *know* who you are. Why d'you think I've been freezing you out? I'm trying to *protect* you!'

Such utter conviction leaves me smiling stupidly. I am exasperated now, and beginning to think perhaps I really *have* done something to upset her. 'At least tell me your name,' I reason. 'Whatever it is that you think I've done, we're both stuck here for the time being.

173

If I knew what to call you, then neither of us would feel so alone.'

I wait for some kind of response, but she isn't the first to break the silence.

'Hobbes! Put your hands in the air and shut your damn mouth! If you so much as breathe another word it'll be your last. Now get down on your knees.'

I'm about to comply, only to be shoved violently between the shoulder blades. The impact jars my spine, and yet I can sense the guard behind it has just held back from really laying into me. Nevertheless, I'm spread-eagled in the snow within seconds, suffering the familiar sting of the plastic restraints binding one wrist to the other. The dogs must have picked up on the drama, given the surge of barking. As I'm hauled to my feet, I catch sight of the girl I've risked so much for just to share a few words. She has also been restrained, though the guards have seen fit to allow her to stay on her feet. We exchange a brief glance, before the guard escorts me from the airstrip. As the shock of what's just happened begins to sink in, amid the din from all the dogs, I hear a voice call out behind me.

'*My name is Beth!*'

I hear her clearly, but there isn't much I can do to respond. I just fix my sights on the cannery, and hope the snipers in the watchtowers don't have me in their cross hairs. For if they do, they might wonder why this detainee suddenly looks so pleased with himself.

24

'Get to the back of the cage, Hobbes! Get back there right *now!*'

As soon as the two guards crashed into the cannery, I knew they were coming for me. It's the same pair who escorted me to the interview room. On this occasion, however, things are very different. When the first guy starts yelling at me, it feels like time slows down. I take a moment to register that they really are addressing me, and then show them the palms of my hands.

'It's OK!' I say. 'I'll do whatever you want.'

'Then do it!'

The first time they came for me, these two showed great restraint. They were courteous but ultimately unconcerned that I would present them with any difficulties. Right now, though, I'm faced with a pair of snarling animals. One draws his baton as the other unlocks the gate, then points it into my face.

'One wrong move, and you can kiss your teeth goodbye.'

I'd only been brought back in from the cold a few minutes earlier. The guard who caught me talking was evidently annoyed, but I hadn't considered it to be a huge deal. As there was no pressing reason for me to be here any more, I guess I found it hard to recognise the rules. Certainly Williams related to me in a way that suggested I was just helping them out with their enquiries. Nobody had charged me with anything, after all, and yet now here I was being hauled into a double arm lock. With my shoulder still tender, the assault makes me howl.

'Go easy,' I protest. 'You don't have to be like this!'

'Keep your mouth *shut*, Hobbes!'

At once, the pair rush me towards the side door. Held down as I am, with my head forced forward by a terrific pressure between my shoulders, I find it hard to move my legs. I lose my footing, midway across the space, but that doesn't stop them from dragging me onwards. I feel panic as much as pain, and fleetingly laugh, despite myself. This level of intimidation just seems so ridiculous, degrading and unnecessary. I try to look up in vain, feeling vulnerable as the crown of my head leads the charge. Instead, I see only the tiles beneath me rushing by, and a skewed view of the one detainee not watching this drama unfold.

McCoy had been returned to his cage during my

short time outside. It's the only thing I notice as they drag me through the cannery. There he is, curled up in the corner, his lank hair stuck over his face.

'Where are we going?' I ask through gritted teeth, upon which my arms are levered further backwards. 'Please, there's no need to be like this!'

The pair bundle me into the corridor, and then switch to simply dragging me along when my footing slips once more. This time, they don't stop to knock at the interview room door. It's already open, with both Commander Stagger and Arty Dougal awaiting my arrival.

'Take a seat.' Stagger is toying with a pair of binoculars when he says this. He winds the strap tight around the spine, and then places it on the table in front of him. 'We need to speak.'

My escorts practically throw me into the opposite chair, and stay right beside me as I gather my wits. 'I've told you everything,' I say, addressing Dougal as well, who is simply sitting there staring at me. 'I've no reason to lie.'

The blow from behind hits me square between the shoulders. It knocks the breath right out of me, but the shock is what leaves me reeling. Before I can protest further, the guards have hauled me upright in my seat. Across the table, Commander Stagger considers me for a second, and then slips a photograph from under his papers.

'Who is this?' he asks calmly.

It's Beth. I recognise her immediately. The photograph is a still from a CCTV camera. In the picture, she's on the move and searching for something. She looks very different, in a quilted jacket with some logo on it that's too small to recognise and a matching baseball cap. It's the frown that leaves me certain that it's her, even if much of her face is hidden under the bill of her cap.

Aware of the recognition in my expression, Commander Stagger repeats the same question: '*Who is the girl in the frame?*'

'She's the only female detainee in the cannery,' I confirm.

'The one you were conversing with on the airstrip?'

'That's correct.'

'What did you talk about?'

'Excuse me?'

Another rabbit punch, this time finding my kidneys, leaves me writhing in the chair.

'We heard every word.' Commander Stagger reaches for the binoculars. 'These are fitted with a highly sensitive directional microphone, Hobbes. The guards in the watchtower even took the precaution of using the record facility when they trained their sights on you earlier. We can play it back if you wish. I'd just sooner it came from you, because I really need a sense of what it's like to hear you tell the *truth*.'

I consider what he's getting at here. I'm also hurting and scared I'll get hit again.

'I asked for her name,' I tell him, grimacing as I sit up. 'She's been giving me frosty looks since I arrived, and I was concerned that she had mistaken me for someone else. I know she's called Beth now, but nothing more. I might've learned her surname, but your boys were too quick to haul me inside.'

'Nelson,' says Stagger, boiling up now. 'Beth Nelson. She's twenty years of age, from Jackson, Tennessee, but you know that part already. Frankly, I don't care if you also know the name of her first pet and any food preferences. I'm only interested in how you came to work together on this job!'

'You tell me,' I spit back in frustration. 'Because that's the first I've heard of it and clearly you don't believe a word I've said so far!'

'*Show some respect to the Commander!*' This time, one of the guards behind my chair belts me hard around the head. It hurts almost as much as the punches that they've landed. Reeling now, and close to tears, I just can't believe I'm being treated like this. Our first encounter had been detailed, but comfortable. I'd been happy to cooperate, and answer all their questions. This time, everything has changed. The only thing that remains the same is the fact that Arty Dougal clearly hates my guts for highlighting a dumb flaw in his system.

179

'Carl,' he says with a sigh, breaking his silence at last. 'Can I call you that?' Just hearing my first name earns him my full attention. I wait for him to speak again, still reeling from the blows. 'Clearly, you're a smart kid. Don't let yourself down now by pretending to be dumb.'

'I'm not!' I blurt. 'I have never seen that girl outside of the camp. I don't even know what she's done to be here! I'm not lying, I swear!'

'Easy now, *enough*!' This is Stagger. His voice cuts us both silent, but I am relieved that he has intervened. I don't like this doughy-faced security expert one bit, and I know the feeling is mutual. 'Hobbes, let's go back to what happened at the depository.'

'I've told you everything,' I say again, sounding as rattled and resigned as I feel.

'Yes, you have,' he agrees. 'Up to the moment where you issued the order for the doors to be opened.'

I sit up, reeling from the blows but curious now as to where he's going with this. 'I sent out the order from the Command Sergeant Major's computer,' I say to confirm, and take a moment to compose myself. 'With the password reset I just accessed it remotely, then found a folder containing procedures on his desktop. It covered everything in detail, and so clearly that even *I* could understand how things worked. In fact,' I go on, 'one of the first things I found out is that the gold *doesn't* just sit inside the depository gathering dust. Sure, samples are taken every now and then to test for purity, but there's a whole lot more movement than that.'

Despite the way I'm feeling, I get some sense of satisfaction from the shift in the way they both regard me.

'Go on,' says Stagger uneasily.

Resting my hands on the table, I lean in and prepare to tell them something they already know. Something nobody outside the system should ever have been wise to. Because, in the wrong hands, it would be invaluable.

'Fort Knox is *not* in permanent lockdown,' I say. 'That's just a smokescreen. A low-level security measure, of course, but just as necessary as all the concrete walls, locks, codes and procedures that deter anyone hoping to rob it. The fact is that bullion bars are transported in and out of the facility according to the demands of the world market. In some ways,' I say, addressing Stagger directly now, 'you could say it's a con trick just like the kind I used to find out the truth.'

In the silence that follows, I worry that I've antagonised the Commander. I can't help feeling on the defensive here, and yet I know deep down that crowing about what I've done is no way to guarantee my seat on the next plane home. Even before Stagger finds his voice, I have begun to shrink back into my seat.

'I am not prepared to confirm or deny what you

have just said, Hobbes. Right now, I just want to know how you opened the damn doors.'

The two guards loom close behind me as he speaks. That he hasn't simply tipped them the nod to hit me again seems like a lucky break. I figure I had better not blow this last chance, and tell him what he wants to know.

'Once I'd read through the Command Sergeant Major's email correspondence, I found an order he'd issued to run a drill some weeks earlier. His diary told me when he'd next be out of the office. When that time came I just sent out the order again. All I did was change the date and insert the right code. He kept a list of them in the folder with the procedures.'

I note Arty Dougal's cheeks heat at this, but keep my eyes on the Commander.

'Who else saw this email?' he asks.

Puzzled, I ask Stagger to repeat the question, and then tell him nobody. It went directly to the key-holders. 'And you're quite sure of that?'

Anxiously, I glance over my shoulder. I want to clear up any problem the Commander might have with my story. I just hope the two guards have finished demonstrating how big and strong they can be.

'The keyholders are depository staff,' I continue. 'They work in the same building that houses the vault. They're bank clerks, basically, dealing in gold bars instead of paper money, and are really just cogs in a bigger machine. According to the details in the procedures folder, when a consignment is due to arrive – under heavy guard, of course – the order comes in for the keyholders to open the door. They stay to observe the delivery and then lock up again. It's the same for the despatches, only that requires more paperwork. It all happens on a regular basis. The flow of gold is kind of fluid. It means these guys have got to be one hundred and *one* per cent trustworthy. The one per cent is where the battalion come in. Their job isn't just to check the vault mechanism, but also to be sure that staff members aren't running scams of any description. And so, at any time the order can come in from the Commanding Officer to open up the vault. The procedure for that drill is very simple. The keyholders just engage the locks and punch in their numbers within a thirty-second timeframe, but critically they must return to their desks again. That's all they have to do, with no questions asked. It's the role of a battalion detail to run a security sweep on the vault. Once they're through, they notify the Commanding Officer, who then issues another order for the keyholders to return and close up again.'

'This battalion detail,' says Stagger. 'Did you notify them?'

'No,' I say in all honesty. 'I was only interested in seeing if the keyholders would unlock the door even if nobody from the battalion was present. In a system as rigid as this,' I add, 'people are reduced to serving basic functions. If they questioned everything, the system would break down. It's the responsibility of the higher ranks to review any change in the way things work. In this case Command Sergeant Major Daniels was in charge of the drill. Only he could modify procedure.'

Commander Stagger consults his notes. 'And as the man himself was on the golf course at the time, then effectively, Hobbes, you created a window of opportunity in which any amount of bullion could go missing.'

'I had nothing to do with that,' I say quickly. 'Though I admit that I was logged on to the main man's computer at the time, preparing the order to close the vault, when suddenly bars started going missing.'

'How did you know?' asks Stagger.

'The floor of the vault is pressure sensitive. Every minute, it calculates how many bars are present. The Commanding Officer has access rights to this cool program that lets you see the weight in real time. It ticks over at the bottom of his screen, so he can keep an eye on things at all times. When I saw the number dropping, I panicked. I just logged off and pretended it never happened.'

I sit back from the table, aware that the silence I've created this time seems shot through with suspicion. Commander Stagger seems to reflect on what I've just said before he speaks again.

'No doubt your message board buddies were mightily impressed.'

'They were freaked out,' I say, quite truthfully. 'They're just kids with an interest in computer systems. Geeks maybe, not master criminals.'

Arty Dougal, who has been quiet throughout, folds his arms across his belly and addresses Commander Stagger like I'm not even here. 'Either this kid is lying through his teeth,' he declares gleefully, and pushes his glasses to the bridge of his nose, 'or he's in for one hell of a shock!'

Commander Stagger doesn't seem to find his point remotely amusing. Instead, he reaches for the photograph of Beth he'd shown me earlier, and holds it up for me to see. This time I note the background in the shot. It may not be in focus, but now I see it in a different light, and my jaw simply falls. For stacked upon pallets behind her, gleaming under spotlamps in what has to be the vault, are countless gold bullion bars.

'Hobbes,' says Stagger, watching me closely. 'Say hello to *Chimera*.'

25

I felt some guilt the one time I had discussed that screen name with Stagger. It was as if I had dragged an innocent bystander into this mess. An online presence who had warned me that I might be getting into something dangerous.

As it turned out, Chimera had been right. Now 'he' had been unmasked as Beth Nelson, the girl who was so unsettled to see me here. Maybe it's the shock, because as soon as I draw breath I move to defend her.

'You must have the wrong person,' I say. 'There's no way she can be a bullion robber! She doesn't look capable of it!'

Even the Commander seems to find this amusing, though he hides it well. 'Five hundred gold bars vanished from the vault that day, Hobbes. With each bar valued at about twenty thousand dollars, someone had done their sums.'

I try to work it out in my head, but Dougal gets there

first. 'That's ten million bucks,' he says, and whistles to himself. 'Lot of money, Carl. It seems your little lady isn't just a pretty face. She's a cool operator as well.'

'But I didn't know any of this,' I plead, and immediately fall quiet. For it dawns on me that my focus on duping a military system was so intense back then that my guard must have dropped. The result? I'd been hoodwinked myself.

People reinvented online all the time. Generally, it's done as a bid to be more attractive and appealing than you are in the real world. That's why it just hadn't crossed my mind a beautiful woman would masquerade online as some geeky guy. Faced with the full picture here, I am embarrassed to admit that my expectations and assumptions have been neatly manipulated.

'You'll understand why we need to be convinced of your innocence,' continues Commander Stagger. 'Obviously such a huge quantity of bullion bars is worth nothing unless you have contacts prepared to purchase them. Now, it's no secret that Beth Nelson took a job with a high security courier company sixteen months before this raid. That's dedication, Hobbes! And to time a delivery to the very moment you opened the doors just goes to show the level of planning and teamwork involved.'

Online, on the eve of the attempt on Fort Knox, Chimera had checked in with me to find out how my plans were shaping up. Thinking back, I remember feeling bullish enough to answer every question. Nothing had aroused my suspicion at the time. By then, the girl behind the screen name had scammed me comprehensively.

'No wonder she's so upset to see you here,' suggests Arty Douglas. 'When you've kept as quiet as she has, the last thing you want is for your accomplice to show up and start shouting his mouth off.'

'The kicker,' the Commander continues, before I have a chance to defend myself against any of this, 'is that the bullion bars are beginning to surface around the globe, and we don't like where we're finding them.'

For a moment, I think Stagger is going to suggest they've found one under my bed. I'm already feeling used and abused. Planting stolen gold on me would be no surprise after everything that's happened.

'How's your geography?' asks Arty, who seems more upbeat now I know the bigger picture.

'I've never travelled far until this weekend,' I say in all honesty. 'Why?'

Commander Stagger clears his throat. 'Hobbes, I am sure you're aware of the detainee in the cage opposite your own.'

'The guy with the headache,' I reply, increasingly unconcerned by the guards behind me. 'Give him some painkillers and I'm sure he'll shut up.'

188

Stagger looks at me irritably. Just long enough to remind me what could happen if I persist with my attitude.

'Christian McCoy is quite a prize for us, Hobbes. His involvement in terrorist events all around the world has made him very difficult to pin down.'

I draw breath to confirm that I know all about him. The only thing that stops me is the realisation that I might bring Williams into a whole heap of trouble for telling me. The man is about to retire, I remind myself. He wants to go home as much as I do. I focus on Stagger, waiting for him to continue, but his attention has turned to Arty. Judging by the way he's scoping me, owl-like, through those glasses of his, I realise the systems guy had seen me prepare to speak.

'Are you familiar with his work?' asks Arty Dougal. 'What can you tell us about McCoy?'

I switch my attention back to Stagger, and pray he won't pick me up on it.

'Judging by what I've seen of him here,' I say, 'the man thrives on causing mayhem.'

Stagger holds my gaze for a moment, testing me, it seems. Finally, with a sigh, he simply nods in agreement.

'We nailed McCoy through an associate in Pakistan. Lately, our man has been busy setting up arms deals for Al-Qaeda, which is why efforts had been stepped up to capture him.'

As he tells me this, I am well aware that Arty Dougal is watching every blink I make. All I can do is fix upon Stagger, and listen to him intently.

'McCoy's arrest certainly came as a relief to the authorities,' he continues. 'But it also brought a great deal of concern. Firstly, because the funds McCoy had passed to his arms buyer in Pakistan amounted to a substantial sum. But more immediately – and this is where you come in, Hobbes – because half of it took the form of gold bullion bars.'

I take this information on board without a word. With every turn this interrogation takes, I feel like I'm being dropped deeper into a hole with the bottom still out of sight.

'All I did was open the doors,' I say again, and for a moment I'm too choked to continue. 'I'm really sorry for the trouble this has caused, but you have to believe me when I say I knew nothing about it.'

'We want to believe you.' Arty Dougal's soothing tone fails to hide how much he's relishing my predicament. 'We really do, Carl. But it's tough. Y'know? A kid like you and a lady like Beth. You'd make a great team, don't you think? It's just a shame you chose to pool your talents to help her betray an entire nation. Nobody likes a traitor, Carl. An *American* traitor is about as bad as it can get, and you're tarred by the very same brush.'

'But I don't *know* her!' I find it hard to contain my

anger now, despite the threat of another punch between the shoulders.

'Like you didn't know anything about McCoy?' Stagger raises his voice to match my own. 'Hobbes, I looked you in the eye just now, and asked what you could tell us about him, and you lied through your teeth.'

I am lost for words for a moment. All along I'd questioned whether Williams had been instructed to brief me, and now Stagger had confirmed it in so many words. It was only following my last conversation with the special agent, in which he'd left me thinking we'd genuinely bonded, that I figured I was just being paranoid. Now I knew the truth, it felt like a betrayal.

'Listen,' I reply, reasoning with him now. 'You can use Williams to play games with me all you like, but I am not protecting *anyone* here. For all I know Beth *may* be working in league with McCoy, but *I've* never even seen her until now!'

Even before I finish speaking, I realise exactly why I've been brought all this way. The trap I'd just walked right into was nothing compared to this. I stare at Commander Stagger, spinning recent events into a whole new story in my mind. I think about my conversation with Beth on the airstrip. That we'd been given the freedom to speak seemed slack at the time. Now I knew that the guards had been equipped with fancy binoculars fitted with microphones, I realise they were just waiting for us to start talking. I sit up straight, still facing the Commander in disbelief.

'You set me up!' I hiss at him. 'You wanted to find out what I would say when I thought I was alone with Beth!' I slap my palm on the table. 'You were hoping we'd talk about the job, weren't you? Did you think we'd discuss what happened to the gold, perhaps? Well, the evidence must be on your tapes. All I did was ask for her name!'

'Although she knew yours already,' states Arty. 'You guys clearly have some history. Just tell us all about it, Hobbes. Because if she's alarmed that you're here on account of your big mouth, you're certainly not using it here!'

Everything he says just winds me up now. It's clear that no explanation is going to satisfy him. Worse still, he's revelling in it.

And that's why something snaps in me. For one crazy moment, I forget all about the two guards behind me, and just explode.

'*What do you want me to say?*' I yell at him. 'Should I hold up my hands and admit that I'm a terrorist? Would you like me to confess that I opened the vault knowing the gold inside would be used to fund atrocities? Next, you'll be suggesting that I personally groomed Grimstad into strapping on a bomb belt. Doubtless you found the odd bullion bar lying around the Paris cell when you raided it in connection with the embassy bomb plot. Why don't you mark me down for that one, too?'

'*Are* you a terrorist?' Arty enquires calmly, relishing my outburst. 'Did you plan the heist with Beth?'

I narrow my gaze at him, teeth clenched, and breathe out through my nose.

'Screw you,' I tell him. 'I've helped you all I can.'

The tension in the room seems to fracture at this. Commander Stagger winces, and touches his temple, while Arty Dougal turns to him and demands some action.

'Are you going to let a detainee speak to me like that? *Are you?*'

Stagger tells him to relax, and gestures for the guards to make ready.

'You're here to be processed,' he tells me, with some irritation. 'Whatever your involvement, we need to be sure that we have every last *atom* of information from you. You've told us how you cracked open the vault, and I'm grateful for your cooperation with that. But now we need to know about the money. We want to know the people involved in such a large-scale operation, and how so many bullion bars could end up in the wrong places all around the world. Because, if you're hiding knowledge of terrorist involvement, Hobbes, it could cost lives.'

I sigh, practically groaning. 'I know *nothing* about that. How many more times do I have to tell you?'

'Until I am satisfied that you're telling the truth,' answers Stagger, and lifts his gaze to the guards behind me. 'Take him to the Fridge,' he orders. 'Maybe once he's cooled off he'll want to help us out some more.'

26

I am too fired up to show any fear. The guards must know it, because they tackle me now like I might well resist them. I've been hurt enough times since my arrival to know what to expect. It just doesn't lessen the shock or the pain. With my arms pinned behind me, they simply drag me head first along the corridor like a sack of potatoes. Even if I wanted to work with them now, I couldn't pick my feet up to match their pace. I can barely see where we're going, but at the far end we swing around and then come to a sudden halt. I hear a jangle of keys, the sound of a lock mechanism turning over. Without a word, I'm flung through the open door. Sprawled on the concrete floor, I turn to see them coming at me in silhouette, with no time to protect myself.

'*This*,' yells one of the guards, as he stamps upon my lower back, 'is for being a wise guy with the Commander just now.'

'On your hands and knees!' the other one orders, despite the fact that his colleague has just flattened me. '*Do as I say!*'

Groaning through the force of the blow, I pick myself up, only to be grabbed roughly by the wrists and hauled towards an iron ring bolted to the concrete just in front of me.

'This kid is dead,' I hear the first guard mutter. 'He'll never make it through.'

As he speaks, the other guard snaps out several wrist restraints, and deftly binds me to the ring. He then orders me to stand, which is next to impossible, and does the same thing with my ankles. It leaves me bent double and panic-stricken, but too afraid to protest. All I can do is fight for breath, and hope they don't punish me when I sink into a squat.

'Comfortable, Hobbes?' the guard who kicked me snarls. 'Get used to it.'

The pair withdraw at this, slamming the door behind them. They take the light away, too. It's completely black in here, but for a dim glow coming in under the door. At first I worry someone or something might be in here with me, lurking in the darkness. All I can be certain about is that it stinks of bleach and urine. I can hear a stiff wind blowing against the wall behind me, and the muffled sound of dogs barking in the distance, but nothing more. Then I hear the iron ring tapping, and realise it's because I'm shaking violently.

There isn't much I can do to stop it, however. They've bound me so tightly to it that I can't shift away. I test the restraints. There's no give in them whatsoever. My wrists and ankles feel like they have been fused to the floor.

For a moment I just squat there helplessly, and try very hard not to let the knot in my throat grow tighter.

The more I dwell on what has just happened, the more it feels like I'm in the hands of a school bully turned psychopath. Somewhere, somehow, a line has been crossed and I'm trussed up on the wrong side of it. If I can only break free from the ring, I tell myself, I know that I could also shake off feeling so vulnerable. I also feel stupid for getting myself into this mess. Ashamed, in some ways, too. As it is, I have no control over the situation, and no information to offer that could possibly improve things. I have told them everything about my involvement with Fort Knox. At least I think that I have, and begin to wonder if perhaps I am missing something myself.

In the solitude, I reflect on the madness that has overtaken my life since I first knocked on those bank vault doors, and try to make some sense of it. I think about Beth Nelson, and the revelation that somehow she had targeted me online. My reputation as a hacker really didn't extend beyond the members of the message board. I try to remember how long Chimera had been posting. It must've been a while back, because I

197

considered the name to be a familiar feature of the community. I had just assumed that a young male hacker was behind the screen name. One who had taken a shine to my style of work. A lot of the people who swapped ideas and strategies on the board really liked to get their hands oily with computer code. Personally, I just preferred to beg, borrow or download software that helped me detect an unsecured system, and relied on my wits, phone or email to slip through the net. Thinking back, I was flattered by the attention Chimera paid me. I guess I pictured a fresh-faced kid who just rated what I did. We certainly had a connection. I liked our conversations. They had a spark to them.

Only now I knew who was behind them all, that spark took on a different glow entirely.

Reflecting on some of the spin-off chats we had shared, not just about hacking but about music, video-games and favourite films, I have to recognise what a great job Beth did. She hadn't crashed into the community, or invited any suspicion from her postings. She had made friends with me, pure and simple. In suggesting Fort Knox as a target, as if plucking the name at random, and then appearing to have second thoughts, she had pulled off exactly the kind of confidence trick that was often debated on the board. I even wonder whether she learned the strategy from something I'd mentioned online, which makes me smile to myself.

I really had been properly fooled, and for that she deserved my respect.

What troubles me, however, is how a young American woman like this could channel millions of dollars into a terrorist network. Somehow, she hadn't just forged a connection with me but also with McCoy. Robbing the Federal Reserve probably marked her out as a folk hero in some quarters. It was where the gold had ended up that would earn her no friends back home. What she has done surely won't help her chances of getting through this. Now that I have been caught up in it all, it also seems the possibility of my own release is slipping further from reach.

I feel sick, just thinking about my situation here. One hour earlier, I had been looking forward to heading home on the next flight out. Now, I can't shake the thought that I would be left here to rot. One of the guards had said himself that I was dead already. I keep hearing the threat inside my head, repeating it over and over. In fact the only thing that stops it is a sudden, shocking leg cramp.

I cry out in pain, but can't move to ease it. Now I realise those guards knew exactly what they were doing binding me down like this. All I can do is tough it out, but that's not easy in my mindset. In desperation now, I even consider a way of escaping that wouldn't physically get me out of here, but just might keep me from being crushed by the experience.

In Drama classes, we sometimes carried out a warm-up exercise that involved projecting ourselves outside of our bodies. It seemed like a joke at the time. Now, however, bound up like a pig awaiting slaughter, it helps me deal with the pain no end. I visualise myself unfurling feathered wings, and then, inch by inch, rising up and out of this windowless environment. No longer bound by chains or even gravity, I see the cannery below, the courtyard and the buildings surrounding it. Rising higher, taking in the compound fence and the airstrip now, I am reminded of the fact that the elements rule out here. The camp may be governed by a sense of law and order, but nothing can stop the punishing conditions from laying siege to it. If I were in the party deciding whether or not to close the place down, I'd start by questioning why it was opened in the first place.

An imaginary layer of cloud is just beginning to mesh beneath my view, when a scream brings me crashing back to reality.

I open my eyes at once, and recoil against my constraints when a second cry breaks the silence. It's coming from the room next door, though I am powerless to get my ear to the wall to be sure. The third scream is followed by a howling protest.

'*My God, no! Please. Don't! I'm begging you!*'

It's female, I realise, and that brings one name to my lips.

'Beth?' I call her name out loud, struggling in vain to get free. 'Beth Nelson! It's me, Hobbes! What's happening?'

I can't believe that nobody has come running at the noise. Something truly dreadful has made her cry out like this, and I am overwhelmed once more by a sense of helplessness and anger. Next thing a light spits on and off above me. Just a flash at first, but then it repeats, and within seconds a bright strobe lamp bracketed to the roof is hitting my confines hard.

'Stop this!' I yell. 'Stop this, *please!*'

The light combines with the din from the next room to thoroughly disorientate me. I keep yelling Beth's name just so that she can hear my voice. Because whatever horror she is suffering in there – and the wailing and screams do not let up – I need her to know that she is not alone. I don't care who she is, or the fact that she had used me to rob that gold depository. Nobody deserves this kind of abuse. *Nobody*. Combined with the strobe going off above me, so rapidly now that each flash feels like glass shards puncturing my pupils, I am aware that this whole terrible turn of events has been orchestrated to break me down.

And that is what makes this assault on my so-called partner in crime so impossible to bear.

By the time the guttural protests tail off into sobbing, my cheeks are wet with tears.

'Beth!' I call again, my eyes smarting badly from the

relentless switching between darkness to light. 'I'm here for you, Beth. Do you hear me?'

The silence that follows makes me think at least she is aware of my presence on the other side of the wall. I'm just hoping it will give her something to cling on to when the screaming starts again.

This time, I am torn between just collapsing into my shackles and shouting at the top of my voice. I curse the animals responsible, and then, finally, sink into a heap of despair. I squeeze my eyes shut but it doesn't make things more bearable. Every invasive flash of light forces me to confront the fact that there is no escape from this. I am ashamed to even think that I would cover my ears if I could, anything to shut out the noise, and then something happens that does exactly that. It only lasts for a second at most, but totally rewires my understanding of what's going on.

For the generator falters, dimming the lights in the corridor and killing the strobe completely.

What it also serves to do, however, is cause the screams to slow and drop in pitch. I look up, aghast in the dark. Then the flashing strikes up once more, along with that faint chugging sound from the courtyard. Immediately, the din through the wall comes back up to speed, and I know for sure that what I'm listening to is a tape recording.

experience in the Fridge. Me? I had come out stronger.

'Everything good with you, Hobbes?' The guard observes me closely. He's not quite as tall as I am, and so I make the most of it by staring him down.

'You know the way back to your cage,' his colleague says, and jabs his thumb towards the corridor behind him. 'Let's go.'

This time, I walk freely between them. I may be unsteady on my feet, but I make it all the way back to the cannery without assistance.

I am aware that my return earns a great deal of attention. North and Cortés both stop what they're doing and turn, though I simply look through them. In particular, I see Beth Nelson clasping the mesh of her cage, peering across the space at me. She doesn't look like someone who has just endured hours of torture and sadistic humiliation. I nod at her, unconcerned by what the guards on the gantry might make of it, and grin openly when she does likewise. I may not have encountered this girl before I came here, but after everything I've been through in a bid to prove that very fact, I now feel a strong connection with her. In the cage to her right, McCoy has his head buried in his hands. No matter how closely the two of them might have worked pulling off the Fort Knox robbery, he seems locked in his own world right now. Oblivious to his surroundings, he's rocking back and forth on the balls of his feet, clutching at his temples. It makes him look kind of disturbed. I figure the guards are still holding out on his request for medication. Grimstad is observing me, too. For someone who has been secretly skipping his pills, he looks remarkably sedated. He watches me pass with those half-hooded eyes of his, a trace of dried blood still visible on his cheekbones. Despite his appearance, however, he doesn't look so insane to me. I greet him with a brief nod.

And he responds by winking at me.

It's so unexpected that I look away wondering if I imagined it. Under normal circumstances, I would never dream of exchanging pleasantries with someone who had tried to blow himself up and take hundreds with him. Here, though, we're sharing an experience. It doesn't exactly turn us from cell mates to soul mates. Just something in-between.

By the time the guard slams the gate of my cage shut, that familiar simmering silence has returned to the cannery. I sit on my mat, contemplating my surroundings. Beth meets my eye this time, as does the marksman when I glance up to see if we are being watched. I look back at her. Wisely, she doesn't so much as shrug.

For hours I just sit there, watching for patterns in the guards' behaviour. It may not get me out of here, but understanding how the systems work puts me in the frame of mind to find a way through them. I came here believing that my full cooperation would earn my freedom. Now that strategy has failed, and in view of my treatment here, I'm ready to consider the alternative.

Throughout this time, the guards who escorted me back return to pick off a detainee from the opposite row. They flank the guy on the way out, but bring him back later in a double arm lock. The next detainee to head out for interrogation doesn't return at all. The guards who had come for him simply return to collect another prisoner. *Welcome to the Fridge*, I think to myself, and hope he makes it through.

When Agent Williams enters through the main door, I sit up straight. Williams flips his collar down as he makes his way across to me, his shoes leaving wet prints across the tiles. He unbuttons his coat along the way. Briefly, I glimpse a holster under his arm. It reminds me that we are not equals. We might have spoken like that at times, but I have no authority here.

'You knew,' is the first thing I say, when he drops down to speak with me. I'm not just thinking about the information he fed me on McCoy. I'm guessing he was also aware that my conversation with Beth would be monitored as we cleared the runway of snow. 'I just can't defend myself here,' I continue, and this time I don't care if anyone is listening. 'The way I see things, my only way out is to admit to something I didn't do. You must've seen that this would happen to me right from the start!'

206

Agent Williams gives me this pleading look, and asks me to keep my voice down.

'It's out of my hands, Hobbes. I'm your escort, not your interrogator. I just want to be sure you're holding up. Beyond that, I simply follow orders.'

The side door opens as he speaks. I glance over his shoulders, and narrow my gaze. 'Here's your boss,' I mutter.

Commander Stagger steps across to speak to North and Cortés. He seems agitated. I even wonder if he's only just learned what went down in the Fridge. Having seen only one female in this place, I was bound to conclude that Beth was behind the screams I heard. As soon as the power dipped, however, revealing the true nature of what I was hearing, so something transformed inside of me. Throughout my time here, I had always felt like I was in the hands of the good guys. Now, it seems to me that the boundaries aren't so clear cut. I've witnessed good and bad on both sides, which makes it so tough to know who to trust.

'Hobbes, will you level with me?'

I look through the mesh at Agent Williams. 'Go on,' I say.

'*Are* you holding back any information?'

I hold his gaze for a beat before speaking. 'What do *you* think?'

He smiles after a moment, and reaches up to loosen his tie. 'I think if it was down to me, I'd say you've earned a *window* seat on tomorrow's flight home.'

As he tips his head to ease the knot, I notice movement in one of the cages behind him.

Thomas Grimstad is sitting quietly, with his legs crossed and his hands in his lap. Beth Nelson is lying on her side, staring into space. What grabs my attention is McCoy. He's no longer holding his head in his hands. He's slumped backwards, shaking violently from top to toe as if an electric current is passing through him.

'My God!' I breathe, noting the foam bubbling from his mouth. 'Help him!'

Agent Williams registers my alarm, turns to see what I'm looking at, and is up on his feet immediately.

'*Medic!*' he yells, scrambling across the tiles now. 'Get a medic right now!'

At once, the quiet erupts into chaos. With no key to open the gate to the cage, Williams is shouting at North to get over here right now. Cortés looks like he's caught in the headlights of an oncoming car, until the Commander yells at him to fetch the damn medic himself. North joins Williams now, along with another guard, but it's hard to see what's going on. A scrum quickly forms in front of McCoy's cage, then swiftly parts as Williams drags the detainee clear.

McCoy is still bucking and writhing like a marionette in the hands of a child. North attempts to pin him down by his shoulders, only to curse aloud at the blow he receives from a stray elbow. Beth looks shocked, witnessing the scene from such close quarters. Whether or not they had worked in league on the depository, I know just how she feels. This is the first time I've ever witnessed anyone suffer a seizure. I can't help thinking that it should never have been allowed to happen.

'There's blood!' Beth is the first to notice it erupting from his mouth. North recoils from the sudden spray, as does another guard who has come to assist.

'He's bitten into his tongue!' Despite being splattered, Williams is suddenly alone in his struggle to keep the man from harming himself. 'This is a bad one!'

Another guard comes crashing through the side door now, with Cortés close behind. He's carrying a white box striped with red crosses. Commander Stagger directs them to the scene, but the pair never make it that far.

In a space this vast and empty, a gunshot sounds like a lightning strike. I can't even work out where it's come from at first, let alone who's behind it. I just shrink instinctively, as Cortés and the guard dive for cover, and then look up in horror.

28

Across the floor, I see McCoy on his back still with Agent Williams kneeling over him. Except Williams is no longer attempting to help the man. Instead, McCoy has the agent's handgun in both hands, and is aiming it at a dark bloom on Williams' shirt. He isn't twitching or writhing at all any more, but this isn't some miraculous recovery. McCoy has faked the whole thing.

Williams peers down at his chest, eyes and mouth open in disbelief, only to be sent sprawling sideways as the man underneath him springs into life.

'Nobody move!' Seizing the moment, McCoy wheels around with the handgun braced in both hands. As he moves, what looks like a flaring match-head appears to go off at his feet. My ears are still ringing from the first gunshot, which is why it takes me a moment to realise that one of the guards on the gantry has just scrambled to fire off a round. It's clear he isn't going to miss a second time, but McCoy responds by finding Stagger

210

with his handgun and freezing on the spot. 'My bullet will reach his skull before yours reaches mine!' he yells, spitting blood with every word. 'Drop your weapons, all of you!'

For a moment, only silence fills the space. Then, without taking his eyes off the mercenary threatening to cut him down, Commander Stagger addresses his men.

'Do as he asks,' he tells them calmly, though nothing can hide the tension in his voice.

From the gantry, the first rifle falls through the air. As it clatters onto the floor, so another one follows. Throughout this, Agent Williams remains quite still. His limbs are arranged all wrong, with one leg underneath him and his left arm outstretched towards Grimstad's cage. I see no rise and fall of his chest. Just blood pooling underneath him. I can't believe he might be dead. I can barely even process what is taking place here.

McCoy waits for the last guard to surrender his weapon, and then mops at his mouth with his sleeve. His jumpsuit looks more like a butcher's apron now. Even his teeth are scarlet.

'Man, that hurt!' he complains. I watch him step back towards Williams' body, his gun trained on the Commander still, before hurriedly swapping it for one of the assault rifles dropped by the guards. I don't know anything about firearms, but this one looks like it might let off more than one round with the squeeze of a

211

trigger. 'Now I want anyone *not* in a cage to form a nice queue in front of the main doors.' McCoy slings the rifle's strap around his shoulder, and holds it low at his hip. He then turns to find the Commander. 'I believe you call this a *process*. I want it done in the next ten seconds, else there'll be more killing.'

Of all the military personnel in the cannery, Commander Stagger is the only one who doesn't leave his position. He simply stares penetratingly at McCoy, despite being at the wrong end of a gun.

'Is this a breakout?' he asks calmly. 'You'll never make it.'

McCoy looks to the cages behind him. 'A *breakout*?' he says, as if playing to the audience. 'Commander, you're the one who has me classified as a mercenary. This isn't a breakout. This is *work*! Now, look lively. You're holding up procedure.'

Stagger glowers under the bill of his cap at this man before him. 'The detainees are my responsibility,' he growls. 'I am *not* abandoning them.'

McCoy runs his finger and thumb down the tracks of his moustache, considering his position, it seems. Finally, he spits another plug of blood between his feet and braces his gun to fire.

'Let's get going, Commander,' he says with a note of irritation, but Stagger simply stands his ground.

'I leave when every last detainee is back in my charge. Anything less would be a dereliction of duty.'

In response McCoy's knuckles whiten where he grips the gunstock. His finger stays curled around the trigger, but then he drops his stance. Second thoughts, it seems.

'So speaks the captain of this ship,' he sneers, and breaks away to shepherd the last guard into line.

Judging by the hammering that strikes up from the other side of the main doors, however, it seems that help has just arrived.

'*Open up!*' a voice demands. '*Is everything under control?*'

McCoy touches a finger to his lips and turns to face the hangar door. 'Ignore them,' he whispers across to the guards gathered there. 'Here's how I sign you out. One by one, I want you to step out of the secondary door and get the hell out of here. Don't stop in the courtyard or turn around. Just walk on through to the processing area and hope I don't plant a bullet in your spine. Is everyone clear on that? Good.'

Without pausing for breath, McCoy singles out the medic at the head of the queue, and orders him to step up to the door.

The man looks panic-stricken, but does as he is told.

Judging by the gathering voices outside, it sounds like every last soldier in the camp heard the gunshot and came running. McCoy must sense this, because he suddenly opens fire on the main hangar door. I watch with my heart in my mouth as bullet holes pepper an outline around the cowering medic. When McCoy is finished, he invites the poor man to trigger the door release. The guy scrambles to oblige him. The secondary door pops open. From my cage, I can only see a section of the courtyard outside, but it appears to be deserted now.

'Run along now, soldier,' he orders the medic, 'and tell everyone hiding out there to back away. Else your buddies in here will take turns receiving a bullet between the eyes.'

McCoy follows the medic to the threshold. He watches him exit, and then directs the rifle with one hand at a point above the front building. It's the communications tower, I realise, just as bullets spray from the muzzle of McCoy's gun. I hear glass crashing out from up there, and figure the smoked-out windows have just been targeted. 'Just in case anyone was thinking of issuing a mayday!' he bellows into the ringing silence that follows. 'Let it be known that I can see into the tower now. You can try to get up there if you like, but mark my words, you'll come down in a body bag!' Stepping back now, McCoy shoves another guard out into the cold.

Before that one has cleared the generator, he has already pushed out the next in line.

I watch them leave in turn, struggling in vain to work out just what McCoy has in mind here. Grouping the guards in the processing area across the courtyard might get them all in one place, but it didn't get *him* out of the cannery, let alone this icebound camp. Stagger himself had stressed how deadly this environment could be. If McCoy is intending to make a break for it, he'll effectively sign his own death warrant.

And that's when his exit strategy comes to me. As a hacker, you need to know how to get *out* of a place as much as get in, and I guess the same goes for mercenaries. The difference between McCoy and me is that I would never contemplate sinking to the depths I fear he has planned.

If I'm right, then more lives are going to be lost, and in the cruellest of ways.

Within the space of a minute, all but two guards are left in the queue: North and Cortés. North is first to approach the threshold. He looks like a parachutist preparing to leap into the void. Then McCoy tells him to wait, and North turns round with an expression of pure dread.

'Let me go,' he pleads. 'I have a family.'

This serves to amuse McCoy no end.

'You should've thought about that when I asked for medication,' he tells him, and tightens his grip on the weapon in his hands. 'You know how grouchy some people can get with a headache.'

The way McCoy mocks him like this makes me fear for North's life. Agent Williams remains sprawled on the floor way behind him, but McCoy hasn't given him a second glance. He's more interested in the two remaining guards, and also the Commander, who attempts to intervene on their behalf.

'Send them on their way,' he asks. 'These men were only following orders.'

'Good,' replies McCoy. 'Then they'll help me with a little task first.' McCoy gestures with his weapon for the pair to stand aside from the door. 'You see those fuel drums roped off under the generator?' he says, pointing with his gun. 'I want you to collect one each, also some of that rope, and bring it all back to me.' North and Cortés glance at the Commander, who gives his consent with a nod. 'Do they need your permission to *pee*?' asks McCoy as the pair hurry into the courtyard. He watches them go, nodding to himself. 'I'm impressed by your authority, boss. Lucky for me I didn't shoot you first.'

As McCoy says this, still watching the pair outside, Commander Stagger creeps backwards by a step. One of the assault rifles dropped by the guards lies just behind him. I grip the wires of my cage with my fingers, and hold my breath as he takes another step closer to it.

Just as he reaches down, a voice from a cage some way down my row calls urgently to McCoy.

'Where are you going?' The Pitcairn mercenary speaks breezily and without turning. He's standing just inside the door, peering out into the half-light with his gun held close. 'Boss, you had better come right back before things get bleak for you.'

I see Stagger's shoulders sag. He hangs his head, as I do, and abandons the bid.

North is the first to return. Judging by the way he shoulders the drum, I doubt very much that it's full. Cortés struggles with his load, however, and resorts to rolling it over the threshold.

'Too heavy to handle?' asks McCoy. 'You'd better pop the cap for me.'

Cortés does as he is told, only to jump away when McCoy kicks the drum over with his foot.

'What are you doing?' hisses Commander Stagger, as the fuel inside spills across the floor. 'That's highly flammable!'

'Oh really?' McCoy steps carefully around the pool, and orders the two guards to lie down in it. Cortés draws breath to protest, and that's when McCoy starts yelling. '*Do as I say, dammit! I'm in charge now! Obey* my *orders!*'

The ferocity of his voice is startling. As the pair drop to the ground as directed, the fumes begin to creep into my cage. I feel dizzy and sick as it is. This just makes things a whole lot worse. I still think I am wise to McCoy's plan, and yet I could never have guessed he'd stoop so low in executing it. One of the guards, I think it's Cortés, is sobbing now as he rolls from side to side. His fatigues are soaked, but McCoy isn't content until every last drop has been drawn into the fabric.

'On your feet,' he says finally. 'And pick up that

drum before any more fuel leaks out. Don't you know it's explosive?'

With the gun trained on them still, McCoy stoops to collect one length of rope. He then instructs North to sit with his back to the drum, and orders Cortés to strap him to it using the rope.

'*What?*' A look of disbelief crosses North's face. Once again, McCoy is quick to yell at him. It's clear he's losing patience. This time, they don't even glance at the Commander. North just drops down, his hands raised in surrender, pleading with McCoy to stay calm.

As soon as the task is complete, McCoy orders the Commander to tie the remaining drum to Cortés. Stagger stands his ground at first, but moves in quick enough when McCoy starts to torment Cortés with the gun.

At this point, much to McCoy's displeasure, Cortés begins to weep.

'Hell's teeth, man. Be brave!' McCoy waits for the Commander to finish, and then orders him to stand aside. Next thing he circles around the two men, as if conducting an inspection. He pauses only to rip the key fobs from their belts, and then gestures towards the door with one hand. 'You're free to go,' he tells them. 'If you can get off the floor, that is.'

For a moment, Cortés and North simply gaze up at the mercenary. Cortés is the first to make a move. Still sobbing, he struggles to get onto all fours, and then slowly raises himself into a standing position.

McCoy waits for North to join him, the pair both drenched and terrified, and then braces his weapon as if to pull the trigger. 'This one is for all the suicide bombers in the building!' he calls over his shoulder. 'For whatever reason you messed up, and let's face it you must have failed to end up in this place, I want you to watch my two friends in action here. Why?' he finishes, with a flourish of his gun. 'Because they're going to show you how it's done!'

29

One bullet. That's all it would take to explode a fuel drum. Drenched from head to toe in generator fuel, North and Cortés would stand little chance of survival, and nor would anyone else within the blast zone.

Commander Stagger makes all this quite clear. His desperate warnings go ignored, however, as McCoy dispatches the two men, side by side, across the courtyard.

'Stand up straight, fellas,' he calls after them, straining now to see them over the top of the generator. He lifts up on his toes, holding the rifle at shoulder height now. The smell of petroleum hangs heavily in the air. 'It's important that I keep you in my sights!'

'For pity's sake, lay down your weapon!' Commander Stagger hasn't moved since McCoy foiled his bid to grab a gun. One step out of turn now, and he must know his men will pay for it. 'It isn't too late to put a stop to all this!'

'Oh, I've only just started.' McCoy continues to splatter blood with every word he speaks. I remember what he has done to himself to catch Williams off his guard. A shiver runs through me, for he's clearly bitten down deep into his tongue. 'Boss, relax a little. You're making me twitchy, and your boys out there don't need that right now. I just want them to keep walking, all the way through the processing area, and through those big blast doors.'

'But conditions out there—'

McCoy cuts short the Commander's protest by shouting more encouragement across the courtyard. 'You're doing good, guys! I see your buddies over there are clearing quite a space for you both. What I'd like you to do now is ask them to drop their weapons, turn around and make an orderly exit.'

This time, Stagger reacts with outright fury. 'You can't do that,' he snaps. 'They'll freeze to death!'

McCoy glances from the courtyard to the Commander, smiling to himself. 'Boss, it was you who put the idea in my head! If you hadn't stressed how suicidal it would be to spend a night under the stars, I'd have lined them up in the courtyard just now and shot them all. By letting them run around inside the compound grounds we get to put your warning to the test. We could even lay some bets down on how many survive to see a new day, if you like.'

Stagger doesn't respond at first. He simply keeps his

eyes locked on McCoy. I might have worked out just what the mercenary had in store, but it's no less shocking to hear him outline his plan.

'There *is* no chance for survival out there,' retorts Stagger.

'There's always a chance, boss.' This time, McCoy turns to address him directly. 'Without hope, how do you think these guys you keep under lock and key get through each day?'

'Every man you send out there will *die*!'

'Oh, absolutely they will,' confirms McCoy. 'If any of them make it through the night, I'll despatch them good and proper in the morning before making my own goodbyes.'

Either the Commander is lost for words, or he has no time to reply. For McCoy switches his attention back to the open door, and cheers.

'Well done, boys! I knew I could rely on you two to follow my orders.' He turns back, grinning. 'You really should see this,' he tells the Commander. 'Your men are dropping their firearms just like I asked. No heroics. Nothing. They're even leaving with their hands held high. You've trained them to do exactly as they're told, boss, and I'm impressed. It's a beautiful sight.'

I don't need to see them for myself to picture the scene in the processing area. I imagine that the sight of North and Cortés coming across the courtyard with

222

drums strapped to their backs must've persuaded most of the guards to retreat. The gasoline smell is strong enough in the cannery to make me feel like retching. It certainly would have reached their noses before the two drenched men got close. Judging by McCoy's glee, I reckon a scrum must be taking place to get through the main doors before the threatened bullet turned the space across there into a fireball.

'Hey, boys!' McCoy calls out finally. 'You did good. As you're the last to leave, I'm going to give you a fighting chance. You now have ten seconds to ditch those cans off your back and get through the blast doors before I test if they live up to their name. One . . . two . . . three . . .'

'No!' Commander Stagger rushes forward, only to freeze when McCoy swings around, still counting briskly. 'Four . . . five . . . six . . .'

He gestures for Stagger to back away, before bringing the gun back around and taking aim.

'Seven . . . eight . . . nine . . . ten.'

'*Don't shoot!*'

It takes a moment for me to recognise my own voice. All this time, locked away inside the cage, I have watched control of this camp slide from the Commander to McCoy with a sense of helplessness as much as fear. Now, just a second from witnessing yet more killing, my intervention leaves me feeling totally exposed.

'Say that again, Hobbes?' McCoy glares across at me, his finger still locked around the trigger.

I breathe out in a whimper when his eyes lock on to mine.

'Just don't shoot them,' I say quietly. 'You don't have to do that.'

McCoy seems to reflect on this for a moment. Then he flashes me a grin, and I know he is fooling with me.

'You're right,' he says. 'I don't *have* to do that. But you must admit it would be fun to try!' He finds the gun's front sight again as he says this, and lets off a brief burst from the magazine. The noise is totally blown away, however, by the detonation that can be heard going off across the processing area. The blast wave spreads right through the cannery. I bury my face in my elbow, hearing McCoy whoop gleefully at the destruction he's just caused.

When I look up, however, the noise has just muffled considerably. McCoy faces me, looking crestfallen.

'Damn it, Hobbes, after the way North and Cortés treated us, I'd have thought you'd be *pleased* to see me single them out for an early death. If you hadn't bleated at me just then, I'd have brought them down *before* they followed their buddies through the blast doors. Thanks to you, my boy, I imagine there are more than two dead men on the other side now.' He glances back outside, up on his toes again, and then promptly comes back sounding calmer. 'Although you got to admire the strength of those doors. A little blackened, but they appear to have locked shut just nicely. At least nobody will be coming back inside without an invitation.'

McCoy may be fooling with us once more, but Commander Stagger is clearly in no mood to humour him. 'Before you unleashed hell on those poor souls,' he says, 'you said yourself that hope never dies. I just pray you're right.'

'Prayers won't help them!' McCoy breaks away from the cannery door now, flaring up all of a sudden. 'Hope might be what gets people through tough times, but it counts for nothing out there, Commander. This is one of the most godless environments known to man, as you were so keen to tell us on our arrival! If there's any hope to be had, my friend, perhaps you should thank Hobbes for speaking up just then. If that explosion picked off more of your men than I had planned, that means there are less out there facing up to the fact that they're about to freeze to death.' McCoy stops at this, and begins a slow handclap. One he directs at me. 'So, well done. Congratulations, young man, for sparing so much misery. I should be mad at you, but I guess I must have a conscience after all!'

My heart hammers, but not in fear as much as anger now. Another detainee begins to clap, uncertainly at first, but then picking up the pace. He's actually *applauding* what McCoy has done. Others quickly join in: shouting wildly and rattling their cages. I glance at

Beth. She is kneeling at the front of her cage. Her head is bowed, in apparent despair, but I can't help thinking she could also be mourning the loss of the man on the floor before her.

When it comes to the question of who stands as a force for good or bad out here, McCoy has just redrawn the boundaries. For the first time since this uprising began, I know for sure which side I'm on.

30

McCoy takes centre stage in the cannery, soaking up the attention. I could be at a prizefight, such is the noise. It's impassioned but also primal and raw. This reaches a crescendo when McCoy frogmarches Commander Stagger to his former cage and slams the gate closed behind him. I'm not frightened any more. What just happened to North and Cortés was inhumanly cruel, and I can barely take in the sight of the body bleeding out on the floor over there. I want to smash my way out of this cage and see if anything can be done to help Williams, and it's this sense of frustration that turns me to fury.

Before McCoy faked the seizure, I had been weighing up my chances of escape. I was just so mad at how I'd been treated that it seemed like a way of fighting back. Watching the guards at work inside this cannery, evaluating the system in operation here, I'd told myself that there had to be a way. Even if it looked impossible,

227

I couldn't lose sight of my belief that no system was entirely secure. Then McCoy had proved my point, and in a way I could never have imagined. Listening to him now, having seen him execute the first part of his plan so mercilessly, I realise I'm not the only one with his sights fixed on the next flight out of here.

'This is a great day, my friends,' crows McCoy now. 'We came here as enemy combatants. We'll leave as *freedom* fighters. To achieve this I need recruits, beginning with a pilot. I know for a fact that there are a couple in this cannery. I've read files on all the detainees who can help me, in fact. So, can I please have a volunteer?'

'Me . . . please!'

From the row opposite, a detainee quickly raises his hand. He doesn't speak English naturally, but his eagerness is clear. McCoy spins around on hearing his voice, and calmly turns the rifle on him.

'*Lying* to me won't save you!' Once again, the thunder of automatic gunfire resounds around the cannery. The detainee slams into the back of his cage, as if yanked violently from behind by strings, and then sinks to the floor with his eyes rolled skywards. I catch my breath, but can't stop staring at McCoy. It's clear he's demonstrating his authority here, but there's an element of utter madness in his methods. 'Even if you *were* telling me the truth,' he snarls after a moment, addressing the dead man, it seems, 'you must've done *something* unforgivable to be here. Some might say

228

you actually *deserved* every bullet!' He turns his back on the cage, his rifle slung low still, and locks his eyes on me. I see them glitter as he grins, and then pinch at the corners. 'How about you, Hobbes? Refresh my memory. Have *you* earned your wings?'

I shake my head, struggling to find my voice at first. 'I can't help you,' I say eventually.

McCoy walks slowly towards me, sizing me up, it seems. What's so chilling is that every time he's fooled around like this today it's ended in death. 'How can I be sure you're not just being a coward, boy?'

'I can't fly a plane,' I say quickly. 'I really can't.'

Outside my cage now, McCoy slots the barrel of his rifle through the mesh. I freeze when he does this, on my knees in front of him. A smell like fireworks comes off the muzzle, also some heat when he touches it to my throat.

'Look me in the eyes, Hobbes, and say it again. You can consider this a lie detector test, if you like.'

I look up to find him staring at me, and sense that whatever I say will be the wrong answer. I hold his gaze, close enough to smell the edge to his breath, thinking all I can do is remain silent. And then, from nowhere, it seems, a voice reaches across the cannery.

'I can pilot a plane for you.'

McCoy blinks at me, a smile spreading slowly under his bandit's moustache. Without a word, he withdraws the gun from my cage and turns to find the volunteer.

'*Beth*, my lovely. I wondered when you might lower yourself to speak to me once more.'

His response confirms what I had thought. These two have a past of some description. Going by the way Beth flares up at him, it's evidently not a close one.

'You set me up, McCoy. I wouldn't even *be* here if it wasn't for your lies.'

McCoy pretends to look hurt, spreading his arms wide. 'I approached you with a business deal. I guaranteed a buyer for every last bullion bar, and delivered the goods without involving you.

'But you never told me who!' She pauses there, as if suddenly aware that this is a very public exchange. 'I am not a terrorist, McCoy. I may be a thief, and a good one at that, but had I known about your *buyer* when you first approached me, I would've gone straight to the authorities.'

'The authorities are right here.' McCoy nods at the Commander. 'Is there any more information you'd like to hear from these two, boss? I know you've been giving Hobbes here a hard time, but you're wasting your breath. Beth played a game with him just as I played a game with her. The difference between them is that Beth figured she stood to make a million bucks from the robbery, and Hobbes . . .' He trails off there, and turns back to shoot me a pitiful look. 'Well, Hobbes got to talk online to a hottie, even if he didn't know it at the time.'

230

I catch sight of Beth looking at me. I see some guilt in her expression, but none of that matters now. Too much blood has been spilled here. Right now I really don't care if she's been duped as much as me. I just keep my mouth shut and watch McCoy cross the floor once more.

'Beth here has brawn as well as beauty. She comes from hardworking stock.' He faces her through the meshing of her cage as he says this, but is clearly addressing us all. 'For three generations, her family have run a wheat farm in the Tennessee Valley. Beth took over the crop dusting after her father lost his sight in one eye. It's been a few years since she last ran a sweep over the fields, but then you don't forget how to ride a bike either. Same difference, far as I can see.' He pauses there for a moment. 'So, I know you can fly a plane. It's in your files, after all. I'm just offended that you didn't volunteer sooner.'

'Another man's life never depended on it before,' Beth replies, glancing in my direction.

McCoy shoots me a look as well, resting his rifle tip over his shoulder now. Through the cannery walls, outside in the compound, distant shouting can be heard. The men out there sound agitated, almost panic-stricken. McCoy picks up on it and smiles to himself.

'You know what?' he offers Beth finally. 'I've given this a great deal of thought, and even though you can fly I can't trust a *traitor* at the controls.'

Beth looks stung all of a sudden. 'I am *not* a traitor!' she hisses at him. 'If anyone is guilty of treachery, McCoy, it's you. When I showed up at the drop-off to collect my share of the money and found the cops waiting for me, I just *knew* you had tipped them off.'

McCoy steps aside from her cage when she says this, as if to invite everyone to listen and judge for themselves. 'So I didn't want to cut into my profits from the job,' he tells her. 'What can I say? I'm a mercenary.'

'You're a traitor and it's in your blood!'

'Oh, you could say I'm genetically primed to overthrow the system,' he adds, reminding us all of his genetic link to the Bounty mutineers. 'That's why I'm the best in the business.'

I glance at Stagger when he says this. Catch him removing his billed cap to mop his brow. He looks all wrong, locked away inside McCoy's former cage, as if he's been shrunk down, while the man responsible for imprisoning him has grown by several inches. Even so, he doesn't look ready to give up on anyone just yet. As McCoy doubles back, pacing between the two rows now, he finds the Commander glaring at him.

'You have no reason to swagger, McCoy. The consequences of your actions will be severe.'

'Uh huh.' McCoy responds like he couldn't care less. He simply switches back, and scans the cages in my row. 'Now, there's one more pilot present here at this party, and he's my man. Above all, I know *he* won't give me a hard time,' he adds, glancing back at Beth. His attention comes to rest on the detainee in the cage at the far end. The man looks very scared, but contains it by simply staring at the floor. McCoy advances towards him, then crouches at his level. 'I know you understand a little English,' he says softly. 'I'm not going to hurt you, OK? I'd fly the plane myself if I had to, but I read your files and you're good. Flying under the radar is something you can do in your sleep, am I right?' Slowly, he inserts the key into the lock, and opens up the gate. 'C'mon, man,' he continues, standing now with his hand outstretched. 'I'm offering you a lucky break, here. The plane I have in mind can take maybe a dozen passengers, max. This guarantees your seat.'

Cautiously, with his eyes fixed on McCoy's rifle, the detainee crawls out into the open. McCoy offers his hand. The man accepts it as he climbs to his feet, and then grins when this figure who has just set him free claps him on the back.

Immediately, more voices call out to be released. McCoy invites the freed detainee to collect one of the guns dropped by the guards, and then sets about opening up the neighbouring cage. At once the appeals become more urgent. Not everyone is crying out to be released. Some, like Grimstad, watch impassively, while several actively beg to be left alone. McCoy considers each request. Working his way from one end of the row to the next, it's clear he's picking off those who can be

233

of use to him. On reaching my cage, however, he simply walks right past like I don't exist. He does exactly the same thing on crossing to the row opposite, blanking Grimstad, Beth and the Commander. As he makes his final selection, ignoring the angry howls of those who had been hoping to join him, a sense of dread begins to build inside me. For every detainee McCoy lets loose picks up a weapon before joining the gang now massing on the floor. I see one of the more excitable in their number hold a rifle aloft with one hand. He cries out victoriously, and lets off a round into the vault above.

Several others join in this insane celebration, reeling off shots that pound my eardrums. One of the freed men catches my eye. For a moment I think he might turn his gun on me. He certainly levels it in my direction, only to break off and scatter with the others at an almighty burst of automatic weapon fire.

'That's *enough*!' McCoy stands at the heart of it all, having brought silence to the cannery once more. He brings his rifle back down across his chest, and orders everyone to the door. 'Fortunately, the nice boys outside have left us their recreational quarters. After being cooped up here, it's only right that we unwind before taking our leave, don't you think?' Crossing the floor himself now, McCoy opens up the door into the courtyard, and then gestures for the freed men to move out. After a moment, while they try to judge whether this is a trick or not, the first detainee takes up his offer. 'Be sure to bust that poor guy from the Fridge,' McCoy tells him. 'He deserves to come with us. And if you find any military hiding out back there,' he adds, raising his voice to be heard over the sudden scrum, 'kill them on sight.'

'And you?' The detainee appointed to pilot the plane is the last to leave. He stands humbly before his saviour, speaking in a language that is evidently not his own. 'What will *you* do?'

'Me?' McCoy paws at the nape of his neck. 'Buddy, I'll be right along.' He turns to scan the cages, shouldering his weapon now in the same way that I'd carry a schoolbag. 'I just got to finish the job first.'

31

Camp Twilight housed the mercenaries. Warriors for hire if the price was right. That's what Commander Stagger had announced when we first arrived out here. Listening to what McCoy just said, desperately trying to take stock of our situation, I feel a knot of fear tighten in my guts.

For McCoy was claiming to be on business. Whatever that meant, I can only think it's going to be murderous.

With the last freed detainee gone, the first thing he does is lock up the side door. It takes a few attempts to find the right key on the fob, but McCoy works methodically and without any sense of haste. Muffled gunshots can be heard from the front buildings. I just hope this is celebratory fire, and not cold-blooded killing.

Finally, with the door secured, McCoy returns to the centre of the cannery. He's whistling now, the rifle slung behind his shoulder, turning in a slow circle as he reaches the centre ground. I remember how the Commander had made his first inspection with a similar sense of calm. There is no hint of the craziness McCoy had displayed on the flight out nor in his first hours here. If all that unbalanced stuff was an act, then what I'm seeing of him here is even more chilling. I glance at Agent Williams. He is dead, I am sure of it. McCoy had shot a man who believed he needed help. Through my eyes, that marked him out as more than dangerous. That was an act so calculated it touched upon pure evil.

'I've seen some places,' McCoy says eventually, still turning to address us all. 'But this one is as close to hell as I'd ever care to be.'

'Hell is where you're heading, buddy. That's for sure.'

Stagger's comment draws McCoy full circle.

'Then I'll be among friends,' he says, and directs his attention towards the abandoned white medibox. Squatting before it, he rummages around for a moment, finds a snap pack of pills, and knocks back several. 'You know,' he says, and pauses to swallow them down, 'I really *do* have a headache. I'll be honest, it kicked in when I first accepted this job. I mean, how exactly do you get inside a remote detention centre like this? I asked myself the same question over and over again. When it came to me, the answer was so simple I booked my ticket straight away!'

I remember what Williams had revealed to me about McCoy's capture. It seemed so slack for a fugitive such as this to make a call from a hotel landline. Now I consider what he's just told us, however, and realise he's been playing the authorities from the moment he dialled out. He must have known that the weapons buyer he had financed was under arrest in Pakistan. By calling him directly from a landline and with the phones inevitably bugged, McCoy had effectively handed himself in. The way Stagger is reading his boastful expression, I sense that he has just reached the same conclusion.

'You *purposely* sacrificed your liberty?' The Commander is clearly finding this hard to accept. 'That's insane!'

'My brief is to catch up with someone.' McCoy is still crouching before the medibox. The pistol he used to shoot Williams is lying on the floor nearby. It draws his attention like a dropped wallet might. Having moved to retrieve it, he checks the magazine for bullets and faces the Commander once more. 'There's only one place the individual in question could've been processed, in fact, and that's here.'

'But why?' Stagger cuts to the question on my mind. This time, McCoy responds by crossing in front of Beth's cage, and drawing up before the one beside it.

'Because the bounty on this man's head is too good to refuse.' He slams the magazine back in place, addressing Grimstad directly now. 'I read in the press that you stirred up threats of retribution from the black metal community, Thomas. All I can say is that the people who hired me to come here aren't big fans of the genre. They've probably never heard of it, in fact. What interests them is the fun you had trying to blow up a concert hall.'

For the first time since we've been locked up here, the Norwegian appears to register the fact that he is being spoken to. He has sat passively throughout the whole appalling episode, but this gives him quite a start.

'Leave him alone!' protests Beth. 'Leave us all in peace!'

McCoy shrugs. 'It's just like the Commander told us. There are people in this world who want people like us dead. Some of them are wealthier than others. Take those who wish to silence young Thomas. They don't care who he tried to take out with his bomb belt. They are intrigued, of course, as to how the hell he got hold of the explosives, but then the best cells operate independently nowadays.'

'The *Paris* cell?' Stagger says out loud what has just come to my mind.

'The only concern my clients have,' McCoy continues, 'is that Thomas is silenced before he cracks and talks about his connections. And as they have come into a lot of money lately, thanks to Beth and Hobbes here,

239

I have been offered enough of the spoils to make what seemed like an impossible job irresistible.'

All I can think is that McCoy must have been offered *millions* to take a risk like this. Millions *I* made happen. At any other time, I would be horrified. Right now, every emotion I feel is bound up with an instinct for survival. I have Beth to thank for drawing McCoy's attention away from me a moment ago. I just can't think of anything to offer that would help the detainee now suffering from his attention.

'So, Thomas,' the Pitcairn Islander continues, 'is there anything you'd like to tell us before I earn my dough? C'mon, you don't just wire yourself up to explode in a public place without some kind of agenda. You can tell us, Tommy-boy. Just as long as you're safe in your cage and I can be sure you won't respond by trying to bite chunks out of my throat.' He trails off there for a moment, which only serves to remind me of the poor official Grimstad had maimed during his initial interrogation. 'Speak up, man,' McCoy continues, pressing him now. 'If you like, you can call it a final confession.'

For a moment, all eyes turn towards Grimstad. With his head bowed, and his greasy black hair flopped forward, it's hard to know what's going on inside his head. Then he looks up, as if surfacing from a dream. In fact, it's clear from the way he regards McCoy that he's totally tuned in to what's happening. I see him draw breath, and when he speaks I know I am not alone in being lost for words.

'Everything was staged,' he says, in a completely different accent to the one I'd expected. 'My codename is Victor. I'm a deep cover agent for the United States Government.'

32

At first, McCoy looks genuinely shocked. He takes a step back, as if knocked off his guard, only to recover with a grin. Judging by the way he chuckles to himself, I figure a mercenary like this must thrive on the unexpected. He clearly places great faith in surviving by his wits. Something like this can only serve to stretch him.

'Commander?' he says, seeking some kind of confirmation.

If Stagger is as dumbstruck by the revelation as I am, he does well to keep it to himself. He simply stares at the figure in question, who continues to speak in what has to be a natural American accent.

'Thomas Grimstad does not exist,' he says. 'The suicide bomb attempt was a staged operation. Even the story about his attack on the interrogator is a fabrication. It was simply designed to cook up maximum publicity.'

McCoy considers what he has just heard. He rakes his hand through his long, slick hair, stopping at the crown.

'In view of your silence,' he says, addressing Stagger directly, 'I'm guessing this is news to you?' The Commander remains tight-lipped. 'The question is, do *you* believe he's telling the truth?'

Stagger switches his attention back to the detainee in question, who brings himself to the front of the cage before addressing McCoy.

'The operation was designed to wake up the Norwegian government,' he continues. 'Since 2001, they have grudgingly allowed us to use this cannery as a detention centre. We're on an island that belongs to them, you see. A remote arctic archipelago—'

'Svalbard,' McCoy cuts in. 'A desolate bunch of ice-bound rocks midway between Norway and the North Pole. Geo coordinates seventy-eight zero zero north, twenty zero zero east. I know *precisely* where we are, in fact, as do my clients. Now get to the point.'

I had figured out for myself that we must be in the Arctic Circle. Even so, the level of detail McCoy just offered is breathtaking. I knew the importance of planning, but this took things to a whole new level. If he'd masterminded his whole operation with such care, then surely there was no way of stopping him. Even something like this couldn't dent McCoy's confidence, though the man claiming to be a deep cover agent seems suddenly less sure of himself.

'We need the ongoing support of the Norwegian government in the fight against the War on Terror.' He looks to the floor, as if debating whether he should continue at all. Finally, he makes his decision. 'When they first provided us with this site,' he continues, 'we argued that the infrastructure wouldn't be fit for our purpose. Nevertheless, we did our very best to make it work, despite repeat requests for a larger, more suitable location elsewhere on the archipelago. When negotiations failed, it was decided that an alternative means of persuasion should come into effect. We might be a long way from home here, but our ability to detain our enemies and gather intelligence from them is an issue of national security. And so Thomas Grimstad came into existence. He acquired a birth certificate and background, of course, before being dispatched onto the mainland with a carefully faked bomb belt to remind those who make such decisions that terrorism can strike nearer to home. By leading the Norwegians to believe one of their own had links to the Al-Qaeda cell genuinely apprehended in Paris, we succeeded in renewing our relationship.'

'Mission accomplished.' McCoy retreats from the cage, nodding in approval it seems.

'Naturally, they want to be sure this isn't some kind of torture camp, which is why we invited them to form the decommissioning party. Once they see that conditions aren't suitable for us to effectively process a national threat like me, we can look forward to a much-needed upgrade.'

'So you're locked up here for the sake of appearances.' McCoy continues to face the man in question, listening closely despite the distance. 'You had to be seen to be put on the rendition flight, am I right?'

'That's correct.'

'That's *bull*!' McCoy spits back at him. 'If you were telling the truth then the Commander here wouldn't be trying so hard not to look like you've just dropped the biggest bombshell of them all! Nor would you have been so quick to break your cover, man. I've come across plenty of deep cover agents. Hell, I've even killed a few in my time, and none started singing as quickly as you just have.'

'That you killed them tells me I had no choice,' he answers calmly, and then lowers his attention to the body on the floor in front of his cage. 'I can tell you that Agent Williams was party to my identity. Having completed my primary objective in Oslo, I received instructions to covertly observe the running of the camp for a few days. Having taken such extreme measures to persuade the Norwegians that we deserve a better site, we can't afford for their members of the decommissioning party to witness *anything* untoward.' He pauses there, considering the dead man still. 'Williams was expected to brief Stagger later today. Once he'd presented him with the code words and the contacts to confirm my identity, the plan was for me to alert the Commander to any areas for concern that may not have come to his attention. Without Williams' assistance, we could never guarantee a clean sheet before the party's arrival tomorrow. The poor guy was due to fly out with me early next week,' he adds ruefully. 'Not that he was wise to the exit plan himself.'

'Is that right?' By now, McCoy has recovered his poise. 'How convenient that Williams can't confirm your claim, huh, Thomas?'

'Like I said, Thomas Grimstad does not exist.'

'And I've come all this way to make sure of exactly that.' Still facing the undercover agent, McCoy finds the medibox once more. 'So, where does that leave me? What do I have to do to earn my money now?' I see him pick out a syringe package first, followed by a clear tube. It contains a liquid, with a plastic cap. McCoy sinks the needle through it, and withdraws the liquid into the syringe. 'I promise this won't hurt. A little sting, and that's it!'

'What is that?'

Stagger rises up on his haunches in a bid to see more clearly. McCoy merely shows him the syringe, turning next so everyone can see. 'It's military-grade anaesthetic. Something to numb the pain.'

'What pain?' Whether or not he's just concocted the story to save himself, the man I know as Grimstad seems more switched on than ever before. Even so, he must sense McCoy is in complete control here. For Grimstad falls quite still, with his eyes locked on the Pitcairn mercenary as he settles in front of his cage.

'Now be cool. It's just a needle. You're not scared of needles, are you?' McCoy shows him the pistol in his other hand, and then sheer menace enters his voice. 'One wrong move and I'll kill every last person in this cannery, leaving you until last.'

With no choice now, he doesn't retreat when McCoy opens up the gate. Nor does he protest when McCoy reaches in, pops open the throat of his jumpsuit and eases it clear of his left collarbone. He just submits like this is something he must do to spare us all. I look away when McCoy sinks in the needle near his neck, and then hear him offer congratulations on staying so calm.

'Just take a breath, OK? It's all over now. Now, that didn't hurt, did it? I promised you no pain, and I'm a man of my word . . . whoever you may be!'

Without warning, having addressed the guy so calmly, McCoy leaps upon him like a wildcat. He stands no chance in the face of such aggression, and tumbles to the floor of the cage. With one forearm rammed against the man's throat, McCoy uses his free hand to press the gun to a point below his right shoulder blade. In the struggle now, I see him angle it downwards by several degrees, as if searching for a particular spot. I cry out for him to stop, as does Beth and several other detainees, but the sudden shot kills all protest.

247

With a bark like a dog, his victim snaps his head back, both eyes bulging, and then sinks to the floor. A small red circle forms where McCoy continues to press the muzzle. It's no bigger than a coin. Somehow, it even holds its shape when the Pitcairn mercenary eases Grimstad into a seated position and then withdraws from the cage.

'That's it! All over now!' He slams the gate shut on the shocked, groaning man, locking it down again. 'I apologise if I was a little rough with you just then, but I couldn't afford to shoot wide. An inch or so out and you'd have died instantly. You see, rather than killing you outright, I thought you deserved a couple of hours to make your mind up about your true identity. As far as I'm concerned, you're Thomas Grimstad, and I'm just following orders so I can be sure I get paid. But if you're *really* a deep cover agent, there's time now for you to convince these guys and die with a clear conscience.'

'You haven't killed me yet,' grunts the man he's just shot, who then curses under his breath.

'Oh, you *will* die,' McCoy replies with complete confidence. 'That round I just fired? The bullet passed clean through your airway. The reason you're not bleeding out like a stuck pig is because the artery I nicked is draining into your lungs. It's a technique I picked up from the Japanese Yakuza some years ago. That way, if they wanted to send out a message, their victim would have enough time to stagger back and deliver it before drowning on the inside. In this case, I just bought you an extra hour of life, and without any pain, but I promise you one thing: it's fatal. If I thought I was gambling with the bounty on your head, I'd have shot you through the heart. The fact is there's *nothing* anyone can do to save you. This is it, man! You've just earned yourself a toe tag. I guarantee it!'

McCoy might be relishing this moment, but I'm appalled by what I've just witnessed, as are many others around me. His victim, meanwhile, responds to the details of his death sentence with little emotion. He stares at the floor, supporting himself with one hand, taking deep breaths in and out. His face looks a little more washed out, perhaps, and I think that his eyes are beginning to glass over. I just hope this is down to the powerful tranquilliser in his system, because he seems unnervingly at peace.

'You're sick!' This is Beth, glaring at McCoy from inside her cage. 'Nobody deserves to die like that.'

McCoy nods to himself, as if in agreement. 'Sick but rich by a whole heap of bullion bars, my dear. And don't forget *you* supplied the funds that paid for the hit. There is blood on your hands as much as on mine.'

Beth's jaw slackens by a notch. Her face reddens, and for a moment I think she might cry. For someone who possessed the guts to break in and out of Fort Knox, it's a shock to see.

249

McCoy notes her response with a chuckle as he crosses in front of her cage.

'I selected you, Beth, because you look like the last person who would stage a robbery. You're a sweet girl. Nobody would suspect you couldn't be trusted. Not least your employees. I figured it would take me several months to persuade you that my plan was foolproof. That it only took a matter of weeks tells me as much about your guts as it does about your greed!'

'Oh, you were good,' she says, staring right through him. 'You had me suckered, and I admit I wouldn't have come close to pulling off the raid without your help, support and guidance. But right now, after everything that's happened, I will not give you the satisfaction of seeing me shed a single tear.'

McCoy shrugs, totally unconcerned. Then, with a nod to the Commander, he makes his way towards the main door. Midway, he stops – as if reminded of something that had slipped his mind. He turns one more time and gestures at the deep cover agent he's just shot.

'If my friend here grows a little nervous, maybe when the Reaper starts clawing at his shoulder, remind him that he's got a pile of stay-calm pills stashed away some place.'

He glances in my direction as he says this, and tips me a wink. If I had assumed I was the only one to notice Grimstad dodging his medication, McCoy here just demonstrated that his eyes were wide open throughout the whole thing too. As he prepares to leave the cannery, some of the detainees McCoy has passed over begin to yell and slam their fists against the meshing.

'You guys just sit tight,' he tells them, raising his voice to be heard. 'I think I've demonstrated this centre is in no fit state to contain enemy combatants. Once I'm gone from here, let's hope they see fit to transfer you some place warmer, huh?' He pauses to haul open the door. The rush of cold air cuts through the cannery. All of a sudden, I cannot wait for this fiend to leave us.

McCoy steps out into the courtyard. He faces us in silhouette, surveying the carnage he has created. 'I'm locking you up for your own safety,' he tells us, and begins to close the door. 'Let's not forget that some of the world's most wanted are on the loose out here!'

33

Agent Williams had a wife and son. A guy about my age, so he told me. He hadn't left them, as people sometimes say when a family man has passed away. McCoy had stolen him from them.

For several minutes after the Pitcairn mercenary makes his exit, nobody breathes a word. We all hear him return and secure the doors with what sounds like a chain, but it doesn't prompt a response from anyone. Even those detainees who would have gladly taken up arms with him just sit there reflecting on events. Altogether, in the aftermath of what has happened here, it feels like a wake.

The body on the floor is the focus of attention. It looks as if it has been washed in here by a freak wave. All the firearms that littered the floor have been swept up by the escapees. If a rescue team burst in right now, they'd wonder what the hell had happened. Judging by the way Williams is lying, he seems to be pointing towards the man claiming to be a deep cover agent. It makes me wonder whether perhaps Williams really *did* know something about him. What's weird is that the guy isn't behaving like he's next in line to die. In fact, he's the only one here who seems entirely tuned out from his surroundings. He could almost be in the same zombie-like state he arrived in. I tell myself this must be down to the tranquilliser, rather than play-acting. Even so, it's hard not to suspect that Thomas Grimstad had attempted to spin a story to save his life, and failed.

'I'm sorry!' Beth is the first to break the silence, and when she does it sounds desperate. 'I feel responsible for all of this. But I swear McCoy fooled me. Right from the start, he sold the whole thing as a business proposition. He convinced me that his buyers for the bullion came from the world of fine art, mining and finance. He even recommended that I recruit a hacker to help me, and suggested the board where I found Hobbes.'

I don't respond to this. In different ways, McCoy has worked everyone here to his advantage. What fires me up, though, are the casualties he's left behind. The sight of Agent Williams' body is totally unsettling. So too is the presence of the man who has just confessed to being some kind of state-sponsored invention, but received a bullet through the lungs all the same. Finally, I turn my attention to the detainee who had attempted to earn his freedom by claiming he could fly a plane. The one McCoy had gunned down in cold blood. Stagger, I notice, seems oblivious to them all. He's crouched inside the cage beside Beth's, with his knee raised to meet his chin, and his hand pressed flat to his brow. Events haven't just overtaken him here. They've left him for dead as well.

'Unless we do something,' I call across to the Commander, 'more people are going to suffer. Not only have you got men freezing to death outside, just think about the kind of misery those creeps are capable of unleashing on the wider world. Every single one of them is a high risk mercenary with blood on their hands. It's why you locked them up here! Now my guess is that when that inspection party touches down tomorrow, McCoy and his men will stop at nothing to commandeer the plane. God alone knows how I've managed to find myself among such dangerous animals, but at least I'm not like them. Why? Because after what's happened I know we can't allow a single one to get away!' I pause for breath, aware that my emotions are getting the better of me. 'So why don't we finish feeling sorry for ourselves, and work out how we can turn this thing around?'

My outburst serves to switch all attention to me. I feel foolish all of a sudden. Foolish and very scared. Even so, I hold the Commander's gaze, demanding an answer from him.

'I admire your optimism,' he says finally. 'I guess it's understandable in a kid your age.'

'McCoy didn't give up!' Beth might be addressing Stagger but she's staring directly at me. Having shown such remorse a moment ago, I'm pleased to see her sense of determination return. 'The odds were stacked way against him escaping from his cage, but he did it, and so can we.'

The Commander sighs, and shifts uncomfortably. 'These cages are practically indestructible. Even the bolts that hold them together have been welded for extra security. McCoy may have scammed his way out, but that's not an option for the rest of us. Without a key, and in view of who is on the loose out there, all we can do is hope that these cages can *protect* us.'

I loathe the silence that hangs over this place. It drops down at every opportunity, poisoning the air somehow. But I've had enough of it this time. I've seen too much to just sit here and hope for the best. I want to get out, even if I can't get away. Grasping the mesh with both hands, and despite what the Commander has just said, I shake it as hard as I can. It doesn't shift, of course, but that only prompts me to start beating it from the inside with my fists. Finally, having spent just some of the fire inside me, I come to rest with my head bowed. And then I chuckle to myself.

'I'm here because I can get into places that are

supposedly off limits to the outside world. Now I'm stuck inside one for real, and I can't get *out*.'

'Hobbes.' I hear Beth call my name, but am too despondent to respond. I just stare at the floor, lost to this bitter thought, until she orders me to look her in the eyes.

'I got you into this,' she calls across the space. 'I'll find a way to get us out.'

'What we need is a guardian angel,' I say, if only to keep the silence at bay. 'I just doubt anything like that could ever find us in a place this godforsaken.'

I break from Beth's gaze, dwelling for a moment on the prone body just out of her reach, and then close my eyes to think.

A moment later, when I look up with a start, I see the corpse has shifted a notch.

When it moves again, I blink to focus on the bigger picture, and register who is behind it.

'Grimstad,' I say without thinking, and have to remind myself who I'm addressing here. 'What are you doing?'

At first, I think it must be an illusion. For, despite the steel meshing, he's worked his arm through to grasp the dead agent's hand. In doing so the cage has cut into his skin like cheese wire, stripping it raw.

'It must be the anaesthetic,' says Beth, switching to the corner of her cage to watch. 'He *can't* be feeling that pain!'

256

Like Beth, the remaining detainees in the cannery strain to witness the detainee at work. Stagger repeats my question, demanding to know what is going on, but the man doesn't even blink in response. I don't like to think that McCoy has only injected him with a *local* anaesthetic. That means the man is feeling this acutely. With one final heave, he hauls Agent Williams' body in front of his cage. That's when I realise his objective, just a moment before he searches Williams' blood-soaked jacket, and plucks out a set of keys.

'*Yes!*' I punch the air, euphoric. Other detainees are quietly celebrating, while many simply observe with questioning faces. Commander Stagger is among them.

'Drop the keys!' he orders, showing no sign that he regards Grimstad as anything other than a threat.

I look questioningly at Stagger. 'But this is it! This is the break we need!'

As I speak, the man claiming to be a deep cover agent finds the right key. With the gate open, he grits his teeth and draws his hand back through the mesh. Witnessing such an act of self-mutilation, it's hard to think this is anything other than a man capable of carrying out a suicide bombing. But even if this *is* the young Norwegian who struck fear into the heart of his country, I simply can't believe he's in a state of mind to kill right now. Under the circumstances, I'm prepared to take the risk.

'Hey, over here!' As soon as I call out to him, Stagger

appeals for me to shut up. I ignore him, for I have the detainee's full attention. The bullet wound has opened up a little, blooming through his jumpsuit. I can't ignore his forearm either, skinned as it is and glistening in this light, but nothing is as shocking as the rate at which all colour is draining from his face. Crescent shadows are forming under his eyes, which shrink by a fraction when he dips through the gate of his cage, and rises up into the glare of the flood lamps. He stares at me, his eyes hooded more than usual, and I can't help but be gripped by a sense of dread. If this man really *is* working for the US Government, so deep under cover that even the Commander has only just learned of his presence, then he must have been picked for appearing to function on a different level from anyone else.

Then he steers his attention to Beth. Immediately, Stagger's next petition to the man sounds desperate.

'I want you to bring those keys directly to me, *is that understood*?' This time, looking at the way Grimstad observes Beth, I share the Commander's alarm. She doesn't move, as if faced with a predatory animal, even when he crouches to unlock the gate.

'That's an order!' Stagger yells, but his authority has gone.

With her eyes fixed on the figure that has just selected her, Beth edges from the cage. Cautiously, she stands before him. I see her eyes drop to his bullet wound. She reaches up to touch it with both hands. The man who's just freed her doesn't flinch.

'I can dress this for you.' She looks up into his eyes, and then gestures at the medibox. 'Your arm needs attention too.'

He declines by folding down the sleeve of his jump-suit, and then steps around so he's facing my cage with Beth. 'There's no time to waste.' He speaks with difficulty, his shoulders heaving with every breath he takes. More immediately, I detect just a hint of Scandinavian in his accent. 'As a dying man, I have one last request, no?'

I regard him warily, wishing I could be sure of his intentions, whoever he may be.

'Just so long as it doesn't involve bloodshed,' I say.

His lips shrink from his teeth. An untimely smile, of sorts.

'That depends on your skills,' he replies, moving towards the gate of my cage now. 'And whether or not you can trust me.'

'I want to trust you, Thomas. Really, I do.'

'Please,' he insists, holding my gaze as he slips the key into the padlock. 'Call me Victor.'

34

Beth embraces me just as soon as I leave the cage. I am so surprised that I just stand there for a moment with my arms at my side.

'What's this for?' I ask.

She looks up at me, eyes shining. 'For everything,' she says, which sounds to me like an apology, and then she breaks away.

The detainee who has just freed us from our cages is not looking at all well. His lungs are working hard, and his lips have begun to go blue. He's in such a bad way that I see no reason why this agent, code-named Victor, should be anything other than truthful with us. He may scare me still, but I have to believe his story.

Commander Stagger has yet to drop his guard, there inside his cage, but now I'm on the outside I don't feel so tense.

Victor is still holding the key set in his hand. I offer

to unlock the other detainees for him. Immediately, he withdraws from me by a step, and his hand curls into a fist.

'Nobody else can help you, Hobbes,' he says, and faces the Commander's cage. 'Would you agree with that?'

Their eyes meet for a moment. Stagger's concern turns to puzzlement, and then some understanding softens his expression. 'You've released Hobbes for his talent as a hacker, right? Based on what I've learned from him during our interviews, I'm thinking you're also aware that he knows how to exploit the weakest part of any secure system.'

'Your observation would be correct.'

'And Beth because she knows how to exploit that talent in *him*?'

Given how she had manipulated me to help her rob Fort Knox, I have to accept that he's right. Even so, I find it hard to meet the girl's gaze. At the same time, I regard the Commander's interpretation as a licence to begin working freely on a plan to fight back against the man who caged him.

'If Hobbes can find a way to access the communications tower, and send out a mayday,' continues the deep cover agent, 'then it will be over for McCoy. After that,' he finishes, addressing everyone present, 'we'll just have to hold out hope that help reaches you before he does.'

'McCoy has secured all the doors,' says Beth after a moment, and gestures at the keys in his hand. 'Those won't get us out of here.'

For a second, I see defeat come into the face of this dying man. He takes a breath, as if to steel himself, and turns to me.

'A *back* door,' I say without thinking, for I have to give him something. 'As a hacker, one of the first things I do in evaluating a system is seek out a back door. We're talking about a software program installed in secret by the system architects, giving them access at any time. It's often dressed up to look redundant, but basically anyone can use it once they learn of its existence.'

Beth looks around as I speak, wasting no time, it seems. With a grin, she settles on a point over my shoulder.

'We'd better just hope that the sea ice under the cannery can hold our weight. It might take a miracle for us to bring McCoy to task, but none of us can walk on water.'

I turn at this, see the steps down at the rear with the winch hanging just behind it.

'That trapdoor hasn't been used in years,' says the Commander pessimistically. 'It's entirely rusted in.'

'Well, let's put that to the test.' Beth heads for the rear of the cannery, leaving me to face the deep cover agent.

'What can we do for you?' I ask, still reeling from what he must be going through.

'Just promise me you'll never give up,' he says, with an unnerving sense of calm. 'And if we do make it out onto the ice, start looking out for yourself instead of me.'

'You want to come too?' I can't hide my surprise. 'Why?'

'I might've accepted a bullet just now, but I won't die quietly,' he says. 'Besides, it'll take some hours before conditions outside start to pick off the last of those guards. They'll be well aware of the fate they're facing, however, so you can be sure they won't take kindly to the sight of prisoners running loose.'

'He's right,' Stagger says from his cage. 'Even if they don't have weapons, they still have the dogs. You could be torn to pieces.'

'I'm trained to survive by my wits,' continues this man I had known as Grimstad. 'Even if I'm not firing on all cylinders right now, I can still be of use to you. Because McCoy must be stopped, at all costs, and I have nothing to lose.'

I glance at the Commander, feeling sick to the pit of my stomach. He holds my gaze for a beat, and then stares with great suspicion at the individual who has freed us.

'If a covert operation was running at my detention centre,' Stagger says eventually, drawing his attention, '*I* would have known about it.'

The pair regard one another for a moment.

'You believe I made it up to save my skin, Commander? Well, McCoy's little venture took you by surprise. And that should never have been allowed to happen. I can also tell you I have seen other things occur within these walls that are equally unacceptable. Abuses of power that you really should have known about,' he adds, with some emotion. 'All I can hope is that had I reported this to you as planned, you would've had the authority and the confidence to put a stop to it all immediately!'

I think about North as he says this, and what has just happened to him. Even so, whether he was talking about the behaviour of one rogue guard, or the entire system in operation here, nobody deserved to die for it.

'Let me out,' Stagger demands. 'I can take over from here.'

Solemnly, the injured man shakes his head. 'When you refused to abandon these detainees, sir, you just about started to earn some respect from me. They need you to stay with them in case McCoy comes back before we can reach him. Besides, I've spent time with Hobbes and Beth. They're the only two people I can trust here. If I freed you, Commander, that would be one more person on the loose I'd have to regard as a threat.'

Stagger's shoulders slump at this. I sense he's aware of his utter powerlessness here.

264

'You don't have to do this at all,' he says finally. 'For your own safety, I recommend that you return to your cages.'

Beth's mouth tightens as he says this. 'If we give it our best shot,' she replies, 'we might just save some lives!'

The trapdoor doesn't budge. I pull hard on the iron ring, but it's rusted into the frame. I try one more time, straining with all my might, and then let it drop back. Stagger regards the three of us from his cage, looking both tense and resigned. Beth is standing at the top of the steps, with the deep cover agent beside her.

'It isn't going to shift,' I tell them.

Beth focuses on the door, and then lifts her gaze above my head. I follow her line of sight, see the old winch hook hanging over me, and grin sheepishly at her.

'What are you? The brains behind this operation?'

She skirts the step, and reaches for the pulley chain. 'Seems so,' she replies. 'Though what we could really use right now is some brawn.'

I can't be sure if she says this to put me down or fire me up. Either way, I join her straight away, and together we lower the winch. The agent codenamed Victor heads down the steps to snare the ring with the hook. It fits beautifully. He gives us the nod to pull it up. This time, I ask Beth to stand aside.

'Let me do this,' I say.

'Are you trying to prove yourself to me?' she asks, tipping one eyebrow.

I grip the chain, one hand over the other, and give a silent prayer that I'm not going to need any help.

The cold takes my breath away. It rushes in when a crack appears in the seam around the trapdoor. For a second, it feels like I am trying to open an airlock. One more heave on the chain, I think to myself, and we'll all be sucked out into the void.

'That's it!' Beth clenches her fists when the trapdoor finally gives way. The plunge in temperature is incredible. The heating system in here may be fierce, but it's no match against nature. A shiver runs down my spine, but there's no way that I can simply lower the winch now and close the trapdoor again.

I join the other two at the open hatch. The ocean is a good drop down. It's really just a fractured floor of ice, furrowed in places like a badly ploughed field, muted in the grey light, and punctured by the concrete stilts that support the cannery. Water swells and recedes through the fissures, but it's the sounds that grab me. The constant splitting, popping and cracking we can hear is a reminder of the stresses at work within. My eyes are streaming from the cold by now. I realise we have to act, one way or the other.

'No system is impenetrable,' I say, and face them both across the hatch. 'But I have to tell you that I have *no* idea how we're going to get back inside the building.'

'Yes, you *do*,' Beth counters. 'Every time I looked out from my cage I could see you were thinking things over. And the work you did on Williams was something else. I heard every word. He may have been briefed to feed you slivers of information, but by the time you'd finished he was eating out of *your* hand. So just take one step at a time, Hobbes. You can pull this off,' she says to finish, and turns to the third in our number as if seeking reassurance.

In his tranquillised state, I notice the wounded detainee's pupils have opened right out. They make his eyes seem unnervingly black and penetrating.

This man is on our side, I have to tell myself. *He's a deep cover agent, not the angel of death we all believed him to be.*

'In these conditions,' breathes Victor, 'I estimate we have less than an hour to get you back inside. Any longer,' he adds, and grits his teeth on easing himself through the hatch, 'and I may not be the only dead body out there.'

35

As soon as my feet break the thin film of water, I know there is no going back. I am the last to drop, having guided the other two down as best I can. My knees absorb much of the impact, but that doesn't stop the ice pack from groaning. Once again, I'm reminded of how hopeless my pumps are out here. I take a sharp intake of breath, hear a crack then a pop, and wonder if we'll ever make it onto solid ground.

'Don't move!' I hiss, and my breath turns to vapour in an instant.

I can feel the ice splintering beneath us. My arrival on the surface, it seems, is threatening to open it up. I know not to panic or move without thinking things through. Online, if I enter an authorised zone and find it's wired with an intrusion detection system I hadn't anticipated, the most effective response is to simply stay put. The temptation might be to turn and run, but that's when mistakes are made. Instead, by staying cool, you can work out a way to bypass the system or fool it into thinking you're friendly.

'I don't like this,' Beth whispers. 'I don't like this one bit.'

Beside her, the deep cover agent keeps a bead on me like some ghastly bird of prey.

'What do you suggest?' he asks, in a way that makes me think he actually has an idea. That he doesn't go on to offer it, leaves his question feeling more like a test. The air is quite still out here. It amplifies every sound. I hear dogs, and wonder if they've picked up on our presence.

'We can't just head for the shoreline. Not until we've established where the guards are located, and how we're going to tackle them. Until we see what state they're in, we won't be sure what kind of threat they present.'

'Right now the biggest threat lies beneath our feet.' Beth looks nervously at her pumps. She picks one foot after the other from the water, as troubled as we all are by the cold. Inside the cannery, thanks to the relentless heating, my jumpsuit had been damp with sweat. I can feel it freezing to my skin.

'We need to spread our weight,' I say finally, and turn to look across the bay. 'So let's follow different paths, and regroup over there.'

The wreck of the trawler is partially obscured by ice debris. Mostly this takes the shape of huge splinters.

They jut from the surface like a timber floor in the aftermath of an earthquake. 'If we can make it across without being spotted,' I say, 'it'll give us a clear view. What's more, if it can support a ship that size I'm sure it'll take three passengers.' I face around again. 'Are you sure you want to do this, Victor?'

I find him staring at the boat, still struggling with his breath.

'Now we're on the outside,' he says, and offers me a look, 'that codename feels like wishful thinking.'

I don't disagree. In this brutal cold, the odds of coming through this on top are stacked high against us. I just don't know whether this means he would rather be addressed by his assumed name.

'Grimstad?' I say hesitantly.

A wry smile crosses his lips. 'You should know that *I'm* your greatest threat right now,' he says. 'No matter what you call me.'

I trade glances with Beth. When I look back, he isn't smiling any more. Even so, I think I understand him.

'You're the heaviest,' I say. 'The one most likely to compromise the ice?'

With a nod, but not a single word to confirm what I've just suggested, he moves off. As he heads out from under the wharf, I note the dark red circle on the back of his jumpsuit. The exit wound makes me realise that the bullet has passed clean through his body as well as his lungs. It's also evident to me he's in a hurry. I just don't want to think about why.

'What do you make of him?' asks Beth, watching him go.

'Frankly, I don't care who he is. I'm more concerned that we don't follow in his footsteps.'

Beth faces me side on. 'Amen to that,' she says.

We pick our way out of the shadow of the great wharf, moving in an arrowhead formation. I realise that the light has faded considerably since I worked on clearing the airstrip of snow. I can still see where the sun is lurking, behind the seaward horizon now, and yet it feels more like a polar night. Stars prick the dusky sky, forming clusters and patterns I would never see from home. But this is no time to stop and stare and instead I focus on placing every footfall on solid ice. Moving in a straight line is impossible. We're all hunched low for cover, and follow any path that opens up to us. I feel like a pawn moving across a chessboard. Every move we make might be our last, and yet we hope for the best. The legs of my jumpsuit are splashed through now, while my fingers and toes are beginning to throb. I chance to look behind me, just to check how far we've come, and catch my breath at the arc of colours combing up across the sky. I see what looks like an aura of blue and violet, shimmering in waves like nothing I have ever seen before.

'What *is* that?' I gasp.

271

Beth is just a few metres away from me, looking towards the seaward horizon. She glances over her shoulder, looks up smartly at this spectral curtain, and grins.

'The northern lights,' is what she says. 'But what I'd really like to see more than anything right now is the inside of that communications tower.'

The trawler is much larger than I had thought. The wheelhouse is situated near the prow, but up close I realise that a long rear deck must be entirely submerged under the ice. In spite of his gunshot injury, the figure up ahead moves towards it as if blinkered to everything else. I realise the spectacle in the polar sky has distracted me, and now he's really opened up some distance between us. Dwarfed as he is by some of the ice debris, from wind-chiselled breakers to tumbledown blocks, he appears to shrink on approaching this great vessel. But then something happens that prompts me to break into a sprint. He vanishes completely. Just drops away from sight. All I hear is a crack and a splash, and know just what that means.

'*Grimstad!*' Beth surges forward with me, having called out the first name that sprang to her mind. We barrel across the ice pack, closing in together, un-concerned by the risk of being spotted, and there he is again: an orange torso flailing in slick black water. It's clear the ice floor here has cleaved in two. A sheet of it is floating freely behind him, while the one he's clinging to is threatening to tip right over on top of him. 'Don't move!' I yell. 'We'll get you out!'

Beth races around the edge of the pool to reach him. As she does so, I notice that in places a crust of pack ice remains intact where the bulk has broken off underneath. I realise what this might mean but it's too late to help Beth. For the crust just shears away from under her feet.

'Keep going!' I urge her, though she doesn't need to be told. It's as if she's just sensed that some water-borne predator is about to punch through the surface, and simply throws herself clear. I negotiate the other side as carefully as I can. Once more, our combined weight causes cracks to spread out all around. Grimstad is facing me now. The ice sheet is almost vertical as his weight pulls him down. For the first time, I see some desperation in his eyes, and grasp the hand he offers me. With Beth's help, we drag him off the sheet, and keep heaving until his free hand finds a surface that supports him. Another sharp cracking sound accompanies his escape. This time, we don't hang around to consider how lucky we've just been. It's only when we clamber onto the rear of the trawler, trapped as it is in a thick band of ice, that I get an elevated view of the pack. It may have laid siege to the coastline, trapping this wrecked vessel, but the way it breaks into trenches of open water behind us makes me realise that there's no way out from here.

The poor guy's soaked through and shivering violently, as we all are. Unlike Beth and me, each with our hands tucked under our armpits, he makes no effort to keep the cold from attacking. It's like he's walking in his sleep, with no real sense of where he is or even what has happened to him. As all this was his idea, however, I have to believe that despite the acute shock he must be in, he remains switched on to the dangers we face.

I had expected to feel the effects of our sub-zero environment, but this is really severe. If it weren't for the adrenaline pumping through my system, the conditions would've got to me by now. We've been outside far longer than we were on crossing from the airstrip to the compound. Our jumpsuits weren't wet then, either. If the wind got up now, I fear it would kill us instantly.

'Do you need to rest?' Through chattering teeth, this is the first thing I ask Grimstad once all three of us are hidden from view behind the trawler. A dull ache has overtaken the feeling in my feet. My soles had been stinging as we crossed the pack. Now they just feel like they're giving up on me. We're gathered behind the wheelhouse, which looms over us. The slanting deck disappears beneath the ice we stand on, which has also consumed half the net winch. Beth sits back on what's visible of this big metal spool, and draws her knees up tight. Grimstad remains on his feet.

'Not until the job is done,' he says. 'And I'm sure you'll appreciate that time is precious to me now.'

The door to the wheelhouse is located over my head, angled more like a skylight. I test the handle. It doesn't move, which is no surprise given the ice caked into the joints and seams. I look around to see if there is something we can use to get inside, only to find our soaked and wounded accomplice is one step ahead. As I investigate behind the winch, he clambers around the side of the wheelhouse and carefully frees up a length of metal tubing.

'What's that for?' asks Beth, with a note of caution in her voice. The way Grimstad is brandishing it prompts me to ease away with her, but he just stops and shrugs.

'Who cares?' he says. 'But it might just help us here.'

This time, we have more luck. It takes a couple of blows, with a pause between each one to be sure we haven't been heard, until finally the ice seal cracks and the door flaps open. I haul myself inside, and then help Grimstad in as carefully as I can. Beth joins us without assistance, and for a moment all three of us take in our surroundings in silence.

It feels more like a rocket capsule than a wheelhouse, with the seats tipped back and the control panels facing down at us. More immediately, it provides no shelter from the cold. Just as I am thinking that we've simply found ourselves a place to die, I turn and find myself face to face with something that might save us. For

275

hanging on hooks behind the captain's chair are several fishermen's oilskins.

'It's a sign,' says Beth, and sets about tearing them free.

These foul-weather coats are fleece-lined, I discover. I help Grimstad climb into one, carefully easing his wounded arm into a sleeve, and feeling some relief that it covers up that ghastly scarlet stain on his chest. Seeing the gunshot injury one last time reminds me of what we've left behind in the cannery. My shock at the bloodshed back there has been overtaken by a need to survive, I realise. With Agent Williams in mind, as much as all the others who had suffered at McCoy's hands, I turn around now and focus on the task we face.

'It *is* a sign,' I confirm eventually. 'We're going to see this through.'

The wheelhouse windows are blanketed by frost and snow. Even so, they must have been used for military target practice at some point because they're riddled with bullet holes. The quarter light to our right has been transformed into a spider's web of fragmented glass, with a missing section in the middle. Using the wheel as a foothold, I lift myself up and peek through it into the twilight again. Ignoring the curtains of luminous colour sweeping up to the stars on the horizon, I find a clear view of the cannery and the compound.

'What do you see?' asks Beth.

'The searchlights are working,' I report, noting the

beams that sweep across the grey snow. 'But I don't see anyone in the watchtowers.'

'If they're locked out,' suggests Grimstad, 'then perhaps it isn't just the main gates that are operated from the communications tower.'

I turn to the kennel block. A row of lights can be seen glowing through the side grille over there. It's the heat lamps, I realise, and on hearing muffled barking I realise all the dogs are confined in the warmth. That they aren't on the loose should be encouraging, but it's the activity outside the block that troubles me more. I can't see much from this angle, but it seems I have located the surviving guards.

'My God,' I whisper. 'Oh no.'

The way they huddle under the porch over the front of the block, it's evident that they're powerless to open the door. I figure Grimstad must be right. Accessing the communications tower and throwing whatever switch controlled the block was key to their survival. Looking at them now, it's evident that many of them haven't made it. There can only be a dozen figures out there at most, but it's the evidence of their desperate bid to keep warm that's so unnerving.

'What is it?' asks Beth.

'Dead men,' is all I say at first. 'The guards have scraped together a kind of snow ring, but I see corpses on the inside with them. Corpses stripped to the waist.'

'They've dragged them across from the blast.'

Grimstad speaks with some confidence, despite a rising rattle from his chest. 'For a few hours after death, the human body still produces a certain amount of heat. They're simply trying to insulate themselves, with what little material is available within the compound. Not just spare clothing but flesh and bone as well.'

I draw breath to suggest this means we now have one more urgent reason to reach the communications tower, only to be stopped by a volley of coughing.

'*Thomas!*' Beth is at his side in an instant. Even if she half suspects he's no deep cover agent, she throws away all caution as he fights to recover his composure. The sound is awful, a reminder that the man is basically drowning from the inside, and has little time left.

'Don't wait for me,' says Grimstad between breaths. 'The guards must think if they can survive the night, the temperature will lift enough at daybreak to give them a fighting chance. As McCoy has plans to ensure they're all dead by dawn, you have to find a way to take control, Hobbes, and fast!'

'Me?' I take a sharp intake of breath. 'But we've reached this far as a team!'

'You got me into Fort Knox,' Beth reminds me. 'Compared to the security measures in place at the depository this has to be a walk in the park.'

'I was at home when I broke into the depository,' I remind her. 'There were no armed mercenaries on the loose in my bedroom.'

278

'Just do your thing, Hobbes.' The man at her side sounds impatient all of a sudden. 'You can work out a way.'

Looking back at the headland now, I scan the wing between the front building and the cannery. It's fringed by a shadow over the snow that appears to ripple. The spectral ribbon of light in the sky is responsible for the effect, I realise, but only the perimeter building commands my attention now. It makes me think of a system firewall. That ring of control that stops you breezing in from the wild world and plundering the goods within. Usually, a firewall is an impressive piece of software that proves impossible to penetrate. Sure enough, the wall is way too high to scale, and all the windows are barricaded with bars.

As a hacker, that's why my first move would be to contact the weakest human operative inside and trick my way in.

The problem I face here is that every individual manning the new system in there is heavily armed and trigger-happy. There are no IT grunts inside. Not even a military hierarchy. Just enemy combatants preparing to commandeer a plane. Which is why, I realise, there can only be one target.

'McCoy is our man.' It comes to my mind so instinctively that I say it out loud without thinking.

'*McCoy?*' Beth sounds surprised, but presses me to explain myself.

'Think about his mindset,' I say, climbing down from the quarter light now. 'He's a veteran mercenary. There's nothing that can intimidate him. Even Grimstad's revelation didn't throw the man. If anything, he *thrives* on raising the stakes, because ultimately he's bored.'

Beth has listened with interest, until now. 'Oh, so he's just phoning in this job? Doing it in his sleep? I don't think so, Hobbes!'

'It's a tough mission for McCoy,' I agree. 'But Williams himself spelled out every conflict that has earned the man his stripes as a formidable soldier of fortune. Now that tells me he's at the top of his game, with nothing more to challenge him. It's why he seizes every opportunity to fool around, if only to entertain himself. That whole charade about recruiting a pilot? A man lost his life for McCoy's amusement. It helps him to prove he's in charge, of course, but it's also his Achilles heel. Ultimately, he *cannot* resist the chance to liven up the proceedings, and that's our way in. By encouraging him to play up like that, we'll gain control over the situation because we know exactly what follows.'

'Bloodshed.'

Beth's comment stalls me for a moment, simply because she's right.

'I know how we can draw him to open up the blast

doors,' is all I can promise her. 'It'll get us in, but it may not get anyone out.'

She smiles through chattering teeth. 'Under the circumstances, that sounds like a plan!'

Slumped against the pilot's chair, the deep cover agent behind her meets my eye. He's breathing with such effort now that his shoulders fall and rise each time.

'There's just one obstacle in our way,' I admit reluctantly, because I know this is a tall order. 'I need the help of the guards out there. I just don't know how to convince them we're trying to save their lives. Those guys are freezing to the bone because some prisoners staged an uprising. They'll take one look at us, even in these oilskins, and seek some kind of payback.'

'They're your problem as much as your solution, am I right?' Grimstad eases himself upright. I watch him move with some effort across this cramped space, and then reach up for something I hadn't considered useful.

'It's a distress flare,' I say, as he grasps it from the hook. 'The nearest settlement is over one hundred kilometres away,' I remind him. 'Firing that off would be pointless.'

He responds with a smile, and then closes his eyes. He doesn't open them immediately, however, staying like that long enough for me to look with concern to Beth.

'Help me out of here,' he says finally, and I see that

he is with us again. This time, his pupils have contracted a little. It restores some colour and warmth to his eyes, and I can see at last that he is genuinely human underneath. 'If we have only one shot at getting you back inside,' he adds, holding my attention still, 'I had better make this count.'

I think it through, working out how this could possibly help us, and break into a grin.

'You know, one of the oldest tricks in the hacker's handbook involves setting off printers remotely. The sight of so much paper spewing all over the floor never fails to draw people from their monitors. As a distraction, it frees you up to access a desktop unnoticed.'

Grimstad turns the flare-gun in his hands as he listens, and then lifts his hooded eyes once more. 'And if you're spotted?'

I consider the question, aware that Beth is watching me intently. 'If you're spotted,' I say, addressing them both now, 'they pull the plug.'

36

When the flare goes up, illuminating the compound, my first thought is how dark it has become. With snow and ice covering the landscape, my eyes must have adjusted to what little light is available. It may feel like a very deep dusk, but way out here I figure that actually means we are long into the night. I also realise that doesn't give us long before McCoy unleashes the second strike of his mission. I think of the plane he's preparing to welcome, and the party on board with no idea that they're about to descend into hell.

Watching the landscape now, I see shadows spread in every direction. They continue to lengthen, as the bright source of light begins to float to earth. Beneath it, I trace the winding column of smoke back down to ground level. There on the shoreline, with his arms spread wide as if to welcome those guards now scrambling over the snow towards him, stands a man they believe to be a killer without conscience.

'Thomas Grimstad,' I say to myself, but the name no longer sticks.

'Grimstad is dead,' says Beth, pale with cold. 'Even if he can't convince the guards that he's a deep cover agent, let's just hope they listen to him. Otherwise, all three of us could be facing an untimely end.'

I consider her outlook, aware that there's just so much I don't know about this girl. By rights I should be furious about what she's done to me. I could blame her for everything from my incarceration here to the state of my feet and my fingers. Under the circumstances, however, it feels like we're united against an army.

'Are you ready for this?' I ask.

Beth crouches beside me, braced to make her move. She doesn't answer, focused as she is on the figure doing all this for us. We're midway between the trawler and the shoreline, on solid pack ice, as far as we can tell. The seabed must rise sharply from this point, because the ice contours that hide us drop away in scale. It's here that our dying accomplice has asked us to wait. We'll know when to make our move, the deep cover agent had said, and left us without a smile or a nod. Had it not been for Beth, appealing for him to hold back a moment, it might have been the last words I ever heard from him.

'You could be making an almighty sacrifice,' she had said, taking both his hands. 'And I want you to know that this *convinces* me you're no suicide bomber.'

284

He had nodded when she offered this, finding no argument, it seemed. 'I'm pleased it's taken time for you to be so sure. It means I was good at my job, but it plays hell with your mind. You live out the role so intensely you begin to fool yourself at times.' He stops there for a moment, recovering his breath. 'Back in Oslo, when I touched the battery to the wires on my bomb belt, I felt more alive than ever before. Those kids in the crowd? I regret having to scare them so acutely, but in facing death I believe I left them with a lust for life. Of course, I never dreamed it would end here for me,' he had finished. 'But at least I know that I'll go out with a bang!'

Without hesitation, I had reached out to shake his hand.

'You'll be doing it for noble reasons here.'

His grip was surprisingly strong, but it's the way he stared right through me that gave me one final pause for thought. 'I'll see you on the other side,' he had said, and turned away, flare-gun in hand.

'It's weird, but I can't shake off his final words.' Beth shares this with me as the first guards arrive at the shoreline. The deep cover agent drops down to his knees in front of them, both hands on his head now. We're too far away to tell if he's following orders, or offering himself to them. Either way, with the flare burning out on the ground, I am ready to break cover for the position we have agreed.

'I think that was his intention,' I say. 'I believe he intended to scare the living daylights out of us, so we stay on our toes and see this thing through.' I glance at Beth, whose attention is fixed ahead. I note the frost forming in her hair and lashes, which only serves to remind me of the other threat we face out here.

'Well, I'm scared,' she says, through chattering teeth now.

'Me too. I'm terrified.'

At this, the flare tapers and dies. I see the glow leave one side of Beth's face, but I hold her gaze for a beat. I'm sure I know what she's thinking, and indeed she speaks it, word for word.

'Makes you feel alive, doesn't it?

'Just like the man said,' I agree.

By now, all the surviving guards crowd around the figure they believe to be Grimstad. They look ragged, desperate, enraged. If he is attempting to explain the situation, none of them look like they're listening. I see him slump sideways, as if passing out or reeling from a kick perhaps, only to be hauled to his feet by two of them. At once they begin to drag him back to the kennel block, towards their makeshift, macabre shelter.

Back out on the frozen shallows, meanwhile, his two fellow escapees make their bid to honour this window of opportunity he has just opened for them. I am aware that we only have until they reach the kennel block before one of them turns. If we can make it across to the main building in that time, and lose ourselves in that undulating shadow, we'll at least be halfway there. Even if our man fails to convince them that we're acting in their best interest, they'd never have time to lynch us if we chose to go ahead without their blessing. They'd pay a price, of course, which is why I hope and pray this deep cover agent can get through to them.

My feet are so numb now that I can no longer feel them hit the ice pack. It's an effort to make them move, and I'm worried Beth must be in trouble too because she reaches out for me to drag her by the hand. We stay low, splashing through melt pools as we cut in towards the shoreline. There are no coils of razor wire to stop us here. The high fencing runs into the grip of the ice by a short distance. Even so, there's nothing to prevent us scrambling up the snow-covered shingle and into the compound. It's as if the military knew damn well that the pack ice was unstable beyond the shallows. I could only think they had never considered that anyone would want to bail out from the cannery and then promptly switch back again. It was a simple security flaw, but one I had come across in front of a computer. You set up a system to prevent one threat, only to find it opened gateways for another.

Then again, I'd never encountered a system that relied on nature as a deterrent.

The snow is even harder to cross than the ice. It's frozen into ripples and drifts, threatening to trip us up.

My eyes are streaming, and I'm struggling to ignore the voice in my head that keeps telling me this is suicidal. Despite all this, in full view of the kennel block now, we cannot afford to slow down. I don't have to look to know that the third detainee out here in the open remains the sole focus of attention. I can hear guards grilling him and arguing among themselves. For such highly trained military personnel, they sound more like desperados than the band who forced them out here. It doesn't sound promising, and yet they haven't just killed him on the spot.

The dogs may be locked inside, but they sense our presence as we leave the ice pack behind. I grasp Beth's hand as tightly as I can, pray the volume doesn't build any more, and lock my sights on the main building's side wall.

'Hurry!' As soon as we hit the shadows, I drag Beth low and face the block once more. 'Two minutes,' I say, watching one of the guards get right in the face of the deep cover agent. They've reached the kennel block now. Judging by the way he and several others suddenly spin around I judge it's just been revealed that we're out here somewhere. 'We agreed to give him two minutes from now to try and persuade them we can help. So long as they don't spot us, we still have the advantage. I just need to see him raise his hand as planned. Otherwise, we draw McCoy out on our own terms.'

'And those guys pay the price.'

'Unless they calm down soon,' I say, 'they'll bring him out before we're ready. Whatever happens, we should be prepared to move quickly.'

Beth doesn't respond at first. When she does, I sense some defeat in her voice.

'There's something I have to tell you,' she says. I turn to face her. 'Carl, I've stopped shivering.'

The Commander himself had outlined the symptoms of hypothermia. I only have to look at her expression to see she's close to being overwhelmed by cold here. I've been trying hard to ignore the fact that I'm freezing up, but fear I can't be far behind.

'Don't you dare give up!' I urge her under my breath. 'You're the one who knows how to press all my buttons, just like the Commander said! Without you, we're both finished!'

For a moment, I think her evident frustration might turn to tears. Her expression tenses, but she holds it back. 'I'm just so tired,' she says. 'But I know what will happen if I rest here a while.'

'I'm *here* because of you,' I remind her, cupping her chin in the palm of my hand now. 'The way I see it, Beth Nelson, and as you have said to me yourself, that means we're in this *together*! Now, you possess more courage and guts than I could ever hope to have. Who else would've had the balls to breeze into Fort Knox and help themselves to a haul, huh? Show me what you're made of. Show me *now*!'

She smiles faintly, and closes her eyes for a moment.

'That's another thing you should know,' she continues. 'When I delivered the stolen bullion to McCoy, I found my own private buyer for several bars. The money is in an offshore account now. I figured I needed an insurance policy in case it all went wrong.'

'Money isn't much use to us out here.' I draw her close to me, hoping to share what little body heat I can. 'Unless we burned it to keep warm, of course. Besides, I'm not interested. I never opened the doors to get rich, just like I told the Commander.'

'You're one of a kind, Hobbes.'

'No, I'm just a scared kid who wants to see another day.'

'Make that moment happen for us, Hobbes, and I'll share the money with you. What do you say? Fifty-fifty. Equal partners.'

I'm about to stress that she's coming with me no matter what, only to freeze at the sound of boots creaking through the snow. Beth tenses in my arms, but it's too late to hide or even flee. In the space of a heartbeat, a figure rounds into view. He just appears from the front of the main building, and comes to a dead halt before us.

'*Cortés?*'

Beth catches her breath as I say this, and I do just the same. For the man is burned terribly and clearly in shock. With his jacket hanging from his shoulders in blackened ribbons, he simply stands there, moving his mouth without a sound. Judging by the livid injuries striped around his neck, scalp and ribs, it's clear that a blast has gone off behind him. However, there's no sign of the oil drum that McCoy made the poor devil strap to his back. It makes me think the Pitcairn mercenary must have targeted just one of the two guards as they fled. Cortés has suffered badly, but with no sign of North I can only reach one conclusion.

'H . . . h . . . h . . . he . . . hel . . . *help me*!'

Cortés' lips have lost all colour. Ice crystals have formed on every crease and crevice of his face, but it's the blank stare that troubles me most of all. I rise to my feet, helping Beth to do likewise. He doesn't even blink. All he does is inhale sharply, and repeat his plea.

'It's OK,' Beth assures him. I take him gently by the shoulders, struggling not to look as repulsed as I feel. Cortés shrieks just as soon as I touch him, which forces me to haul him low. I cover his mouth, feeling bad about this but with no choice now. I hadn't spotted him among the other guards earlier. Either he's only just picked himself up, or has been so traumatised that he's simply been wandering the compound.

'We'll help you, Cortés. I can get you shelter and warmth, but first you have to help us.' I pause to gesture at the kennel block. I've struggled to keep one eye on it throughout, and the deep cover agent has yet to raise his hand. 'I want you to go tell your colleagues to shut the hell up and listen to that man. He's trying to help them. So long as they do as he says, they won't risk taking a bullet in the next couple of minutes. Is that understood?'

I wait for Cortés to acknowledge this. Even if his senses are beginning to shut down, the nod he offers tells me that he understands. Finally, I turn my attention to Beth. 'You're coming with me,' I order her, and help her to her feet. 'You needed me for the raid on Fort Knox. I need you for this.'

37

Everyone makes mistakes. Even those at the top of their game. When it comes to working out the weakest human point in a system, it isn't just the grunts and the rookies who can screw up. In different ways, the veterans are equally vulnerable. After all, when work becomes routine it's only natural to skip the humdrum tasks or leave them for later.

In McCoy's case, he really should have killed every guard once he'd rounded them up in the processing area.

Instead, in a bid to make murder more interesting for himself, he'd ordered them from the building to face the arctic elements within the compound. He hadn't tripped up here. If the cold didn't kill those guys overnight he still had time to pick them off and clear away the evidence before the plane arrived. Nothing could go wrong in that respect.

But the fact that some are still alive *right now* is my

key to get back inside. For just as the sight of a detainee on the ice has drawn the surviving guards into the open, so the guards have the potential to draw out McCoy.

Without a word, Beth and I watch Cortés reach the kennel block. His arrival causes the volume to rise by a notch, and then settle sharply. This is encouraging. It suggests he has confirmed the deep cover agent's claims. In a moment, there will be time for them all to make as much noise as possible. Several guards turn to look in our direction, but I don't rise to my feet until I see that hand raised high.

'Let's go.' I help Beth up from the snow. 'Isn't breaking and entering what you do best?'

The front of the compound building remains largely obscured by steep banks of snow. It's a sign of just how vicious the wind can be coming off the tundra. The communications tower looms ahead, cutting into the polar sky. The beacon on top of the mast up there continues to flash, which at least tells me that McCoy hasn't shot out the power along with the windows. Right now, however, my focus is on reaching that space cleared for the blast doors. I try to ignore how scorched it is, a mark of the explosion, while the weak natural light helps to soften what is clearly blood spillage. Most striking of all is the silence behind us. Even the dogs inside the kennel block have been made to fall quiet. It's only once we've crossed the gap and scrambled up the drift beside the blast doors that I look back. The guards stand in front of their desperate shelter, seemingly oblivious to the cold now. They watch us intently. Men with nothing to lose.

This time, it is my turn to raise a hand. A second later, a cry goes up from among them. One swiftly joined by many others. From our position, within the space of a minute, it has gone far beyond the noise they'd made before. This sounds more like some kind of last stand – which is exactly what I want McCoy to hear.

'Listen!' Beth is on her belly beside me. 'Say your prayers, Carl!'

Beneath the din, coming from within the main building, I hear cursing. A moment later, the blast doors crash open. I shrink back a little, but the figure that emerges doesn't pause to look up or around. McCoy is wearing full battledress. He's also carrying a shotgun and a semi-automatic rifle. Each looped over a shoulder. The first thing he does is use the shotgun to jam the door open. Next he locks and loads the second weapon, before stalking into the open. A harsh light shines out from the processing area, in contrast to the gloom he's facing. I see him swing to face the source of the noise, muttering now about how little he can see.

But before his finger finds the trigger, as briefed by the detainee outside the dog compound, the guards break from their position and throw themselves into the snow.

'*Will you please die quietly!*' A spray of gunfire punctuates his orders. '*If there's any more noise, next time I won't waste my bullets. Is that understood? Good!*' A moment later, I hear boots retreating from the snow, followed by the sound of the blast doors slamming shut again.

By then, Beth and I are safely on the inside, but facing no less danger.

out across the snow. Just as I fear he might come through the door, that shadow snaps away, which tells me he's bound for the recreation wing. 'It was right there, jamming open the blast doors! Hobbes, we could've gained a weapon just then and locked McCoy in the cold!' I'm looking around as Beth continues, aware that security cameras monitor the courtyard. I feel euphoric at having got this far, but we can't stop now. Only one of the four cameras can pick us up on this side, I realise, and claw my fingers into the snow. If McCoy's appointed anyone to monitor them, I reckon their priority will be to watch the cannery doors opposite. If any of the prisoners are going to appear, that's where you'd expect them to come from. Even so, I really don't want us to be in the frame should they reverse their view. Beth is still fuming over the gun. She notes me scoping out the camera, and mutters that we wouldn't *be* in this fix if we'd picked up the shooter.

'Think of yourself as a Trojan worm,' I say to explain. 'The kind of malicious software program that sneaks onto a computer in the form of an email attachment.' She frowns, as puzzled as she is cross, but listens anyway. 'The worm's potency lies in the fact that the user doesn't know it's in the system. By the time the damage has been done, it's too late to do anything about it. Beth, if we had shut McCoy outside his men would've been on the case as soon as they realised he was missing. Not only would they open up the blast doors for him, they'd be wise to the fact that intruders are in the building. More importantly, unlike me, *they* know how to use their weapons.' As I say this, I finish scraping a snowball together, and take aim at the camera. Beth shoots me a look.

'So you're going to take them on with *that*?'

I grin at her, focus on my target, and hurl the snowball as hard as I can.

The second attempt makes contact. The impact is enough to swivel the camera away from the doors. I just wish I'd been the one to throw the successful snowball.

'I told you I couldn't do this without you,' I say, as Beth examines her palms. Her hands are raw and swollen from the cold.

'Listen,' she whispers, falling still quite suddenly. 'Can you hear that?'

She tips her head. Under the hum from the generator, behind closed doors somewhere, we hear laughing. It's the sound of men in high spirits, which rules out those locked up inside the cannery. I judge it to be coming from the recreational wing. In McCoy's frame of mind, I picture him regaling his men with some wisecracks about how he's just given the guards something other than frostbite to worry about. If I'm right, it means we're free to make our attempt on the communications tower.

Signalling at Beth to stay where she is, I turn to peek back inside the processing area. I don't want to place myself in any more danger. It feels safe here in the courtyard, surrounded as we are by four walls. But then I know that unless I keep moving I will freeze in fear as much as from the cold. Still crouching with my back to the wall beside the door, I dare to peek into the light.

And almost come face to face with McCoy.

There he is, stomping out of the recreational wing carrying something cylindrical in both hands. I'm so surprised that I simply catch my breath. Had he looked up, he would've seen me. As it is, the man swings away towards the blast doors. He stops just in front of them, and dumps what I see to be an industrial spool of some sort. I step away from the light, angry with myself for making assumptions about what was going on inside that wing. Assumptions and guesswork could get hackers like me into boiling hot water. Indeed, such a close encounter serves as a stiff reminder that I'm not operating remotely in front of a computer screen any more. This is real. And deadly. If I screw up, I will be permanently offline.

Beth is beside me, her back to the wall still. I know she's tuned into McCoy's presence because her eyes are wide as she listens. He's on one knee, ripping cellophane from the spool. Behind him, the blast doors and the wall around it are blackened. Cortés had been lucky to escape through them with his life. Judging by the fragments of fuel tank scattered across the floor here, I figure there is no way North could have made it at all.

Next I watch McCoy whip out length after length of cord from the spool. I've no idea what he's doing. Then, with a moment to spare, I realise he's freed up enough to span the whole processing area. And more.

The doors swing outwards abruptly. I have to duck beside the step to avoid it hitting me in the face, and stay crouched as McCoy strides into the snow with one end of the cord in his fist. On reaching the generator, he hauls out one of the many fuel drums underneath. I'm no expert, but judging by the way he spins off the cap and feeds the end of the cord inside, he's priming it to *explode*.

I glance at Beth. She's hauled her oilskin over her head, and is all balled up looking like rags discarded in the snow. I see her gesturing furiously at me to join her. McCoy is bound to turn at some point. And when he does, I just hope another set of rags isn't going to draw his attention.

By the time he returns to the building, dragging a second drum inside with him, the sound of the door closing is our cue to breathe freely.

'I thought he'd spotted me,' I whisper. 'I really thought we were finished.'

Beth returns my attention to the cord trailing from the door to the generator. 'It seems his mind is on other matters.'

301

The next time my hand closes over the door handle, I am sure that McCoy has left the processing area. Once again his shadow on the snow confirms it. I refuse to guess whether he'll be back. Instead, I move – because unless we seize our first opportunity to reach the communications tower, those guards will be beyond saving.

I crack open the door, and feel warm air draw through the gap.

'Go!' whispers Beth from behind me, some desperation in her voice now.

After so long exposed to the cold, I know we need to be inside. What stalls me is the sight of the fuel drum McCoy dragged through the door just now. It pins the end of the cord to the ground, just in front of the blast doors, but is clearly there for a more sinister purpose.

I look back at Beth, aware that I'm trembling less vigorously myself now, and then at the generator out in the courtyard. There are dozens more tanks under there. My focus extends to the cannery doors behind, and I realise it isn't just the front buildings McCoy has plans to blow up.

'All those people!' I say, aghast.

'They don't stand a chance,' she replies, grim-faced. 'Once that cord has been primed and lit, we all die!'

The very thought is enough to jolt me into action.

'We're still alive,' I remind her, and prepare to move inside. 'And I've no plans to become obsolete just yet.'

39

My pumps barely make a sound on the floorboards. I move fast and low towards the spiral staircase. Compared to the conditions we've just endured, it feels like a furnace in here. My face is hot and my fingers are throbbing badly. I don't know what frostbite feels like, but my feet might as well be in a vice. I even wonder if I might lose some toes when all this is over.

Midway across the processing area, from somewhere in the recreational wing, I hear a voice that reminds me that I stand to lose a lot more than my toes unless I keep moving.

'I don't care if you trained at the same camp! He stays in his cage like all the others . . .'

McCoy. The Pitcairn Islander's mongrel accent is unmistakeable. I spin around to find Beth. She's nowhere to be seen. Then the door swings open from the recreational wing, far sooner than I had anticipated, and the man himself appears.

'Consider yourself one of the chosen few, my friend. I picked you out. You owe me . . .' McCoy has just walked in with another figure close behind. He turns to finish speaking to him, which is the only break I have. 'All I'm asking you to do is stay back to light the fuse. After that, you just walk out the door, salute the nice people from the decommissioning party, and then rush to catch your flight.'

I shrink behind the raised desk in front of the spiral staircase, and hope that Beth has also seen them coming. I can only think that's why she hasn't followed me. I just can't afford to put my head up to look for her.

'But what about the guards?' An Eastern European voice this time, I think. He sounds cautious, even fearful, which only serves to bring some irritation into McCoy's voice.

'We *are* the guards, you dolt! We're not just wearing their uniforms for warmth! As far as the visitors are concerned, you're just another military grunt. They won't give you a second glance. And nor will they question why the snow is littered with corpses, because by then we'll have cleared them away. So long as we keep our heads down when we greet the party at the gate, their only concern will be to escape the cold and get the job done. Just like me, in fact, but for less money.'

I hear the man with him sigh. I judge they're conducting this conversation over the fuel drum, because one of them unscrews the cap next.

304

'Using gasoline to soak a fifteen-metre, cotton-pleat fuse,' the man with the Eastern European accent says next. 'I'd estimate that gives perhaps two minutes maximum to clear the blast arena.'

McCoy claps him on the back. 'Listen to you, the explosives expert. It's your ticket out of here, in fact! Now, seeing that this night is nearly through, what do you say we invite one of the guys to step out, pick off any survivors and hide the bodies? Everyone has to earn their seat on the plane, after all.'

I wait until their footsteps fade to silence before rising from my belly. My feet had been visible from behind the counter, I realise. Mercifully, McCoy has been too busy briefing his explosives man to notice. I pick myself up and find that I am shaking uncontrollably once more. Just then, across the processing area, a door clicks open. With no time to hide this time, I simply spin around helplessly, before breathing out again.

Beth creeps in, coming out of the cold at last, and checks both ways as if preparing to cross a busy road. She finds me standing behind the counter now, the spiral staircase behind me. Unlike me, she's trembling just ever so slightly. In her case, I take this as a sign that she can make it after all. Touching a finger to my lips, I gesture at the open hatch above.

For I can hear activity in the communications tower. It's barely audible, but sounds just like radio chatter to me.

305

Beth doesn't need to read my mind to know what has to be done. If we can get a mayday out, on any wavelength, McCoy and his bid for freedom will be over. It doesn't guarantee that *we'll* get out alive, of course. If anything, it *lessens* the likelihood. Silently, I volunteer to go first, only to pause at the first step.

For our chances of survival may be slim, but having overheard McCoy those guys outside are as good as dead. The thought pricks at my conscience. If they haven't frozen to the bone already, at any moment some cold-blooded killer will head outside to hunt them down.

I turn to face Beth, aware that boots can once more be heard approaching the recreational wing door. There's enough time to get up into the communications tower, but my mind is made up.

'We can't stay here,' she whispers, switching her attention to the door.

I grasp her by the shoulders, and ask her to trust me. 'There's unfinished business outside,' I tell her. 'If I'm not back in a couple of minutes, get up there and raise hell, understood?'

Beth has no time to reply. For the door swings open, forcing us to duck behind the desk again. I catch sight of the man appointed to carry out the massacre. I figure it has to be him because his face displays intense focus, as if preparing for a difficult job. As he comes around to the blast doors, back into my line of sight, I recognise him from the cannery. It's the guy who had been so trigger-happy when it came to celebrating his release. He's kitted out in military fatigues just like McCoy, and armed with two weapons just as he was.

The shotgun to prop the door. The semi-automatic to kill in cold blood.

Without a word, leaving Beth behind the desk, I snake out after the man. This time, I take the shotgun with me, removing it only once I am certain my target won't hear a door closing for the last time in his life.

I feel the cold clamp around my feet, ears and face once again, but frankly that's the last of my concerns. I hold the gun in both hands, surprised by its weight, and the fact that I can even contemplate firing it. The sound of a voice through a walkie-talkie brings me to my senses. I duck around the snow bank, and see my target. He's standing with his back to me, surveying the kennel block across the compound grounds with the radio clamped to his ear.

'This is Fournier. Am starting the clean-up operation, copy? You can tell McCoy that most of them are still alive,' he continues. 'I got my work cut out.'

A response cuts through the static to confirm, but I'm only interested in this guy's voice. The surname sounds French, but his accent didn't back that up. I guess he might be from Algeria, or any one of France's former colonies. Whatever the case, if everything goes to plan I just hope I can pull off his accent.

Then I think of what I have to do to acquire his walkie-talkie, and question whether I am capable of such a thing.

A single guard is standing within the crescent of snow in front of the kennel block. Why Fournier was moved to report a full hand tells me a great deal about the man. In his position, dependent on McCoy to secure his freedom, it's only natural that he'd seize the opportunity to shine for Teacher. The guard he's facing presents no threat to him whatsoever. He's stooped, with his hands folded tight inside his jacket, looking utterly defeated. At first he doesn't appear to even register the mercenary now crossing the compound towards the block. When he does, I'm relieved to see one or two other guards now rise unsteadily from behind the ring of packed snow. I see no sign of the deep cover agent, and just hope he had won the compassion of these men by the time the end came. The guards make no attempt to scatter in a bid to save themselves. Even when Fournier shoulders his rifle butt and takes aim.

And that's because they can see that I am right behind him, with the shotgun in my hands.

'*Freeze!*' I say bitterly, braced for him to wheel around, and when he does, I smash the stock against his temple. The mercenary called Fournier drops like all the bones in his legs have melted away. The way he falls at my feet, with his head bleeding into the snow, I might as well have shot him. Doing it this way, however, I can still live with myself. I look back at the guards in front of the kennel block. The three on their feet appear to be functioning on emergency power. Only one makes a move towards me, and every step is clearly a struggle. In fact, he halts completely on seeing me collect Fournier's weapon. I'm aware that time is precious here, and if I don't start making the right noises McCoy might take an interest.

Which is why I hoist the gun high into the half-light, brace myself to squeeze a trigger for the very first time, and unleash a storm of bullets into the sky. As far as McCoy and his men are concerned, it will sound like those lost souls who survived the night have just been iced in a different way.

The kickback from the weapon is intense, and so shocking that it takes a moment for me to realise that I have just spent all the bullets. I squeeze the trigger again. The mechanism clicks, but the magazine is empty.

I curse myself for being so rash. I should've been more careful. But then I have to maintain the illusion that McCoy's plan is running like clockwork. I reach for the shotgun, thinking at least I have this still. Breaking it open on my knee, I take one look at the chambers and close my eyes for a moment. Even if I had been cut out to squeeze off a round at Fournier, instead of knocking him out, I would've been the one left bleeding out into the snow right now. For the gun isn't even loaded. It really had just been intended as a door prop.

'I'll take care of him, Hobbes.'

I look up with a start. The guard who had faltered when I fired into the air looms over the unconscious mercenary. The way he says this makes me think Fournier may still pay the ultimate price. For I'm facing one of the marksmen from the gantry. It's his unswerving gaze that I can't mistake, despite the fact that a night in this bitter cold has reduced him to a husk.

'Just get him out of sight,' I say urgently, 'and do the same thing with yourselves. You're supposed to be dead and buried now, after all.'

He smiles. In spite of everything. Then he shoots me a look and I know that I can trust him.

'What about you?' he asks.

I wrestle the walkie-talkie from the belt of the fallen mercenary. 'I promised I'd try to give you a fighting chance of survival. I'm going back inside to see it through.'

'Without a gun?'

'It's the only way I know,' I say, aware that I am about to make one of the most important calls of my life. For whoever is on the other end of the walkie-talkie will be waiting for confirmation from Fournier that his killing spree is over. I have demonstrated to myself that I can't handle a gun. But when it comes to controlling a conversation, as a hacker I stand a fighting chance.

40

When Beth sees my face at the glass, she springs from her hiding place behind the desk to ease open the blast doors.

'Where have you *been*?' She glares at me as I slip back into the warmth, but there's no mistaking her relief.

'These mercenaries,' I whisper back at her, cradling my frozen fingers. 'You know how they like to boast about their work.'

Having radioed through the report, mimicking what little I'd heard of Fournier's accent, I'd switched off the walkie-talkie and buried it in the drift outside. Even if someone starts asking what has happened to the man in the next few moments, our next steps can kill off any further concerns about him.

With the blast doors closed once more, we turn our attention to the task at hand. From the communications tower, I hear more radio babble chop through white noise. It makes me realise the tower is not unmanned. Someone is up there monitoring the airwaves.

'Whoever it is sounds lonely,' Beth whispers. 'All I've heard is the sound of conversations being chased up and down the dial.'

'Then let's provide some company,' I suggest, and steel myself to see this through.

The staircase is bolted into both the floor and the ceiling, and constructed from fanning metal footplates. I climb the first step with great care. It's solid enough not to creak, and so I lead the way. The chatter becomes clearer as we climb: flight-speak by the sound of it, given the coordinates and codenames coming through the airwaves. Just as we approach the final turn, however, a voice kicks in that causes us both to hold back.

'This is Camp Twilight, do you copy? Good to have you in range at last. It could be day, it might be night. Either way, the stars are shining bright, and we can't wait to share it with you guys.'

I recognise the voice. The words are a little slurred, but I know for sure who is behind it. I just can't believe what it means. As I listen, a fresh wave of anger begins to rise. And that's exactly what I need to drive me on.

With a hand on each rail, I ease myself up the last few steps and rise into the communications tower.

The figure operating the radio is sitting with his back to us. He's hunched over the radio equipment, oblivious to our arrival. The windows overlooking the courtyard are largely shattered. When McCoy sprayed the tower with bullets, he did a thorough job. From such a steep angle, however, he missed the glass on the opposite side, as well as the computer and the bank of levers underneath. It is cold in here, which is why the figure before us is hunched inside a quilted jacket, with a beanie hat rolled low over his ears. His slumped posture is at odds with the breezy greeting he's just delivered over the airwaves. Indeed, he makes no effort to sit up straight when an answering voice cuts through the crackle.

'*Copy that, Camp Twilight. Keep an eye on the south-east horizon, buddy. We'll be with you in under an hour. Be sure to have the runway markers burning brightly.*'

It had to be the pilot of the incoming plane. Judging by his relaxed and upbeat manner, he can't suspect he might be talking to anyone other than a member of military personnel. If this guy in front of us was a soldier in civilian clothes, then the half-empty bottle of whisky and the softpack of cigarettes by his side would earn him a court martial. The handgun and the spare clip might have come from the armoury, but I can be sure he wasn't authorised to take it. I wait for him to sign off the radio, and make my presence known.

'Hello, Arty.'

The systems security expert practically spins off his

313

chair in shock. He swivels right around, and then reaches back for the gun.

'Stay where you are!' Beth is one step ahead of him, and as furious as I feel. She pounces on the weapon, locking back the hammer in a way that makes me think she's handled one before. At the same time, aware that the guards outside will surely perish unless I can open the kennel block, I snap back every lever on the panel beside me. 'Put your hands on your head,' Beth snarls at him now, 'and stay *quiet*!'

Arty Dougal looks stricken. His eyes flit between us. He falls in and out of several sentences, and then submits to her command.

'Miss, keep *your* voice down!' he pleads at the same time. 'I'm trying to put a mayday out here.'

I laugh aloud at this. 'Arty, that's just lazy. You really should've worked *much* harder on manipulating our take on what we just heard. And we heard every word, I'm afraid. Back in your day you might've made a good phone phreak, but times change. People are more switched on nowadays. You need to seriously gain their confidence before you can persuade them to act in your interests.'

Arty swallows as I speak, his eyes wide and un-blinking.

'It's the truth,' he says. 'I'm trying to save our skins here!'

'And *you* accused *Beth* of being an American traitor!'

I snap, cutting him dead. 'That's about as bad as it can get, you said. And now look at you. What the hell is going on, Arty?'

He grimaces. I realise he's holding back tears. Finally, in what sounds like a big release, he says: 'The *money*! I did it for the money. It was too much to refuse, and . . . and you know about my background, Hobbes. I only started working for the military to escape a jail term. I've always been a sucker for an easy payout, man, and he promised me four bars for the work. But you gotta believe me when I say I never thought it would come to this.' He pauses to compose himself. 'It's McCoy . . .' he says finally. 'That man is no soldier of fortune, Hobbes. He's just so . . . so *cruel*!' Arty looks lost for a moment, only for his expression to change with the offer he then springs on us. 'So what do you say we split the dough and work as a team, huh?'

Beth shakes her head, entirely unimpressed. She's so fired up, in fact, that I'm relieved to see she's shivering now. This time, I'm absolutely sure it's down to her hunger for survival rather than any sense of fear, for it doesn't affect her line of sight.

'McCoy came here to carry out a contract killing,' she reminds Arty, peering down the gun sight at him. 'He practically gave himself up to the authorities for the chance to do the job. You must've been able to guarantee that he'd end up in the same camp as Grimstad. Maybe you pulled some strings, requested an

315

interview with him, huh? Whatever the case, he doesn't plan to leave anyone alive, and *you're* responsible for that.'

Tears gloss Arty's cheeks as Beth says this. Even if he's genuinely remorseful, he's half drunk and in such a fragile state that I don't think he'll be any help to us. I glance at Beth, mindful of the incoming plane. 'We really do need to send out a mayday,' I tell her. 'It isn't too late to turn that plane around.'

'I can do that.' Arty dries his cheeks on his sleeve. 'Please.'

'No deal.' Beth keeps a bead on the systems security expert. 'Do you expect us to trust a *traitor*?'

I reach forward to collect the handset, see Arty's attention drawn to a point behind me.

And promptly feel cold steel touch the nape of my neck.

I look up with a gasp, see Beth drop her gun and lift her hands.

'She's not wrong there,' a voice rasps into my ear. 'A traitor is a marked man, in my book.'

41

I dare not turn to face McCoy directly. Even so, I can be sure his finger is tight around the trigger. Meantime, Arty Dougal drops his hands from his head, and spreads them wide.

'Hey, I wasn't actually going to *send* an SOS,' he protests. 'I was humouring them. I saw you coming in!'

'Arty,' says McCoy, and pauses there for a moment. 'Shut up.'

He pushes the muzzle of his gun hard into my neck now, forcing me to bow. 'I gotta say this, though, you guys are impressive. Hobbes, maybe you should work for me. I'm a fair employer – isn't that right, Arty? I only get a little vexed when people fail to do as they're told!' Some anger unloads into his voice now. Arty sobs out loud, clearly panic-stricken, which prompts a pained sigh from behind me. 'OK, calm down, fat boy. Take a slug from the bottle if you must. At least deal with this with some dignity, huh?'

Arty Dougal grabs the bottle. He tips it to his lips as if it contains an antidote to the trouble he's in here. He grimaces when it scorches his throat, and then tugs out a handkerchief to dry his eyes. 'I'm good, boss. You don't have to worry about me.'

McCoy reaches around me, and picks up the radio handset. The coiled wire yawns apart as he draws the handset to his mouth. 'What's the aircraft's call sign?' he asks Arty.

'It's a secure military frequency,' he replies. 'Just press the button and speak.'

I want to tell Arty that he's mistaken. No frequency is totally secure. Then again, as I'm probably the only other hacker within range of this broadcast, and with no means of eavesdropping beyond using my ears, I simply stay quiet and wait for McCoy to begin. 'This is Camp Twilight again, do you copy?' A crackle of static follows. Seconds later, the voice of the pilot breaks through the speaker.

'*Go ahead, Camp Twilight. The coastline has just come up on the radar. I hope you got the heating turned up high.*'

McCoy chuckles quietly to himself. Mindful of all the fuel cans under the generator, I know just what he's thinking. 'We'll have the home fires burning for you, no worries,' he replies eventually. 'But we got a minor problem with the runway. We're clean out of torches.'

White noise spits through the speaker, and then the

pilot cuts in, laughing to himself. '*It sounds like the decommissioning party are arriving just in time. Shouldn't stop us touching down, though. Is the runway visible from the air?*'

I sense from the pressure on my neck that McCoy has turned to look through the smoked glass to our right.

'It was cleared of snow and gritted yesterday.'

'*Then you can rest easy, Camp Twilight. I've landed in far worse conditions. But thanks for the heads up on that.*'

McCoy signs off, and tosses the handset away. 'Shame we're gonna have to lose an experienced pilot,' he says. 'But that's business.'

Throughout this communication, Arty Dougal has been fretting with his handkerchief. I have listened with a rising sense of helplessness, and watched as he twisted it this way and that. Only now, however, as McCoy ends the transmission, do I realise what he's up to. With his eyes locked on the mercenary behind me, I see Arty quietly feed one end of the handkerchief into the vodka bottle between his thighs. Using his thumb, he then stuffs it as far down as he can. I glance at Beth, who must be aware of what he's just done because she draws McCoy's attention.

'If I'm going to die here,' she begins, 'at least let me smoke a cigarette.'

'Don't you know it's bad for your health,' McCoy teases. 'It'll kill you in the end.'

319

Beth drops her hands to her hips and scowls. 'Is that a yes or a no?'

Judging by the quiet snigger I hear behind me, McCoy is enjoying this moment. On the desk behind Arty, I can see a lighter peeping from the top of his softpack of cigarettes.

'Be my guest,' McCoy offers at last. 'Though if the windows weren't blown out I'd make you smoke it in the courtyard.'

Beth reaches for the softpack. She draws a cigarette for herself, and then offers the pack to Arty.

'Don't you smoke, Hobbes?' As McCoy asks me this, I watch Arty draw the lighter from the pack. He strikes it up, touches it to the cigarette in his mouth, but doesn't let the flame go out.

'It's not my thing,' I reply, aware that my body is shielding McCoy's view of what's about to happen. I don't like the look of it one bit, watching Arty lower the lighter now, and yet I have to accept that we have no other choice. 'I prefer fresh air.'

At once, with an almighty *whump*, the handkerchief inside the bottle mouth alights. The flame jumps between Arty and me, which only fuels the move I make to get clear.

'What the—' Caught off-guard, McCoy makes no attempt to restrain me, and simply gawps at what Arty has just done. Arty springs to his feet, grasping the vodka bottle with the flaming wick. He sneers at McCoy through more tears, and shows him his homemade bomb. 'I might be a greedy fool,' he tells him, with a brief, sad smile. 'But I will *not* die a traitor!'

At first I think McCoy might turn and run. Instead, regrouping with a sigh, he attempts to snatch the burning bottle. 'Get rid of that thing, you clown. Stop fooling around!'

'Hobbes!'

A hand on my wrist demands my attention. It's Beth. We're trapped here, I realise, stuck behind the two men as they wrestle for the bottle now. If McCoy figured he was in control, Arty quickly proves him wrong. Several sizes bigger than the mercenary, he slams him against the control panel. I see him wrench the flaming vessel clear from McCoy, who immediately lunges for it again. If the bottle drops, the explosion will rip us apart. With no way of making it past them to the ladder, I grab the chair that Arty has been using, and hurl it at the window facing the compound. The remaining glass collapses from the frame. Beth is first to scramble onto the desk. I grab her hand. She hauls me up with her, just as McCoy breaks loose from Arty. The big guy has the bottle still. By the look on his face, I just know what he's about to do with it. Beth is staring in dread at the void through the jagged frame, but there's no way back now. I hold her wrist tight as we leap into the half-light, as the space we leave behind us transforms into a fireball.

321

42

In this arctic stillness, the explosion cuts through the air like an almighty thunderclap. What glass had been left in the frames spits over us, just as we hit the steep drifts piled at the foot of the tower. The impact is far from soft. I connect with the slope and tumble, amid glass shards and other debris from the explosion. I hear Beth cry out, and then all is quiet again. A second later, the sprinkler system can be heard kicking in. I am winded, bruised and deafened by the blast, but alive nonetheless. I open my eyes, and find myself facing the sky.

The first thing I notice, despite the devastation around me, is that it's brightened by a watt. Whatever happens from here on out, I think to myself, this long night is almost over.

Smoke coils from the communications tower, and an acrid smell fills the air. Next thing, voices rise out of the compound along with scrambled footfalls on the spiral steps. As the hiss of fire extinguishers opens up, I know it's time to move. Judging by the note of panic in the orders being traded up there, McCoy's mercenaries are clearly desperate to put out the flames before the smoke can be seen from the air. I just don't want to be shot should any of them spot us in the snow.

I sit up, wincing at the effort it requires, and find Beth on her hands and knees beside me. The blast has left a high-pitched whine in my ears. It makes it hard for me to hear her cursing. Even so, the grin she flashes tells me that we've made it. We pick ourselves up without speaking, sharing the same sense of urgency. Glass drops from the back of my oilskin. I figure it has saved me from the worst. My ankle hurts where I fell on it, and this return to the cold is just torture on my feet. Despite this, I will not let anything stop me now. Beth looks equally determined. She's nursing her shoulder, and has suffered a fine cut to her temple, but we're both alive.

Without a second glance behind us, we limp as fast as we can towards the kennel block. There's little left of the snow barricade that the guards built in a bid to survive the night. More immediately, thanks to the few who had made it through, the bodies have been hauled out of sight. The area looks well trampled, but offers nothing else to attract attention. That the door to the kennel block is ajar tells me where the survivors are hiding out. The dogs can be heard in their cages, but none of them bark this time. They simply whine and howl. Having thrown a whole bank of switches in the tower, I see that the compound gates are also open. Instinctively, I think about running for the wilderness, and have to remind myself that at any moment we could get a bullet in the back. Like the guards, we need to get inside.

I hesitate outside the door. Even Beth seems reluctant to go further.

'It's too quiet,' she says over the sound of the whimpering dogs. 'And what's with the mutts?'

'We've just jumped out of a tower,' I remind her. 'Crossing a threshold isn't going to kill us.'

I push the door open, and turn to check on Beth. Immediately, a monstrous hand, missing several fingers, thrusts out from behind the doorframe and grabs me by the shoulder. At once I am dragged inside, spun around, and feel a blade press to my throat.

'Get inside with Hobbes, lady, or I'll kill him right now!'

I only caught a glimpse of my attacker before he introduced the knife. He may have been burned beyond recognition, but the threat in his voice is what confirms his identity. It's North. A man come back from the dead, it seems, and sounding utterly desperate.

I can sense him shivering in spasms behind me, while the smell of charred flesh is sickening. He drags me further back to make way for Beth, and then demands that she close the door. 'Who else is with you?'

'*Nobody!* We've just saved your lives!'

North considers what she's just said, and laughs. 'Did you hear that, boys?'

I see Beth look around. At the same time, North drives his knee into the small of my back, and releases me. I fall to the ground and look up to see what has just caused Beth to gasp. 'Sweetheart,' rasps the wretched figure looming over me. 'You're too damn late.'

Sure enough the guards are here, but none are in a good way. Many are simply curled up in the passage in front of the cages, encrusted by frost. Some just lie there, watching North but powerless to act. Others are unconscious, or worse. To my horror, I see Cortés, his prone body strangely contorted, and it's clear he's dead. Whether exposure, shock or burns have claimed him, it's no longer an issue. He looks at peace, at least. Just two men remain on their feet: the marksman who had taken care of the mercenary, and one of the handlers. Neither of them even registers what's just happened to us. They're working frantically to open the cage at the far end in a bid to access the warmth from the heat lamp in there. The handler might have the keys to get to the dogs now the compound door has been disabled, but he's shaking so violently that he can't fit it into the padlock.

'Let me help,' offers Beth, appealing to North now.

I turn to look at him directly, and catch my breath. If Cortés had looked bad out on the ice, his colleague here looks infinitely worse. For there's barely a shred of skin left on the man. It's as if I'm facing a moving hunk of meat. One that can do little more than scope me out through lidless eyes and blow bubbles of spit between his teeth. Confounding my belief that he had been killed outright, I can only think North must've shed the oil drum just as McCoy opened fire. Otherwise, he'd have been blown to smithereens. Looking at what's left of him, however, I wonder whether he had made the right move at all.

'Take your hands off the boy!' This is the marksman, who speaks without turning. 'We can trust them both.'

North seems beyond caring, however, and fails to respond. It's as if the energy he's just spent on ambushing us is all he has left. Frankly, I'm amazed he didn't perish *before* Cortés. Looking at him now, as the shock of it all begins to shut him down, I figure he can't be far behind.

Beth glances at me, as if to check North isn't going to lunge at her, and hurries across to the guards. It takes her a matter of seconds to free the lock. Any other time, I'd have prickled at the prospect of being so close to an attack dog. This one continues to whine, however, clearly unsettled by the way its master drops in under the heat lamp. Frantically, the other survivors haul themselves after him; every man reduced to a desperate need to save himself. I break away from North to check the bodies left in the passage for signs of life. North simply watches with his arms folded tight, as if hugging himself for comfort, but doesn't let go of the blade. I find a wrist, in a bid to search for a pulse, but it's so chilled I let it drop. The guard behind is also dead, and so I crawl to the one slumped against the wall further back in the shadows, and press two fingers to the side of his neck.

Immediately, two hooded eyes find mine. I gasp and pull away. For it isn't a guard at all. It's the agent codenamed Victor. He's wrapped his oilskin around him like a shroud, and now turns his wraith-like face to mine. If he had left us looking close to death, he has moved even beyond that now. It can only be a matter of minutes before his final breath escapes, I feel, and hope he remains in no pain.

'Listen,' he whispers, and again, with more urgency: 'Do you hear that?'

I pull back, tipping my head at the same time. I ask Beth to be still for a moment. And then, despite the whine in my ears from the blast, I pick up on it. Out here, the silence is striking. The air is so crisp that any sound carries from miles around. Right now, far off in the distance, I can hear a low drone, growing louder by the second.

43

North is the first to break the silence. Without warning, moving with stiff, alarming jolts now, he turns to leave the dog compound. I have to fling myself at his charred, blistered body to stop him, and wrestle him to the ground. He doesn't offer much resistance, even when I snatch the knife from his grasp.

'Stay quiet,' I urge, beyond caring about the state of this zombie in my clutches. 'If we step out now they'll cut us all down!'

Beth is at my side, straining to see through the gap in the door. I sense North slacken underneath me, but keep him pinned to the floor just in case. Across the compound, what appears to be a detail of guards exits the main doors. They're tramping through the snow towards the main gates, puffing hot breath into the still air. They emerge in disarray, however, which is no surprise given the effort they must have put into extinguishing those flames. But they're not going to let that beat them and I watch them recover some order. Behind them, the building looks the same as ever but for the blackened, windowless frames of the communications tower and the debris underneath it. I think about the incoming party, the sound of the aircraft building behind the ridge now, and fear that within minutes there'll be nothing left for them to inspect.

'We can't just stay here!' Beth turns and appeals to me, but I'm all out of ideas. There are a dozen armed mercenaries in disguise out there, ready to welcome the party and even direct them inside. They're almost at the gates now, passing level with us. If we break cover now they'll have no choice but to open fire before turning on the new arrivals. I daren't even breathe, let alone answer Beth. Then I spot one figure in particular and feel only despair.

McCoy is among them.

He's in full battledress, just like the others, but it's clear he didn't escape the blast. One side of his face is burned and grazed, and the manner in which he moves makes it clear that he's badly dazed. I only just spot him, because he's using the others as cover for his injuries. A lone man appears from the building behind them. It's the explosives expert McCoy had briefed to light the cord. I picture the flame now, eating its way towards the fuel drums under the generator. Immediately, I think of the Commander and all the detainees trapped in their cages in the cannery. Leaving the blast door ajar, the explosives guy sprints to catch up with the pack. Beth strains to keep track of them as they pass the dog compound and reach the main gates. I stay where I am. I have no reason to watch them begin their walk to the airstrip. I can hear the plane descending now, and figure in minutes they'll be on that flight to freedom.

Staring at the white expanse outside, I feel utterly defeated.

I only find some fight left in me as I hear the aircraft touch down. The engines roar and then settle. In a moment, I think, as soon as it has taxied to a halt, the party on board will be directed straight to the main building.

'We can stop them as soon as they come through the gates,' I hiss, 'but it'll be too late for the guys in the cannery.'

'It's never too late.' Beth turns to face me, and then gasps when another figure looms over us.

'Beth is right.' The deep cover agent stands before us, swaying unsteadily. He slips his hand inside his frosted oilskin, and brings it back sticky with blood. 'I should be dead now, and yet I feel more alive with every breath I take.' He drops to his knees, in what I think is some kind of collapse, only to snatch North's blade from me without warning.

'What are you doing?' Suddenly, I feel totally threatened by this man who has helped us so far. He comes closer with the blade, so close that I can't avoid his hooded eyes. Whatever pain he is in from frostbite or the bullet wound, the tranquillisers have evidently cut his senses off from it. 'I'm not leaving this world alone, Hobbes. I can promise you that.'

The way he says this, with the detached determination of a suicide bomber, sounds to me like a man entirely at peace with his calling. He might well be a deep cover agent, but it's Grimstad who's preparing for this end game.

I switch my attention from the blade to his eyes and back again. Over on the runway, the plane's engines can be heard shutting down. This is followed by the sound of the hatch opening, and voices exchanging greetings.

'You're not the only one with little time left,' I remind him. 'Give me a chance to reach the building. If I can stamp out the flame before it reaches the fuel drums, we can *save* some lives, not end them!'

'Forget about the cannery.' Beth is out of the door now, openly watching what's going on beyond the main gates. 'Think about yourself for once!'

'What?' I am startled to hear her say this. 'Time's running out for those guys. Come on!'

Beth moves away from the door, out of sight again. 'Hobbes, this is our chance to get *away*! As soon as the decommissioning party come through the gates, we have to make a break for it.'

332

I look at her, speechless. 'But I don't need to escape. I haven't done anything wrong!'

Beth laughs, out of nowhere, and repeats what I have just said in a mocking, whiny voice. I should be stung, but know her well enough now to accept she's simply trying to spike me into action. 'Think about it, Hobbes,' she adds, with a glance at the guard I'm still holding to the floor. I let go of him immediately. North makes no effort to move. With a jolt, I realise he has gone. 'Can you really trust the military to clear your name?' she asks. 'As far as they're concerned you're still in the frame for the bullion robbery. With *me*, the all-American traitor. They won't just grant you a pardon, Hobbes. You're in the system now, with plenty more questions to answer. What's more, many of the people who might've spoken in your favour are dead.' She breaks off there, at the sound of boots in the snow, and retreats into the interior shadows. The deep cover agent remains poised with the knife. He touches his lips when I glance at him, but it's the blade in his hand that persuades me to stay quiet.

The party from the plane pass outside just then. I count five men and two women, all in military greens, some chatting in broken English as they head for the main building. All I want is for someone to register the blast damage to the communications tower and hold back for a moment. Maybe they do notice it, because their talk takes on an edge of concern.

333

And then, instead of turning away as I had hoped, they actually quicken their pace.

'You're sending them to their deaths,' I hiss at the deep cover agent, only to fall quiet for a moment. For the plane's engines can be heard engaging once more. 'If we do nothing McCoy will get away with *murder*!'

'Not while I'm still breathing,' he replies, and calmly rises to his feet.

Beth makes way for him, and then urges me to follow. 'Last chance, Hobbes. Let's get going!'

I don't move for a moment. Just stare at her instead. 'Can I trust you?' I ask finally.

Beth breaks into a scowl, but stops short of an answer. For one of the guards crawls back out of the dog cage just then – the marksman from the gantry, I realise – and drops two pairs of boots at my feet.

'Take them.' He gestures at the men behind him. They're huddled under heat lamps designed for the dogs, defeated to the core, but watching us intently. 'We wouldn't have survived without your help,' he adds, as another guard tosses him one pair of gloves after another. He gestures at Beth, who has already climbed into a pair of boots and is poised to break her cover. 'If you want to find out if she can be trusted,' he says, and reaches down to haul the inert body of North under one of the lamps, 'you had better hurry up and follow her. Go, Hobbes. Leave *now*!'

44

In the open air again, with protection for my hands and feet at last, I am torn over which way to run. The party are outside the blast doors. If I chase after them, I think, the explosion will take me out, too. I turn to look for Beth. There she is, flanking the deep cover agent as he stumbles desperately through the snow. They're heading for the hut beside the airstrip. The plane is turning at the apron now, its engines screaming at full tilt. I picture McCoy looking out and laughing, which is why I come around full circle.

'Hey!' I yell at the party, and wave my arms over my head. 'Get away from there. Get away, *please!*'

In the distance I see heads look around, and then face one another as if to question what is going on. They may think it's their pilot manoeuvring the plane behind me, but I know it's McCoy. I appeal to them one more time, pulling apart my oilskin to flash them the orange jumpsuit underneath, and then turn to flee myself.

'Hurry, Hobbes!' Beth has stopped to call out to me. I see the plane swing around to face the runway, preparing to take off. Behind her, the deep cover agent continues to lumber on. He's heading for the snowmobiles, I realise, with Beth right behind him. I race to catch up as he mounts the nearest one. The key must be in the ignition, because he swings it around in an arc of snow. When Beth reaches the next bike, I'm not surprised when she manages to bring it to life straight away. It's no accident that these vehicles are ready to go. Military personnel had left them like this, believing they would be safe outside the compound. I jump onto a third bike, twist the key, and give thanks for human error when it roars.

I bring the vehicle around so fast that the rear sled fishtails for a moment. In response I gun the engine, and strike out after Beth. I'm surprised to see her fan away from the airstrip, and head across the ice field towards the pine ridge, but follow her without hesitation. By now the deep cover agent is moving at full throttle. He's closing in on the plane as it gathers speed along the runway. Hunched over the handlebars, with the tails of his oilskin flapping violently, I watch him race to catch up. I dare not look behind me at the compound. And not just because I'm frightened by the devastation I might see. If I let my concentration slip for a second, this vehicle might just tip. My eyes are streaming in the headwind. Beth is motoring across the snow pack so quickly I think for a moment that she is trying to lose me. I glance one more time at the airstrip, see the snow bike tumbling away beside the aircraft. I almost crash myself when I take it in, and have to look twice as I swear I see a figure like an angel on the plane's wing. He's pressed against the fuselage, and crawling towards the cockpit windows.

Beth doesn't stop at the foot of the ridge. She simply snakes between the trees, the trunks dark as rock against the snow cover, slicing her own path up the incline. I stand from my seat to attack the rise, really fighting to follow her tail-lights through the gloom now. I think I hear the plane lift away from the runway, but my focus is on the struggle to stay upright. A second later, much to my surprise, l realise I have lost Beth. I had chased her up the same path of least resistance, only now I'm in a basin of sorts and she's nowhere to be seen.

I stand again, searching for her as I move, upon which a figure emerges from behind a tree just in front of me.

Beth is brandishing a broken branch like a baseball bat. With a look of grim determination, she swings it around and knocks me from the snowmobile.

I land on my spine in hard snow. The impact drives the air from my lungs. At the same time, my bike throttles onwards, and barrels into a boulder. With a crunch, the engine cuts out, leaving only the drone of the escaping plane to keep the silence from settling.

'Sorry, Hobbes.' Standing over me now, Beth slings the stick away. 'On the inside, you were invaluable to me. But now we're out here, I realise I made you a promise that I just can't keep.' I'm too winded to speak. I fight to draw breath, but as I do she reaches inside her oilskin and draws the handgun she had seized from Arty Dougal. The one McCoy had forced her to drop on surprising us from behind. 'I grabbed it on the way out,' she tells me. 'It would've been unprofessional to leave it behind.'

I struggle to my feet, clutching my ribs where she has hit me. 'I never considered you to be a traitor, despite what everyone claimed. This changes everything, though.'

'Like I said,' she offers, sounding unsure of herself all of a sudden. 'I'm sorry.'

Overhead, I can hear the plane climbing out of the ice fields.

'So now you're going to abandon me? All because you've changed your mind about sharing your hidden bullion haul? You're as treacherous as McCoy!'

'All that matters is money,' she says, retreating from me now. 'It's all that ever mattered.'

'Not to me!' I spit. 'What we've been through to get this far is worth so much more than that!'

Without a word, she climbs out of the gully and disappears from sight. A moment later, I hear the engine of her snowmobile fire up again. I scramble to catch up, stung by her treachery, only to be caught in a spray of snow as she directs her vehicle along an incline between the trees. I'm in no mood to simply watch her go, however, and break into a sprint. The snow and the big boots may hold me back, but I lock my sights on her tail-light, which burns as brightly as the sense of injustice inside me.

'Don't you *dare*!' I bellow. 'Don't you leave me here!'

The trees rise steeply on one side, but to my right, where they drop away, the ice field returns to view. It seems brighter up here. A hint of blue breaking through the twilight. At the same time, in the sky behind me, I hear the pitch of the plane's engines shift. I glance over my shoulder as I run, and see the aircraft scything sharply in the sky. Beth must pick up on it, too, because she looks around in the saddle. Not at me as I close in, but at the banking aircraft.

Then her eyes begin to pinch in horror.

I hear the engines falter as I look around again. My first thought is that the plane is coming back down to the runway. Knowing how determined the deep cover agent had been to catch up with McCoy, I can be sure the Pitcairn mercenary is aware of his presence on the plane now.

Then the aircraft levels out, and begins to bear down in our direction. I watch it grow in the sky for a beat, before a bolt of dread slams through me.

'Beth, *move*!' I turn and charge towards her.

'Jump on!'

'There's no time!' I yell at her to move as the din begins to drown her idling engine. It turns to a scream and then a kamikaze howl, but Beth just hangs on for me with her throttle primed. Daring to glance back just one more time, I swear I see movement inside the cockpit, and know what I have to do.

This time, it is my turn to unseat Beth. Tackling her around the waist, I drag her from the vehicle as the plane's undercarriage sweeps over us. The slip-stream is intense, however. It flips the snowmobile into cartwheels, just as the plane ploughs into the path ahead. A wing catches the lower treetops, wrenching the aircraft around. I watch in shock as it sinks backwards, seemingly swallowed by so many branches. The engines cut out next, leaving the sound of twisting metal and splintering wood.

A silence settles. Just for a moment. Then comes the explosion.

I bury myself in the snow, bringing Beth down close to shield her from the fireball. The flames from the wreckage rise high in blankets, licking the sky, it seems. I smell fuel, and keep low until I hear the roar subsiding. And when I do raise my head, the first thing I do is snatch the pistol from the girl beside me.

'I'll look after this, I think.'

The shock on her face lasts no more than a second.

For then she finds me grinning, and simply looks sheepish instead.

'So, now you're going to leave *me* out here?'

I shake my head. 'Why would I do that? This is no place for a bullion thief, after all. You're a crook, Beth, but you'll never cut it as a mercenary. A real one would've left me for dead just then.'

The crackle of burning branches draws our attention back to the crash site. As the fuel burns off, the compound appears through the thinning flames.

There it is, way down at the shoreline, scored on three sides by the fencing. Despite the shimmering heat, I see some members of the decommissioning party outside the blast doors. They don't look so upbeat and collected any more. It's bedlam, in fact. Two tear across the snow in the direction of the kennel block, while another can be seen simply turning circles in a state of utter shock. Just then, one of their number retreats through the blast doors and into the open. He's holding a rifle, which is trained at the reception area, and is yelling urgently. A moment later, a file of orange-clad figures emerges with their hands on their heads. I realise the detainees have been released for fear that the building isn't safe. What surprises me is that the device McCoy rigged so carefully hadn't gone off once the fuse was lit. I face Beth. She smiles, without looking at me, and I know just why these people are still alive.

341

'From the moment we escaped the cannery,' I say, 'we've only been apart once.'

'When you crept into the processing area,' she replies, 'and I went back to remove the cord from the fuel tank.'

I reflect on this, nodding now. 'I never thought about that.'

She faces me this time. For a moment I think she is about to kiss me. 'I wouldn't be here without you,' she says, searching my gaze. 'When I targeted you for the Fort Knox job, I had no idea we would make such a good team. Not just inside the cage, but maybe even on the outside.'

For a moment I am lost for words. She draws closer. I want to meet her lips, but a sudden cry from below forces us both to crouch out of sight. Another member of the visiting party has found a weapon. He's on one knee at the open gates, with his sights locked on several detainees who have made a break for it. I watch these desperate, dangerous men draw up as the first bullet whistles into the snowfield, aware that we could expect the same response if spotted.

Inside the compound, I see some of the guards emerging unsteadily from the kennel block. Among the decommissioning party members helping them out is a figure in a billed cap. He seems to be directing things, working to regain some control over the camp he once commanded.

'What now?' I ask, considering our own position. 'Do we give ourselves up?'

Beth Nelson sits back in the snow. 'We're a long way from the nearest settlement, with little protection against sub-zero conditions, and the slimmest of chances that we'll escape with our lives. All we have is a pistol, one snowmobile, some hypothermia problems and each other. But as you're the one with the gun,' she adds with a smile, 'only you can call the shots.'

I glance at the compound. The sun is just beginning to pierce the seaward horizon. The first golden bars reach across the pack ice and onto firm ground. I find Stagger down there again. For one such ray of light is flaring against his shades, which marks him out from the others. I even have to shield my eyes from the glare. I realise he must be looking in our direction, though he makes no attempt to sound the alarm.

Unwilling to be spotted by anyone else, I step back to find Beth awaiting my reply.

I consider what I have left behind. Not just an unfinished interrogation at the compound, but my life at home. I think about my father, sworn to secrecy, and whether anyone else has even noticed that I'm missing. Right now, I should be in front of my keyboard. Instead, I'm overlooking what feels like the ends of the earth, alongside a self-confessed bullion robber responsible for shaking my world upside down. It makes me reflect on Beth's earlier question. Thinking back, it doesn't matter whether Grimstad was lying or telling the truth. Either way, the man must have known *exactly* what he was doing when he forced that plane down over our heads. Even if McCoy played a hand in those final moments, I realise something invaluable might now come from it. Because having come so close to death, I am mighty glad to be alive.

So what choice did that leave me? I grin, despite the odds against us.

'Let's get out of here,' I say. 'Who knows? If we keep working together, we might just strike *gold*.'

Acknowledgements

Wholehearted thanks to my editor, Venetia Gosling, for her long-standing support, encouragement and insight, as well as everyone at Simon & Schuster. I'm also indebted to Philippa Milnes-Smith, for picking me up, dusting me down, and keeping my pencil sharp. On the technical front, Jamie Liddall and Muhammad Mulla at Youthnet proved themselves to be worthy system guardians by answering my hacking questions with great patience (and some suspicion).